"I don't know," Mid said. "That seems like a lot of sneaking to me."

"What do you mean?" Meltern asked.

Mid enumerated on his fingers. "First, we have to sneak out of the salvage camp, again. Then we sneak out to The Fel, for a little camping vacation, collect a bagful of rovaldia—"

"—assuming we can even find any this time of year—" Cheff added.

—"without attracting any attention. Next we sneak Carra and the rovaldia back to where we found her, and finally sneak back into the salvage camp, where we pretend to have been there the entire time, all in the middle of a lockdown. Is that it? Did I miss anything?"

"No," Meltern said, "I think you covered everything."

"No disrespect, sir," Mid said, "but don't you think that's a lot of sneaking? How are we ever going to do that much sneaking in that many places, in the middle of the lockdown, and not get caught?"

In the silence that followed, Buttons held Starry Stargazer up to her ear and listened intently. "Starry says, by being very, very sneaky."

Mid buried his face in his hands.

OPERATION LOCKDOWN

Fellstone Tales

Book Two

by

Liam Kincaid

with illustrations by

Daniel Wood

LBME Publishing

This book is lovingly dedicated to:

Mr. G. Hawke

Who provided me a home on the sea
in which I wrote this book.

ACKNOWLEDGMENTS

Thank you to all who helped create this book, including:

Robert L. Graham, Master World Builder, my brother and best friend.

Sarah J, Best Beta Reader ever!

And my Twitch Crew:
  J. T. "Jack" Shennaghy
  FemaleWriter
  Dear Alisa
  EmperorOfFinland
  Mayah Robinson
  NightWriter
  Charlie Stone

A special Thank You to Penney Knightly for the superb diagram of the rovaldia herb in the chapter "Carra Meets Meltern".

And, of course, my grateful appreciation to Lon Böder and Penney Knightly for the many, many hours of brainstorming, encouragement, and support. This book would never have been possible without them.

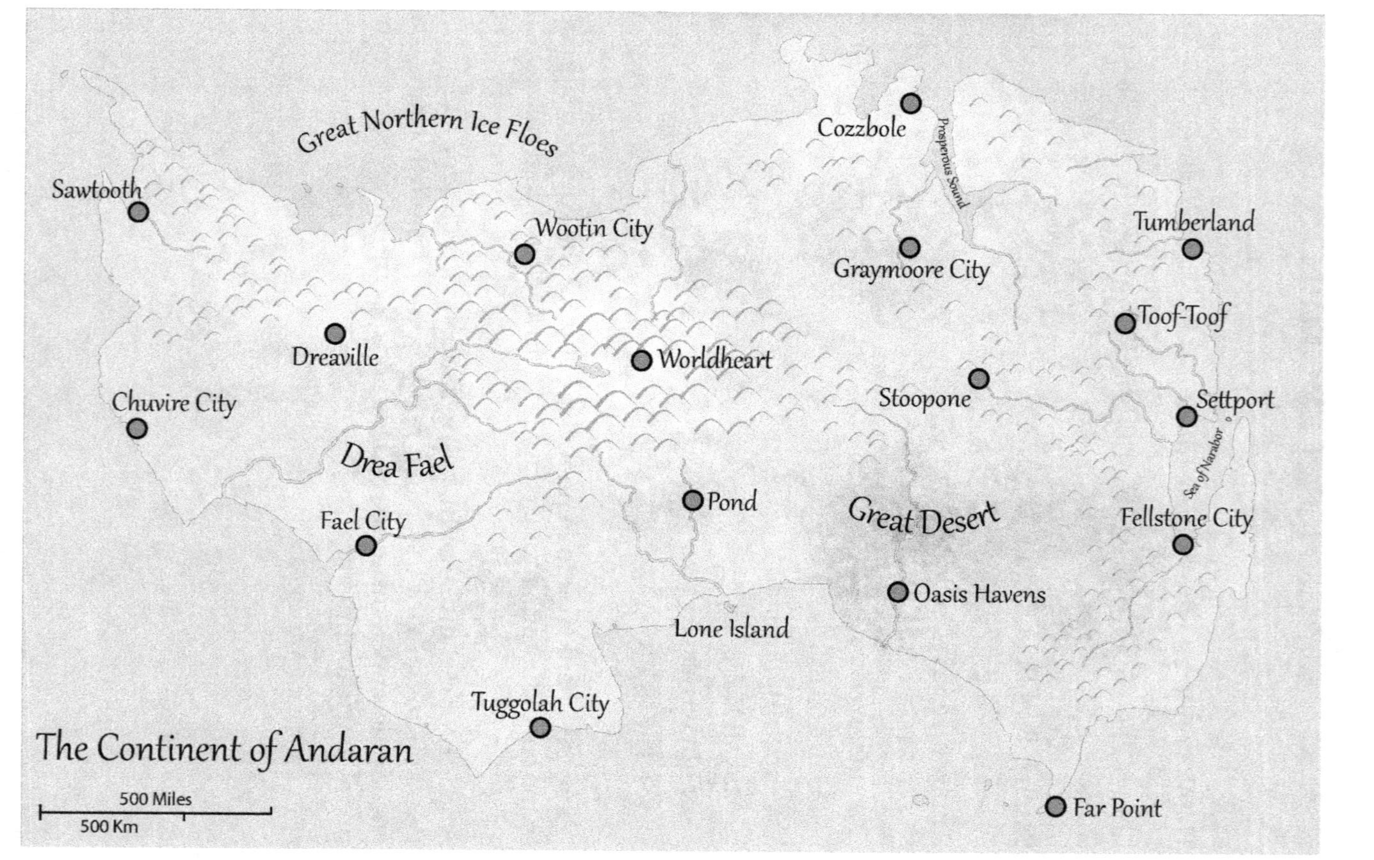

The Continent of Andaran
Great Northern Ice Floes
Sawtooth
Wootin City
Cozzbole
Prosperous Sound
Tumberland
Graymoore City
Toof-Toof
Dreaville
Worldheart
Stoopone
Settport
Chuvire City
Sea of Narubor
Drea Fael
Pond
Great Desert
Fellstone City
Fael City
Oasis Havens
Lone Island
Tuggolah City
Far Point
500 Miles
500 Km

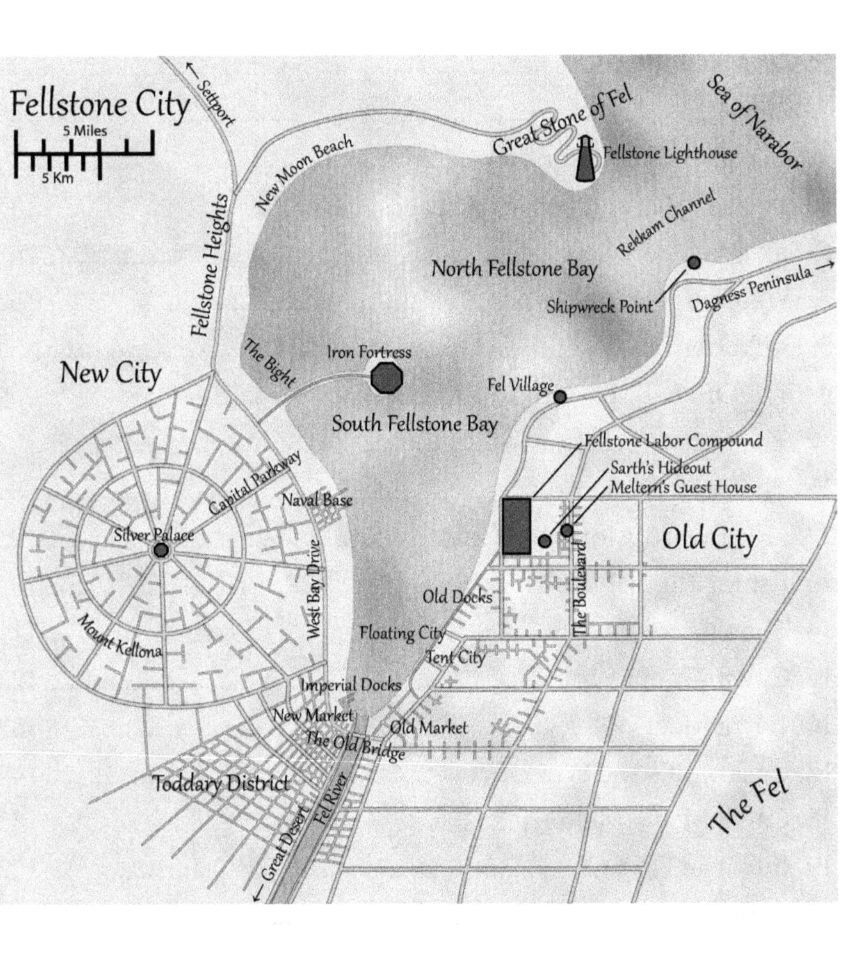

Fellstone City
5 Miles
5 Km
Settport
New Moon Beach
Great Stone of Fel
Sea of Narabor
Fellstone Lighthouse
Fellstone Heights
Rehkam Channel
North Fellstone Bay
Shipwreck Point
Dagness Peninsula
New City
The Bight
Iron Fortress
Fel Village
South Fellstone Bay
Fellstone Labor Compound
Sarth's Hideout
Meltem's Guest House
Capital Parkway
Naval Base
Old City
Silver Palace
West Bay Drive
The Boulevard
Old Docks
Mount Kellona
Floating City
Tent City
Imperial Docks
New Market
Old Market
The Old Bridge
Toddary District
Great Desert
Fel River
The Fel

Table of Contents

— **1** —

A LITTLE EXPLORING

CHEFF DROPPED HIS pencil onto his drawing table. "Finished!"

I looked up from my Library Management textbook. "What's finished?"

"A map."

"*Another* map? Of what this time?"

He put his finger to his lips and beckoned me close. We leaned our heads together. "The BSI's new headquarters, possibly," he whispered. "You know, Books, the one Meltern said we should set up."

The BSI is the Bayside Insurgents, a special cell of the FRM, the Fellstone Resistance Movement. We did the jobs that adult agents couldn't do. Meltern was our boss. At the moment, the BSI had six members: Cheff, Mid, Sable, Buttons, Lery, and I. But we had orders to recruit additional agents.

"Right, I remember. Where is it?"

"Down in the old storm drains, a few blocks north of here." He pointed to a location to the northeast of the Fellstone Labor Compound, our home-sweet-home, in the ancient ruins immediately

13

outside the walls. "I found it a few nights ago, when I was, ehem, 'sleepwalking.'"

"Sleepwalking! You mean you've been hunting again? Are you crazy?" All of Fellstone City had been under a strict lockdown since we rescued Cheff's Uncle Karf from the Iron Fortress a few weeks earlier. "The city's swarming with soldiers and Blue-bands!"

"Not down in the storm drains, it isn't. Don't worry, I haven't been hunting outside the borders of the Labor Compound. But there's precious little game in the storm drains, so I figured, why not do some exploring on the side? I've been keeping an eye out for more exits from the storm drains and a suitable location for our new HQ."

"And you found one?"

"Maybe—that's what we have to figure out. There's this one place that looks promising. It's in a tunnel that I think might go a distance outside the Labor Compound. See?" He indicated a tunnel on the map, across the road from the northeast quadrant of the Labor Compound. "Right about here, I ran across an old, rusted access hatch. I tried to pry it open, but it was rusted pretty badly. It would only budge a few inches. I held my miner's lamp up to the crack and peered inside, but I couldn't see much, only what looked like some old furniture. We need to take a crowbar, force that door open, and have a good look inside. I marked the hatch with chalk." He stood and stretched, then sat back down and leaned close again. "I haven't been able to go exploring for a few days. That big storm we had flooded the tunnels. They're probably dry enough by now, though. In fact, I was thinking that you and I might do a little exploring tonight."

"Tonight? Only you and me?"

"You up for it?"

"Well, I, uh… sure, I guess. Why not? I'll tell my mom that we'll be studying late, and I'm going to sleep over."

Cheff grinned. "All true, Old Son, all true."

* * *

We studied until after Cheff's Aunt Dee and his little sister, Buttons, had gone to bed, then Cheff and I crept down and lifted the trapdoor in the floor of the closet under the stairs. Silently, we descended the wooden ladder into our secret underground room and pulled the trapdoor closed behind us. Before Cheff could get his ancient miner's lamp burning, we heard the muffled sound of the trapdoor opening again in the darkness above our heads. We froze, our hearts pounding. Had the Bluebands discovered us? Or the Labor Compound guards? Or worse, Cheff's Aunt Dee? A diminutive figure scrambled down the ladder and thumped onto the dirt floor beside us.

Cheff finished lighting the miner's lamp and held it high. "Buttons! What—?"

Buttons, Cheff's younger sister, smiled.

"Hi, Books! Hi, Cheff!" She held up Starry, her little stuffed tan pony, and made her wave a hoof at me.

I waved back. "Hello, Starry!"

"Where are we going?" Buttons asked.

Cheff narrowed his eyes. "How is it that you always seem to know when I'm going out?"

"Starry tells me."

"Uh-huh. Of course she does. Why do I even ask?" He sighed. "I suppose there's no point in telling you to go back to bed?"

Buttons shook her head, making her twin black ponytails swing. "Not a chance." She grinned up at him and batted her eyelashes.

"Right." Cheff made a sour face. "Okay, then, let's get going." He handed me a stout metal bar about three feet long with a claw at one end. "Here, Books, you carry this. I'll take the lamp. Buttons, you… do whatever it is you always do."

We crawled through the dirt tunnel that led from our secret underground room to the storm-drain system and eased ourselves down to the shiny wet cobblestones. My small, slender Lildur build made it easy for me to navigate the narrow tunnel, but my spiky hair seemed to attract every particle of loose dirt.

Cheff led the way northward, carefully counting the intersecting tunnels. When we got to the fifth junction, he turned right, eastward. "This way."

We splashed after Cheff down the long, dark storm drain. Again, he counted junctions, six this time, turned left, and headed rapidly northward again for several hundred yards. He slowed down and held the mining lamp up to examine the walls. "Look for a chalk mark, an X."

Shortly, Buttons pointed to a small, white X right below the handle of a rusted metal door. "There it is, Cheff! That must be the one."

"Yep, that's the one, all right. Good work, Buttons. Let me have that wrecking bar, Books."

I handed him the bar and he pried at the rusted metal door.

"I should have brought some oil," Cheff said, "but I didn't expect it to be this hard to open." He worked the bar a few more times. The ancient door creaked and groaned. Flakes of rust and dirt fell to the tunnel floor, but the door wouldn't budge. He rested one end of the bar on the floor of the tunnel and wiped the sweat from his forehead. "It's stuck. It opened farther than this before. It's almost as though… as though someone has locked it from the inside."

He raised the bar again, but before he could begin prying, the door crashed open with a loud thunk! We froze where we stood. A bright light from inside blazed into our eyes, blinding us. A deep voice roared, "All right, you kids, don't move a muscle. You're under arrest. I've got you now!" then broke into insane laughter.

— 2 —

NEW HEADQUARTERS

W E STOOD, PETRIFIED, squinting against the brightness. Then a pair of huge hands reached out of the doorway, grabbed me by my jacket collar, and jerked me through the hatch. The deep voice warned, "Don't move! Don't even think of moving!"

The hands reached out again, and then a third time. Cheff and Buttons appeared beside me. The bright lights still glared in our eyes, making it impossible to identify our captor.

The deep voice boomed out, "What do you kids think you're doing down here at this time of night?"

Cheff shuffled his feet, then said casually, "Finding a new headquarters for the Bayside Insurgents, of course. You'd better not mess with us—we're FRM agents!"

I gasped.

Buttons said, "Oh, Cheff, no! Don't tell them anything!"

"It's too late, Sis." Cheff shook his head sadly. "I'm afraid they already know everything."

"What do you mean, Cheff?" I asked.

"Well—"

Muffled laughter broke out in several places around the room. The glaring lights went out, and we were plunged into absolute darkness. Then the soft room lights came on, and there was Mid, a short round Troh boy, holding a spotlight, laughing so hard that tears were running down his chubby face. Lery, a tall Fessal older than he looked, stood next to him, bent over, his hand covering his mouth. Sable, in her all-black mission outfit, leaned against the wall by the door, smiling.

My head was spinning. "What? Who? How?"

Cheff laughed and punched me on the shoulder. "You should see your face, Books. We got you good this time."

I still couldn't make any sense of things. "But… that deep voice… who was that?" I looked around the room but didn't see anyone else.

Mid held up a strange-looking contraption for me to see. It looked like a big funnel, with a bell shape at one end, and a microphone at the other. He put it to his lips, pressed a button, and spoke. "All right you kids! The jig is up! Come out with your hands up!" His voice sounded as deep as the voice we'd heard earlier—as deep as Captain Utaliak's, or maybe deeper. "I call it the Amazing Voice Changer, or AVC, for short. Watch this!" He turned the knob on the AVC then spoke again. "All right you kids! The jig is up!" This time his voice was high and squeaky, like a mouse. "See? It can make your voice high, low, or anything in-between."

Mid turned the knob again, then handed the device to me.

I put it to my lips and pushed the button. "You're all under arrest!" My voice came out deep and loud.

Everybody laughed.

I asked, "How does it work?"

Mid took it back and pointed to an odd-looking component. "Well, first, your voice goes into here. Then—"

"Later, Mid," Cheff said. "Let's have a look around, and see if we can use this place. It's late, and we have school tomorrow."

Mid reluctantly tucked the device into his tech bag, then handed out flashlights to everyone. "I cobbled these together from spare parts. There's one for each of us."

Cheff accepted his, but said, "Thanks, Mid, it'll make a good spare, but I'll stick with my miner's lamp. It's a lot brighter."

"A lot fussier, too," Mid said, "but suit yourself."

"Wait a minute, Cheff," I said. "How did everyone get here? I didn't see anyone in the storm drains."

"Mid and Lery have been working on their own secret tunnel entrance. It'll be less suspicious if they aren't seen coming to my house all the time. As for Sable, well, I don't know, and I didn't ask. She has her ways. You know how she is."

"Right. So we all have our separate entrances to the storm drains. Except me, that is. And you told everyone about this place—except me. And they all knew about Mid's new toy—except me." I raised my hands, palms up. "You mad at me about something?"

Cheff laughed. "Naw, of course not! I had to tell them earlier so they could meet us here. But I knew you'd be at my house tonight, and then I thought—" He started to chuckle. "I thought—"

"I know, I know. You thought what fun it would be to scare the stuffing out of good ol' Books. Again. And you simply couldn't resist. Am I right?"

He was laughing too hard to answer.

"And I suppose you think that's funny?" I glared at him as hard as I could, but he only laughed harder. Finally, I started laughing, too. "Okay, I guess it *was* pretty funny. But I'll be glad when we recruit someone else, and I'm not the new kid anymore."

"We'd better get moving," Cheff said. "I've already been through the place, of course, before I suggested that we meet here. But I wanted everyone to see it before I report back to Meltern. I've looked at quite a few possible headquarters for the BSI in the last three weeks, and this one seemed the best to me. Let's all have a quick look around and see what we think, then head home. We can discuss the details tomorrow after school. Buttons, you go with Sable. Mid and Lery together. Books, with me."

Buttons shone her flashlight around the room. It was small, and the walls were lined with shelves, covered with dusty, rusty debris of all sorts and sizes.

"It's kind of small, isn't it, Cheff?" I asked.

"It's a lot bigger than it looks," Cheff said. "This is only some kind of store room. Come on, follow me, you'll see." He led us through a door and down a corridor, which opened into what I guessed was the main room.

The place was huge. And filthy. Dark-gray soot and dust covered everything. The circular main room contained a lot of tables and chairs at one end and a big, open area at the other. A platform, perhaps a stage, dominated the far side. A raised area around the edges of the room held more tables and chairs. Doors around the outer wall led to smaller side rooms, many of which also had tables and chairs. After we had explored the side rooms and corridors for a quarter of an hour or so, we met in the big main room.

I asked Cheff, "What kind of place was this? In the old days, I mean."

"'Old days' is right," Mid said, "judging by the furniture. This stuff looks ancient."

"I think it must have been some kind of guest house, or eating place, like Mr. Meltern's," Buttons said. "Why else would there be all these tables?"

"I think you're right about that," Mid said. "Lery and I found a pretty big kitchen through those swinging doors. It's a mess, though."

Lery added, "But I… I think I could… clean it up… maybe. I don't know… if the stove still works…"

"There are lots of little rooms around the main hall," Buttons said. "Enough for each of us to have our own room, if we wanted to. Even Starry and Moka!"

Moka was Buttons' other little stuffed pony, a dark brown one. Buttons claimed that she was Starry's sister.

Buttons made the two little ponies dance in the air. "They're awfully excited!"

Sable pointed to a large open area along one wall. "Training area. Room for equipment."

"Maybe one of the little rooms could be a library," I said. "It would be great to have a safe place to hide forbidden books."

Cheff looked pleased. "Good. Excellent observations, everyone. I agree that this place has some potential and plenty of room for growth. It obviously hasn't been entered for decades, which means it's probably safe from prying eyes. We'll have to be careful to keep it that way."

Mid asked, "Do you know exactly where we are? Where this place is? In relation to the Labor Compound, I mean."

"We'll have to check it out, but I think it's right outside the Labor Compound, across the street from the north wall. I'm not sure what's above it, but most likely it's an abandoned house or business, probably a ruin. We'll have to pace it off to be sure. If it is outside the wall, it'll be a short shot to Meltern's place from here." He took a last look around the room. "Okay, gang, if we're all in agreement, I'll propose it to Meltern for his approval." We nodded. "Good. Then let's meet during morning break tomorrow."

We went down the long corridor to the store room, then climbed out the rusty hatch back into the storm drains, and headed south. Before long, Sable waved goodnight and turned down a side tunnel. When we were closer to home, Mid and Lery turned off, too. A few minutes later, Cheff, Buttons, and I stood together outside the dirt tunnel leading to the secret room under Cheff's house.

Cheff put his hands on my shoulders. "Books, do you think you can get yourself and Buttons the rest of the way home?"

"Sure, Cheff, no problem—we're practically home now. Why? Where are you going?"

"I'm going to report to Meltern."

"Tonight? You want me to go with you?"

"No, I'm going to move quickly and quietly. I'll be a lot less likely to get caught if I'm alone. I'm going to dash out there, report, and dash back home. I need to get some sleep before school. Thanks for the offer, though."

Buttons gave him a huge hug. "Be careful, Cheff. The ponies are worried about you."

Cheff tousled Buttons' hair, then patted Starry and Moka on their heads. "Don't worry, ponies. I'll be extra careful. And if it goes well, I might even bring some meat home for tomorrow's supper. Sleep tight!" He kissed her forehead, then was gone down the tunnel to the south.

Buttons gazed after him, then sighed.

"Be safe, Cheff," I whispered. "Okay, Buttons. Let's head for bed. We have school tomorrow." I boosted her up to the dirt tunnel and crawled in after her.

"Dark-gray soot and dust covered everything."

— 3 —

SCHOOL

THE NEXT MORNING, I woke up in Cheff's bed, groggy and a little bit disoriented. Cheff was still asleep on the floor. I jumped into my clothes and ran home, where I changed into my school clothes, gathered my books, and dashed for the door.

But Mother stopped me. "One moment, Birn Tylandine! Don't even think about leaving until you've had some breakfast."

"But, Mom—"

"No buts, Birn. Sit!"

I sat. Mom set a bowl of soup down in front of me, along with the heel of a loaf of bread. "Thanks, Mom." I tucked into the soup. It was tasty, a little bit spicy, a little bit salty, a little bit sweet. I didn't ask her what the meat was—probably something Cheff had hunted up on one of his 'sleepwalking' trips—I didn't want to know. Over the last few weeks, Mom had learned some secrets of Labor Compound Cuisine from Cheff's Aunt Dee. Mom had been so worn out when we arrived at the Labor Compound that I'd been afraid she might not make it. Aunt Dee had nursed Mom back to health with her wholesome cooking and loving concern.

Mom was a lot better now, and even though she still wasn't coping too well with the death of my father, she kept up with her labor assignments and could even smile a little, now and then.

I finished my breakfast and took my bowl to the sink. "Thanks, Mom, that was *deee*licious!" I gave her a kiss on the cheek and went out the door.

Cheff and Buttons were already waiting for me, and we walked down the street together. Cheff fished a sweet roll out of his bag and handed it to me. "Compliments of Mr. M." It was flavored with cinnamon and topped with dried fruit—yummy! Cheff lowered his voice. "No worries about the you-know-what—Mr. M says the flour and sugar are pure."

Mid and Lery joined us at the corner, as usual, and a few blocks later Sable fell in without a word. I got the same little thrill I always got when I saw Sable. Not that I was in love with her or anything—after all, I'm of the Lildur People and Sable's a Kreff. It's only that Sable is, well, *Sable*: tall, lithe, haunting green eyes hiding behind long black hair, the epitome of silent grace.

Cheff distributed the rest of the sweet rolls, informing each one in turn that the sugar and flour were jexan-free.

I walked alongside Cheff, munching happily, and asked, "So, what did you find out from Meltern last—"

"Shhh, not now, Books. Glance behind us. Snoops!"

Coming around the corner of the block we'd just passed were Miss Averith Brex and five of her Blueband thugs. I dropped back a couple of paces. It would have to keep until later. We walked in silence the rest of the way to school.

When we turned into the schoolyard, my heart sank, as it did every morning.

"What's the matter, Books?" Buttons asked.

"Nothing. Well, nothing much. It's only that the school makes me think of a—"

"A prison?" Buttons asked.

I laughed. "Yeah."

"Well," Buttons said, "that's hardly a surprise. Cheff says that a long time ago, it *was* a prison."

"That's true," Cheff agreed. "The school buildings were a prison before The Fall, or so I'm told. What is now the schoolyard used to be the prison yard."

"From what I've heard," Mid added, "the Basic and Regular School building was the men's prison, and the Advanced School was for women. The admin building was always the admin building."

"What about the Military School?" I asked.

"New," Sable murmured.

Cheff said, "The Military School building was built after Emperor Pallador turned the old prison into a school. It's specially equipped for training Military Officer candidates."

"What kind of special equipment?" I asked.

"Secret," Sable said.

"Of course it is," I said. "Well, that explains why this place looks like a prison, I guess."

"Oh, there's more to the story," Cheff said. "Before Pallador turned it into a school, he used it as—the original Labor Compound."

"He what, now?" I asked.

"In the beginning of Pallador's reign," Cheff explained, "shortly after the Battle of Fellstone City, he turned the old prison into the Labor Compound. When he started rounding up the families of political prisoners—"

"—Like us!" Buttons said.

"—it didn't take long to fill it up, so he made the prisoners start building the Labor Compound we know and love."

"And when he was done with that," Mid said, "He turned the old prison into our school and added the Military School."

"Interesting," I said. "No wonder I feel like I'm in jail every day."

"A sentiment common to students everywhere," Cheff said, "not only in the Labor Compound."

We laughed.

"Time," Sable said.

Buttons held up Starry and Moka and made them wave. "G'bye, boys, see you at break!" She and Lery walked off toward the Basic-and-Regular building. It was her last year in Basic. Next year she'd join the rest of us, except Lery, of course, in Advanced Secondary School. Lery attended Regular Secondary School, training as a professional chef. He had an aptitude for cooking.

We waved back, then went to our respective classrooms—Mid to Engineering and Technology, Cheff and I to Civilian Leadership. Cheff specialized in Factory Management. My specialty was Archiving and Library Management. Across the yard, I saw Sable glance our way as she entered the Military Leadership building.

Cheff and I took our assigned seats in the front row and waited for class to begin. Mr. Rishten, a tall, slender Fessal gentleman with graying hair, sat at his dilapidated wooden desk, adding his customary heaping spoonful of sugar to his mug of steaming felmoss tea. He stirred it vigorously and took a huge swig, just as the starting bell rang. "Good morning, class," he said. "Today, we begin with Chapter Seventeen..."

I wondered what Mr. Rishten would say if he knew that the city-wide lockdown was all our fault. My eyelids drooped while Mr. Rishten droned on and on, extolling the virtues of Emperor Pallador's Torph-relocation program. At last, the bell rang. I closed my Management textbook with a bang and followed Cheff out to the schoolyard.

— 4 —

Special Work Assignment

C HEFF AND I met up with Mid and Lery at our usual table in the break area, in the shade of its rusted tin roof. Little beams of sunshine filtered through a thousand tiny holes, making golden trails in the dusty, sooty air. Buttons came over from Basic School and sat next to Lhuk. Lhuk was Buttons' age, a Torph boy, small and slight of build. He wore an old brown coat several sizes too big for him.

"Hi, Lhuk!" Buttons said. "Where's Squeaky?" She took Starry and Moka from her special pony-carrying backpack and arranged them on the table so they could hear the conversation.

Lhuk smiled shyly, then gently withdrew his pet mouse from his coat pocket. He fed Squeaky a few bread crumbs and set him down on the table.

Lhuk looked intently at Squeaky, who stood up on his hind legs, waved a tiny paw at Buttons, then bowed.

Buttons giggled.

Lhuk spotted Brex and her gang across the yard. He scooped Squeaky up, gave him another bread crumb, and returned him to his pocket.

"That's amazing, Lhuk," Buttons said. "Your Torph Ability is getting stronger, isn't it? Is that why you don't need hand signals to direct Squeaky anymore?"

Lhuk didn't answer, only stared at his lap.

"Don't worry, Lhuk," Buttons said. "I'll never tell. The ponies would be devastated if they sent you out west to the Torph Camps, like your parents." The ponies hung their heads.

Lhuk said sadly, "I'm going to find some more breadcrumbs for Squeaky." He walked off toward the Basic School building.

A few minutes later, Sable joined us. Cheff said, "Scooch together but don't make it too obvious. The last thing we need this morning is *their* attention." He nodded toward Brex, who was assembling her squad of Bluebands for their morning drill. Most of the Bluebands wore makeshift uniforms, according to what they could afford. The only garment they had in common was their royal-blue armband. The Junior Bluebands, not yet old enough to be official, sported lighter blue armbands.

Brex stood stiff and straight in her spotless Blueband uniform, facing her subordinates. Her golden hair, cut in a shoulder-length style, made her flat Torph face seem even flatter, but, more important, hid the natural Torph markings she was so ashamed of. As usual, Brex was conducting some sort of inspection. Also, as usual, Brex looked quite dissatisfied with her troops.

"Let's hope Brex is too busy with her own people to notice us today," Mid said.

Starry and Moka exchanged concerned glances.

When we had scrunched together as close as we dared, Cheff said in an undertone, "After we broke up last night, I went out to Meltern's place. It didn't take long. I traveled fast and I didn't hunt. When I got there, Meltern took me into his… office, I guess you'd call it, or study, maybe. It was a secret office, though—the door was a section of wall that slid open. It was small, and shelves full of all sorts of interesting gadgets and artifacts covered the wall, but I didn't have much time to look around.

"I told him we've been looking for a headquarters, as he had ordered, and that we've also been exploring the storm-drain system. He seemed pleased. He asked me a few questions about our new headquarters and I described it to him, then he said we are authorized to proceed. He wants us to clean it up and said he'll get some gear together for us to move there when we're ready. I tried to ask him about it, what kind of gear, but he said to drop the subject for the time being.

"Then he looked thoughtful and told me he might know the place. He said that if it's the place he was thinking of, it was something called a 'supper club' back in the old days. Before The Fall, he said, it was a fancy eating place with music and dancing and such, all underground. It was called the Undersea Club. He said his father told him that even after The Fall it was nice for a while, the nicest place in town. He remembers going there when he was a kid, but it was getting pretty run-down by then. As times got harder, the supper club closed and was apparently forgotten. Eventually, the buildings above it fell into ruin. It seems that nobody wanted to live or work anywhere near the rapidly-expanding Labor Compound. Anyway, Meltern said it was probably as good a place as any, and better than most. It had 'possibilities,' he said, but he wouldn't say what they were."

"Excellent," Mid said. "I'm looking forward to setting up a few of my own gizmos there."

"I can… can help clean it up," Lery said. "I'm good at… at cleaning."

"Sure," Cheff said, "we'll all pitch in—it'll be fun. But hang on, there's more. I haven't told you the good part yet." He leaned in close and lowered his voice. "Meltern gave us our first official FRM mission."

We buzzed with excitement. Buttons said, "Yay!" and the ponies did a little celebration dance on the table.

Cheff started to elaborate, but Sable hissed, "Wait!" She inclined her head toward the yard. Lhuk was returning to our table. He didn't seem to notice Brex and a dozen of her minions following him.

"Oh, no," Buttons said. She held Starry up and asked, "What do you think we should do, Starry? How can we make that Bad Girl go away?"

Mid laughed. "I have an idea. Hang on. Tell Brex I'm going to the boys' room."

Report book tucked under her left arm, Brex strode up to our group, heels clacking on the asphalt. Three of her thugs swaggered up behind her and sneered at us.

Brex pointed at the retreating Mid and snapped, "Where does he think he's going?"

Buttons looked up, smiled, and made the ponies wave at Brex. "Hello, Miss Brex. It's so nice to see you." She held Moka up to her ear and listened. "Moka says she thinks he's going to the boys' room. I think so, too. He'll be right back, I'm sure."

Brex glared at Buttons, then growled, "He'd better be." She whipped around and zeroed-in on Cheff. "What, exactly, is going on here this morning? What do you all have to whisper about?"

"Nothing much," Cheff said. "We're talking about this morning's class." He yawned. "I was telling everyone what Mr. Rishten said about the lockdown, and how long it was likely to—"

"Shut it, Karfendek. I couldn't possibly care less. But speaking of the lockdown, don't you know that it's now illegal for people to gather in groups larger than three?"

"I heard something about that," Cheff said, "but I didn't know that it included the schoolyard."

"It most certainly does. Especially with a Torph child!" She pointed an accusatory finger at Lhuk. "Go on, get out of here, Torph scum! Scram!" And then to Cheff, "I'm going to put you on report! All of you!" She took her report book from under her arm and flipped to an empty form.

Without looking up, Lhuk trundled off toward Basic School. When he got past Brex and her thugs, he turned and slipped us a wink and a brief smile.

Before Brex could start writing, a deep, booming voice came over the loudspeaker system. "Miss Averith Brex to the Administration Office, immediately. Miss Averith Brex to Administration."

Brex glared at Cheff, then at each of us. "Never mind, I'll deal with you later. But don't let me catch you together again!" She turned and stalked off across the yard, her crew right behind her. When she reached the middle of the yard, she turned to her crew and barked, "Wait right there. I'll be back," then continued toward the Administration building.

As we watched her depart, golden hair flouncing, Mid sauntered back to the table. "Well, that ought to keep her busy for a while, trying to figure out who's looking for her." He sat down next to Lery, who grinned.

We looked at Mid, then Cheff said, "Oh, no, tell me you didn't. You didn't, right?" He looked into Mid's eyes. "You did, didn't you?" He tried to maintain a stern face but started to grin in spite of himself.

Mid said nothing but started grinning, too.

Sable smiled from behind her long, black hair. "He did."

"Did what?" Buttons asked. "The ponies demand to know!"

"Oh, no," I said. "Tell me it isn't so."

Mid didn't answer. Instead, he pulled the Amazing Voice Changer out of his tech bag far enough for us all to see it, then put it back.

Lery started guffawing out loud, slapping his thigh.

I said, "But... but the call came over the loudspeaker system. I heard it. Didn't I?"

"Well," Mid said, "almost. I was standing right under the loudspeaker, the one next to the boys' room."

"Smooth," Cheff said, "rock-smooth."

"Oh, man." I shook my head. "If she ever finds out, you're dead. I mean *dead*."

"Well, then," Cheff said, "I guess we'd best make sure that she never finds out. I'm not going to tell her. Are you, Books?"

"Of course not, it's only that—"

"Save it, Books," Cheff said. "Let me tell you the rest of what Meltern told me before Brex gets back."

"Right," I said. "Right."

"It's this," Cheff said. "We have our first official FRM mission. I don't have all the details yet. All I know so far is that we're to meet an FRM agent inside the Labor Compound, and he'll fill us in."

"An FRM agent *inside* the compound?" Mid asked.

Sable said, "Of course."

"Of *course*?" Mid asked, then thought about it. "Well, yeah, I suppose so. Who is it?"

"I don't know," Cheff said. "I'm as surprised as you are. Meltern didn't say, only that we'd find out when it was time for us to know."

"When's that gonna be?" Buttons asked. "The ponies demand—"

"They can demand all they want to, Sis," Cheff said. "It won't help them this time. But I promise you this: as soon as I know, the ponies will be advised."

Starry and Moka looked at each other, then turned to Buttons and nodded. Buttons nodded back. "The ponies say, that will be acceptable—just this once."

"Good!" Cheff laughed and rumpled her hair. "You know I'd never keep the ponies waiting needlessly."

"School," Sable murmured. "Meltern. FRM."

"Sable's right," Cheff said. "We promised Meltern not to ever mention the FRM at school. We'd better can it for now."

The bell rang, and we returned to our respective classrooms. For the next hour, I pretended to be interested in Mr. Rishten's lecture, but my mind was spinning through a maze of possibilities. Our first official FRM mission! What could it be? Another raid on the Iron Fortress? Another daring rescue? Perhaps from the Silver Palace this time?

Right before the noon bell rang, a messenger knocked on the classroom door, entered without waiting for an invitation, handed Mr. Rishten a small piece of paper, and left without a word.

Mr. Rishten peered at the paper over the top of his black-rimmed glasses, then glanced at me and Cheff. He put the paper face-down on his desk and resumed sipping his felmoss tea.

When the bell rang, Mr. Rishten said, "Birn, stay behind. You, too, Cheff. I have something to tell you. Come on up here." He looked at the message again. "It seems, boys, that you have been selected for a special work assignment. A temporary assignment. You are to be excused from school until next First Day. Ehem. This won't count against your school scores. In fact, according to this message, you are to receive extra credit and a commendation if you complete the work assignment successfully." He shook his head. "I don't know how you did it, boys, but this is a real privilege. Let's see, now, you are to report to one Mr. Z. Bonnovus at the Fellstone Labor Compound Materials Recovery and Recycling Center." He frowned. "I'm sorry, boys, but I don't have a clue where that is. Do you?"

"I do, sir," Cheff said. "It's the Labor Compound junkyard. And Mr. Bonnovus is old Zeek, who runs the place."

"I see," Mr. Rishten said. "Interesting."

"Excuse me, sir," I said, "but when are we to report?"

"When?" He studied the message again. "Why, right now! In fact, you're nearly late already. Well, don't just stand there, get moving!"

Cheff and I scrambled to round up our books and went out the door.

"One more thing, boys," Mr. Rishten called as we left. "Have a great time, do good work, and make me proud. I'm sure you will. I'll see you on First Day next week, and I'll expect a full report."

"Yes, sir," Cheff said. "Thank you, sir. We'll see you then."

"I'm going to put you on report! All of you!"

— 5 —

ZEEK

CHEFF TOOK OFF across the schoolyard in an unfamiliar direction. "Slow down, Cheff," I said. "My legs aren't anywhere near as long as yours."

"Best get moving, Old Son. You heard the man—we're nearly late as it is."

We hustled along a broad avenue through a section of the Labor Compound I'd never seen before. On the north side of the avenue, each huge block contained a single factory with dense, dark, sooty smoke belching from many smokestacks.

On the south side of the avenue were rows and rows of houses, much like our own. I wouldn't have thought it possible, but they seemed even dirtier and shabbier than ours.

Cheff said, "This is the oldest section of the Labor Compound, the first part Emperor Pallador built, almost a hundred years ago. Where we live, in the northeast quarter, is the newest." He smiled wryly. "Be glad you didn't get assigned here. It's a rough neighborhood."

At last, we came to a block that might once have been a factory—it was hard to tell. A dilapidated old wooden fence surround-

37

ed it. Through cracks in the boards, I saw heaps of junk and scrap metal piled high. Cheff turned left, northward, and I followed him to a partially open wire gate. We entered and followed a narrow dirt track with deep wheel ruts.

"I've been here before with Mid," Cheff said. "He comes sometimes to get parts for his… inventions. The office is right down here."

We wound our way through mountains of unidentifiable junk to a small, rickety, wooden shack with a stovepipe in one corner of the roof.

Cheff knocked on the door.

A gruff voice called out, "Come in, come in."

A huge Fruen, taller even than most men of his species, was refilling a teakettle at a rusty old sink. He had the characteristic Fruen white head-stripe and massive barrel chest, and an even bigger belly. He wore a pair of battered dark-green pants over a filthy, one-piece union suit, held up by greasy black suspenders. He had no shirt, and as he bent over the stove, I could tell by the color differential at his waistline that it had been some time since the union suit had been laundered. He sported a battered old black top hat, a once-elegant relic from a bygone era, and five days' growth of thick black whiskers, graying a little around the sides.

"Close the door, Cheff!" the Fruen roared. "Don't let the heat out. It's chilly today. Who's your friend? I don't recall seeing him before."

"I'm Birn Tylandine, but people call me Books."

"Nice to meet you, Books." Zeek offered me a giant paw and I shook it.

"Sit down at the table there, boys, and I'll fix you some delicious felmoss tea."

The old Fruen caught me glancing at Cheff.

"What? What is it? You *do* like felmoss tea, don't you? Of *course* you do!"

He poured us each a cup of the bitter brew. "Well? What are you waiting for? Drink it while it's hot!"

We each took a sip. I tried my best not to react to the bitter taste, but I guess it showed on my face.

"What's the matter? Too bitter for you? Hah! Don't tell me you want some *sugar*, like some namby-pamby schoolteacher, do you?"

Cheff and I exchanged another glance. Zeek couldn't possibly know about Mr. Rishten, could he?

"Of *course* you don't! Sugar is for sissies, right? Bitter is better, right? Of course right! The bitter brew is the better brew, the bitterest brew is the bestest brew. Remember that!"

"Yes, sir. I will." I took another sip and forced it down my throat.

"Come on, come on, drink up! There's plenty more where that came from." Zeek filled the kettle again and set it on the stove, then added a generous portion of dried felmoss. A bitter aroma filled the little shack. He pulled a little metal flask from his hip pocket and splashed some brown liquid into his own cup. "There! That's my secret ingredient. Makes it even more bitter." He turned to me. "What's that? You want some in your tea?"

I shook my head vigorously.

Zeek feigned extreme sadness. "Well, boy, I suppose it's for the best. You see, my secret ingredient is for grown-ups only. You'll have to wait a few more years. Too bad—it's exactly what you need to put some hair on your chest." He laughed out loud and punched me on the shoulder.

The three of us drank our tea in silence. Cheff and I sipped timidly at ours, while Zeek took huge swigs of his. He finished his cup and poured himself another, then he checked our cups, frowning at our lack of progress. After he finished his tea, he took a large timepiece from his front pocket and checked the time. I wondered what he was waiting for.

As I finished my first cup of tea, there came a knock at the door. Mid and Lery entered.

"Well, look who's here!" Zeek bellowed. "My old pal Mid!" He clapped Mid on the shoulder so hard that Mid nearly fell into Cheff's lap, then backed up a step and looked Lery over from head to toe. "And who's this, then? Another new pal? Nice to meet you, boy! I'm Zeek Bonnovus. Any pal of Mid is a pal of mine." He shook Lery's hand vigorously, then looked him over. "My, aren't you a tall one, especially for a Fessal lad. We don't see too many Fessals in the Labor Compound. Someday you'll have to tell me how you got here—I'm sure it's a marvelous story."

To my surprise, Lery shook Zeek's hand firmly. "I'm… I'm Lery."

"Lery, is it? Lery! A fine name! Well, come right in, Lery, and have some felmoss tea. I made a fresh pot."

Mid and Lery found a couple of empty crates, pulled them up to the table, and sat down.

Zeek bustled about, filling teacups for Mid and Lery. He refilled my cup, too, then sat down with us again.

Lery took a huge swallow of felmoss tea and sighed contentedly.

"Good, isn't it, Lery?" Zeek inquired.

Lery nodded.

Mid took an equally huge sip, but choked, hiccuped, and sneezed, spraying felmoss tea all over the table.

Zeek pretended not to notice. "Yes, extraordinarily fine tea!" He casually wiped the table with a filthy rag from his jacket pocket. "Sip it slowly, lad, sip it slowly. It takes time for the hair to grow."

Mid wiped his face with his sleeve. "Hair?"

Cheff murmured, "On your chest. The hair."

Mid looked at his own chest, then at Cheff, and raised his eyebrows.

Cheff looked away, smiling to himself.

There was another knock at the door, and in came Sable and Buttons. I almost fell out of my chair. What was going on here?

"Welcome, welcome," Zeek bellowed. "The more the merrier, right? You must be Miss Sable and Miss Buttons. Sit down, ladies, sit down. I'll get you some tea." Sable sat down next to Cheff, and Buttons came and sat next to me.

"Hi, Books!" Buttons said. "Are you surprised to see me? I'll bet you are. I'm sure surprised to see you." She took the ponies from her special pony backpack and arranged them on the table. "I couldn't find Cheff after school, but Sable said she'd walk me home. Except she had to run an errand first. I guess this is it! The errand, I mean."

"I guess so," I said. I gave each of the ponies a pat on the head. "Hi, Starry. Hi, Moka."

The ponies seemed pleased.

Zeek set yet another full teapot on the table. He poured Sable and Buttons a cup each, then scratched his head. He rummaged around his cupboard and found two tiny cups, then set one before each pony and filled them. "There! Try that, Miss Buttons. That'll put hair on your chest!"

Buttons took a sip of the tea, glanced sideways at the tuft of thick black hair erupting from the top of Zeek's union suit, then pulled the collar of her blouse open slightly and inspected her chest for hairs. She shook her head sadly at Starry and Moka, who seemed disappointed, too.

Zeek laughed and sat down with us. "Well, it seems we're all here. Let me introduce myself. I am Zeek Bonnovus, Salvage Operator Extraordinaire, at your service." He doffed his top hat and made a half-bow from his chair. "I am pleased to meet you all. I've known Mid for a while, of course—he gets parts from me sometimes." He took a deep breath and held it while he looked at each one of us. Then he let it out in a long, contented sigh. He put both hands on the table, leaned in close, and said quietly, "And have I got a work assignment for you!"

Zeek Bonnovus

— 6 —

SALVAGE OPERATION

"As you have likely deduced," Zeek continued, "I run the Fellstone Labor Compound's salvage operation. No doubt you have admired my many magnificent mountains of metal as you came up the path. I collect all the broken equipment from all the factories in the Compound and bring it all here. I save what can be saved, fix what can be fixed, and melt down the rest." He narrowed his eyes and looked at us intently. "It's an important operation, I assure you. Absolutely essential to the functioning of the Compound. From time to time, I receive a special assignment directly from the Silver Palace. And that's why you're here."

"If we're *all* here," Cheff said, "then this must be… *you* must be…" He stopped abruptly.

"That's right, Cheff," Buttons said, "I'll bet Mr. Bonnovus is an—"

Cheff cut her off with a warning glance, then warned the rest of us with his eyes.

Mid laughed. "Oh, stop worrying, Cheff. We all figured it out. This is our first official assignment—I mean, it's got to be, right?—which means that Zeek has to be—"

Zeek's heavy hand fell on Mid's shoulder. "Cheff is right, boy. Some things are better left unsaid. Especially in this place." He pointed at the ceiling of the shack, then at his ears, then put a finger to his lips.

Mid cleared his throat. "I was going to say, this must be our work assignment, and Mr. Zeek must be our boss."

Zeek laughed. "Quite right, Mr. Persil, quite right." He poured himself another mug of tea. "I'm going to be your boss for the next few days. For this special operation, I am going to need some extra help. And that is why I have these." He set five yellow cards on the table, "These are work passes for five helpers of my choice, to be selected at my discretion from the Labor Compound Advanced School and Regular School. The school gave me a list to choose from, and I picked you kids for your various… um… abilities. And best of all, I don't even have to pay you! Imagine that!"

Cheff frowned, but Zeek continued hastily, "Don't worry, Cheff. I *will* pay you, of course. Fair is fair, right? And pay is pay. In fact, I'll see to it that you get a bonus commensurate with the amount of salvage you collect. Okay?"

"Okay," Cheff said, still frowning. "Whatever you think is fair, sir."

"Good! That makes me happy." He looked us over again. "You all look like you could use some extra coin. Except you, Miss Sable, you look just fine."

Sable smiled.

"I picked each of you based on your qualifications. Sable, here, has some military training. I thought that might be helpful out in the wild where we're going. Speaking of which, Lery, I'm a bit concerned about your leg injury. I've noticed that you have a limp. Is that going to be a problem?"

"I don't… don't think… so…" Lery said. "Mid made me a… a brace. It helps… a lot." He pulled up his pant leg to reveal the brace and held it up for Zeek's inspection.

Zeek inspected it carefully. "You made this, Mid?"

Mid nodded.

"Ingenious design," Zeek said. "You think you'll be okay with that, Lery?"

"I'm… sure," Lery said. "I've been practicing."

"Fair enough," Zeek said. "But if it gives you trouble, let me know straightaway, okay? Promise?"

"I promise," Lery said.

Meanwhile, Starry the pony had carefully counted the people around the table. "Excuse me, Mr. Bonnovus, sir, if you don't mind," Buttons said. "You said you have five passes, but Starry counts six of us."

Zeek looked at her kindly. "But, Miss Buttons, I told you that the passes were for Advanced and Regular school students. Are you in Advanced School or Regular School?"

Buttons hung her head. "No, sir, I'm in Basic School, but—"

"Well, there you are, then. I'm sorry."

"But—"

"Quiet, Sis," Cheff said.

"But I'll be in Advanced School next year!"

"Sis, please."

"I don't care!" She stood up and stamped a foot. "This is *so* unfair. If I was old enough to go to the Iron F—"

Cheff jumped up and clamped his hand over her mouth. "Buttons! That's enough! Just because you took a *field trip*"—he glared at her meaningfully—"last month doesn't mean—"

Buttons' eyes went wide, and she stopped struggling.

"All right, now, Sis, sit down and behave yourself."

Buttons squirmed a little under Cheff's hand but allowed him to put her back in the chair. Tears of fury welled up in her eyes. "It isn't *fair*," she said.

Zeek narrowed his eyes and glared at Buttons. "So, little girl, you're going to be a troublemaker, eh? I figured as much. Hmm…" He stroked the stubble on his chin. "I know your type. Let me guess: If you can't come with us, you're going to do something stupid and dangerous, right? Lie, maybe? Try to follow your brother? Is that right?"

Sable smiled, Mid laughed out loud, Lery studied the ceiling, and Cheff forced his grin into a straight face behind his hand. I merely sat there feeling sorry for Buttons.

Buttons lowered her eyes, and the two tears ran down. "I'm sorry, Mr. Bonnovus. I promise I won't do that this time. I worry about Cheff, that's all."

Zeek pulled the filthy rag from his pocket and offered it to Buttons, who took it and wiped her eyes, leaving two dirty streaks on her cheeks. "I understand, Miss Buttons. Of course you do. It's good that you care for your brother and your other friends, too— oh, what's this?" Another yellow card fell out of the handkerchief onto the table in front of Buttons. "Whatever could this be?" Zeek picked it up and examined it. "Why, it seems to be a working pass for one exceptional Basic School student. I wonder who that is? There's a name on it. Let me see, 'Mellabee'—oh, too bad, Miss Buttons. It's for someone else—"

Buttons leaped from her chair and threw her arms around Zeek's neck. "Oh, thank you, Mr. Zeek, thank you! I promise I'll be careful and do whatever you say."

Zeek took her gently, but firmly, by the shoulders and held her at arm's length. His eyes burned into hers. "Yes, Miss Mellabee 'Buttons' Karfendek, you will. And if I hear otherwise from anyone, you go straight home. Understand?"

Buttons said, "Yes, sir, I understand."

Zeek's voice softened. "I'm sorry for teasing you, Miss Buttons, but I needed to emphasize that it is an *extra special privilege* for you to be going with the older kids. It took some extra doing, but

I got permission for you to go along, mostly because the school feels you're too little to be left home alone all day while Cheff is gone. Also, a certain acquaintance of mine, and of yours, whose name begins with an M, said that your... *field trip...* might not have been successful without you. But, I must say, the way you reacted just now makes me wonder if I did the right thing. I think you almost said something about your field trip that you might have regretted later." He pointed at the ceiling again.

Buttons stared at the table. "Yes, sir, you're right. I promise I'll be much more careful from now on."

"See that you are." He smiled and let her go. "There will be other salvage operators there, and they will all have extra help, too. It's a big project. Discretion is absolutely essential. You might even say that discretion could mean life or death."

Zeek let that sink in while he poured himself another cup of tea. "There are other conditions, Miss Buttons: first and foremost, you do everything I tell you without question or hesitation. Second, if you're not where I can see you, you're where Cheff or Sable can see you. No exceptions. Do you understand?"

"Yes, sir, Mr. Bonnovus, I understand. And I'll make sure the ponies understand, too."

"Good, you do that. I'm counting on you to take this assignment absolutely seriously." He waved a meaty finger in front of Starry's muzzle, then Moka's. "I'm counting on you both, Ponies. You must listen carefully to Cheff and Sable and do exactly as they tell you. Understand?"

The ponies nodded somberly. They understood.

"Good. Now, let me tell you a little about the assignment." He rummaged around in a drawer, then spread a large piece of rough, brown paper on the table. With the stub of a pencil, he drew a large square in the lower left-hand corner. "This is the Labor Compound, where we are, up on this hill. See? Down the hill to the southwest are the docks. Now, if you go north from the docks, along the bay, what will you find?" He drew a squiggly line from the docks northward.

"Fel Village, sir, the little fishing village," Cheff said.

Zeek raised his eyebrows. "That's right. Don't tell me how you know that." He continued drawing the shoreline, which turned eastward, curved gently toward the north, then turned sharply eastward again, making a bump that stuck out into the water. He put an X on the tip of the bump.

Sable said, "Shipwreck Point."

"Correct, Miss Sable. This bump is called Shipwreck Point. For hundreds of years, ships have run aground on the rocks of Shipwreck Point, hence the name. There's a narrow passage *here*— Miss Sable?"

"Rekkam Channel."

"Yes, Rekkam Channel, named after the old Barnost Rekkam, the first ship captain who lost his ship there, between Shipwreck Point and The Great Stone of Fel, where the lighthouse is." He drew a little lighthouse across the bay from Shipwreck Point. "The Fellstone Light is supposed to warn ships of the dangers."

Sable said, "Currents. Treacherous."

"Especially during spring tides and storms." Zeek sighed. "I'm sad to say that it happened again, only two days ago, in that big storm we had. A freighter, the Star of the East, got caught in the currents and ran aground on the rocks of Shipwreck Point. It carried a large cargo, mostly ore and lumber from Tumberland. Much of the cargo washed away in the storm, and I'm sure that, by now, looters have carried away most of what remained. However, the ship itself is valuable. It has a steel hull and steel decks, plus a huge amount of copper plumbing, instruments, valves, motors, and so on. Emperor Pallador wants to conserve as many of the resources as possible. I am one of several salvage operators who will melt her down. We've each been assigned our own part of the ship to dismantle. Our first job is to remove the most valuable parts before the Army Engineers start cutting the hull apart, so time is of the essence."

"Great," Cheff said. "When do we start?"

Zeek grinned. "I always love a man of enthusiasm. We'll leave in a few hours. I'd like to get there in time to make camp before dark."

"Camp? We'll be… camping?" Lery asked. "I like… camping. We went camping, sometimes, when… when I was… in the… the…"

Cheff touched Lery's arm and shook his head.

Zeek raised his eyebrows but made no comment.

"Hurray!" Buttons said. "We're going camping!" The ponies gave each other a high-five.

Mid said, "Excellent! I have a few gadgets that I made precisely *for* camping. They're in need of a field trial."

"Gadgets?" Buttons said. "We like gadgets! What are they?"

"You'll see," Mid said, "all in good time."

Sable smiled a little behind her long hair.

Zeek laughed. "Fine, fine, bring your gadgets and try them out." He stood up. "So, now, go home. Pack whatever you think you'll need for a few days. One bag per person, right? Tell your families"—he glanced at Sable—"or whomever, that you'll be gone for a few days, and that I'll try to have you back by evening on Sixth Day, er, I mean, Pallador's Day of Reflection. That'll give you plenty of time to rest up before school the next day, okay?"

"Okay," Cheff said.

"Be back here in"—he checked his timepiece—"three hours. That should be plenty of time. Don't worry about packing food— there will be plenty to eat, courtesy of Pallador's Corps of Engineers. They run the camp kitchen. Okay?"

"Okay," Cheff said again.

"Then get moving! I have plenty to do to get myself ready." He stood up and clapped his hands. "Go-go-go!"

Operation Lockdown

— **7** —

WILLAM THE WHEEZER

ALL SIX OF us made it back to Zeek's well before the three hours were up. Cheff had his utility pouch at his hip, Mid had his tech kit, Buttons' pony pack was bulging, and I had a little backpack Cheff had loaned me. Lery had a small, brown, canvas bag with a thin shoulder strap, plus his enormous pipe wrench hooked to his belt, as usual, and a blanket rolled up under his arm.

Buttons poked around the edges of one of the giant heaps of scrap metal. From time to time, she'd stoop, pick up an object, and put it into one of her pockets.

"What are you doing, Sis?"

"Nothing."

Cheff shrugged. "Well, don't get too dirty too soon, okay?"

"Okay, Cheff," she said, but it was already too late—dark smudges covered her blouse and pants.

"How did Aunt Dee take the news about the salvage assignment?" I asked Cheff. "And about Buttons coming with us?"

"Not well, not well at all. It took some convincing that it was merely a routine work detail and that I would look after Buttons. She made Buttons promise to obey me and stay in my sight."

I chuckled. "Sounds like Aunt Dee and Zeek would get along. My mom was pretty worried, too. I told her it was mandatory, which it is, but that only made her more anxious. I said I'd ask Zeek to stop by if he could and give her an update."

Sable came in wearing her mission outfit. I'd only seen her wear it one other time, the night we rescued Uncle Karf from the Iron Fortress. It was all black, with a utility belt full of mysterious hooks, clamps, blades, and other items. Her long, black hair hung in a ponytail fastened with a black velvet band. She looked ready for nearly anything. I suddenly envied Sable her military training.

Cheff poked his head into Zeek's office but no one was there. We followed the sound of a steam engine past the office through the maze of scrap heaps to a large, metal workshop. The steam engine belonged to an ancient flatbed steam truck.

The old steam truck seemed to be made largely of rust and baling wire. It shook and shuddered and produced great dense clouds of steam and smoke. From time to time, it emitted the oddest wheezing sound. Mid rubbed his hands together gleefully. A cranky old steam engine was exactly his kind of thing.

Zeek stood behind the cab next to the vertical steam engine with its massive twin flywheels, shoveling coal into the firebox.

In the back of the truck, his enormous paws hanging over the edge, was the ugliest dog I had ever seen in my life. He was a weird brown-and-orange brindle pattern. His right eye was blue, his left eye was brown. One fuzzy ear hung down, the other stood straight up and had a rather large notch missing from it, no doubt the result of a canine disagreement of some sort. His large, slobbery jowls were parted in the middle by a snaggle-toothed grin. As we approached, he sniffed the air, then tentatively wagged his kinked tail, which appeared to have been broken in several places.

"Puppy!" Buttons yipped and started for the truck.

"Wait, Sis," Cheff called. "We don't know if he's friendly."

He grabbed for the back of her jacket, but it was too late—Buttons already had her arms around the homely brute and was explaining to him who we were and why we had come.

The dog's tail wagged a mile a minute as he licked Buttons' face, then carefully examined Starry and Moka, whom he apparently found agreeable. He gave each pony a wet lick, then heaved himself up into a sitting position and barked loudly one time.

Zeek looked up and waved. "Ah, children, you're here early. Wonderful, wonderful! We can get an early start. You know what that means, eh, children? We'll be first in the chow line! Did I tell you that Pallador's Corps of Engineers would be feeding us? A feast, that's what we'll be having. A feast, I tell you!" He patted his rotund belly cheerfully.

He climbed down from the truck's bed. "I see you've met Pally already. Well, Pally, what do you think? Will these children be good helpers?" He scratched Pally's ears roughly. Pally wagged even harder and licked Zeek's hand. "Pally thinks you'll be great helpers!"

"Is he named Pally because he's your pal?" Buttons asked.

"He's my pal all right, but that's not how he got his name." He whispered in Buttons' ear, "'Pally' is short for 'Palladog.'"

"Palladog!" Button clapped her hands, then stopped abruptly. "Hey, that's a lot like Emperor Palla—"

"Shhh!" Zeek put a finger to his lips. "We wouldn't want anyone to get the wrong idea, now, would we?" He winked at Buttons.

"We sure wouldn't!" Buttons said and winked back at Zeek, which made him laugh from somewhere way down deep inside.

"Here, give me your gear, we'll stow it in one of these side cabinets. Good. Now, help me put the stake sides on the truck bed."

When all the sides were in place, Zeek said, "Okay, children, I think he's ready."

"Who's ready?" Cheff asked.

"Willam, here." Zeek patted the truck's front fender lovingly. 'Willam the Wheezer.' That's his name. He's a good old boy. He and I have been through the wars together, haven't we, Willam?"

Buttons raised one eyebrow and tugged on Cheff's jacket sleeve. "He's talking to his truck! Do you think it answers him?"

Sable said, "You already know the answer." She reached over and patted Starry.

"Do you think he was actually in the wars?" Mid whispered to Cheff. "I didn't think Zeek was that old."

"It's an expression, Old Son," Cheff whispered back. "It only means they've been through a lot together."

"Yes, that's right," Zeek agreed, as though Cheff and Mid hadn't been whispering. "Willam and I have been together a long time." He patted Willam's fender again. "Well, what are you waiting for, children? Climb in! The girls and Books in front, and the big fellows in the back seat." He walked around to the driver's side.

Mid smiled wryly. He mumbled, "Nothing wrong with his hearing, anyway."

Zeek called across the cab of the old truck, "My eyesight is pretty good, too. Now, hop in!"

Buttons giggled.

I don't know what Willam was originally built for, but he seemed the perfect truck for Zeek. Four persons—five in a pinch, or even more if they were skinny enough—would fit in each of the cab's front and rear seats. Behind the cab, the venerable vertical steam engine stood proudly, belching clouds of black coal smoke. Next came the water tank and the coal bin. The cargo area boasted a hand-operated crane and a large wooden chest full of ropes, pulleys, and other gear. Willam's reinforced rear axle could support heavy loads. A cargo rack on top of the cab offered additional light-cargo storage.

We piled in. Buttons sat next to Zeek. Next came Sable, then me next to the window. In the rear, Lery sat behind Zeek, Mid was in the middle, and Cheff was behind me, next to his window.

Buttons took Starry and Moka from their backpack and arranged them on the dashboard. "They like to see where they're going. And so do I." She strained to peer over the dashboard. "But I can't, not very well, anyway."

"Is that so?" Zeek said. He reached under his seat, pulled out a grimy, dark-green woolen blanket and folded it several times. "Here, sit on this. Is that better? You can see now? Good. Okay, children, are you ready? Let's go!"

He put on a pair of old leather gloves and turned the steam valve, then put Willam into gear. Willam lurched forward, wheezed desperately a few times, and slowly began to roll.

"Here, give me your hand," Zeek said to Buttons. "You can help me with the shifter, okay?"

Buttons glowed and put her hand on the gearshift lever.

"When I tell you, pull the shifter all the way down, like this. See? The gears are like a big H. First gear, in the upper left of the H, which we are in now, is only for getting started. When we have a little speed—I'll tell you when—you pull the shifter straight down to the bottom left of the H. Third gear is at the top right, so you'll have to cross over in the middle. Don't worry, I'll help you when the time comes. And finally, when we're out of town and out on the open road, you'll pull the shifter straight down the right side of the H, and we'll be in fourth gear. You got all that?"

Buttons frowned. "I think so. What's the little 'R' off to the side?"

"That's for Reverse." Zeek laughed. "It's easy, you'll see. Besides, I think Willam likes you."

We turned out of the junkyard onto the broad avenue that ran through the Labor Compound. When Willam had gathered a little speed, Zeek said, "Now!"

Buttons pulled as hard as she could, but the shifter wouldn't budge. Zeek put his enormous paw over her little hand and pulled together with her. The shifter slid down into second gear. Buttons beamed again. "I did it!"

"That is the girl!" Zeek roared. "I think you're getting the hang of it."

Buttons kept her hand on the shifter, even though it wasn't time to change gears yet. The ponies looked proud.

We chugged and wheezed our way to the central avenue of the Labor Compound then turned south. We passed the school and approached the main gate. There was one other truck ahead of us, a routine supply truck. A guard checked the driver's papers, peeked into the truck's bed, then waved him through. After the gate closed again, the guard stood facing us with his arms crossed, blocking our path.

I stuck my head out of the window to get a good look at him. "Oh, no!" I said. "It's Manyard!"

Sable grabbed my shoulder and pulled my head back inside. "Head down," she murmured, then stared at her lap. I lowered my head, too, as did the rest of us.

"Andaran's bones!" Zeek growled. "Just what we need! Buttons, hide the ponies, quick! Children, sit up, sit still, fold your hands, eyes in your laps. Don't move a muscle or say a word."

Zeek nudged Willam up to the guard shack. Out of the corner of my eye, I saw Mid stiffen and his fists clench. Cheff leaned over and whispered, "Easy, Old Son. Today isn't the day."

Mid nodded tersely and froze solid, head down.

The guard, Manyard, swaggered around the front of Willam and stuck his ugly Fessal face into the cab. He looked us over, then barked at Zeek, "What's this all about, Bonnovus?"

"Special work assignment, Officer Manyard, sir. I have the papers here, all in order."

"I'll be the judge of that!" He snatched the papers from Zeek's hand and examined them minutely, once, twice, and a third time. He seemed disappointed that he could find no fault with them. He flung them back into the cab and growled, "Make sure you're back by evening on Day Six. If you come in the day after, I'll have you shot."

"Yes, Officer Manyard," Zeek said meekly. "Thank you, sir."

"Roll out!"

The gate slid open. Zeek didn't wait to be told twice. He put Willam into gear and eased him toward the road. The great iron gate clanged shut behind us.

"Phew! I don't like that man!" Zeek said. "And from the looks of things, you don't either, Mid. Have you had trouble with him before?"

Mid was still rigid so Cheff answered quietly, "Manyard sold Mid's little sister to a rich Fessal woman when they first arrived at the Labor Compound. He hasn't seen her since."

"I see." Zeek pondered. "Mid, you did well to keep still. I can't begin to imagine how hard that was for you. Don't worry, boy, Manyard's time will come. I'll make a mental note that he's due for some… special attention."

The tone of Zeek's voice made me shiver. I didn't know what 'special attention' meant, but I was glad it was Manyard who'd be getting it, and not me.

We came to a stop where the Labor Compound's driveway met the main road, directly across from the bus stop. "Look!" I said. "There's Brex, and Tocette, and four of her Bluebands!" The six of them waited at the bus stop. "Where do you suppose they're going at this time of day?"

Cheff said, "Maybe they have some special patrol duty in Old City."

"Maybe," Mid said. "Hard to tell. Well, I won't miss them for a few days, that's for sure."

"For sure," Buttons agreed. Her hand was back on the shifter. As Zeek urged Willam onto the road, she pulled back hard and put Willam into second gear. "I *am* getting the hang of it!" she said, smiling. "Hurray!"

"…the ugliest dog I had ever seen in my life."

— 8 —

LOCKDOWN

THE LABOR COMPOUND looked much bigger from the outside. This was only the second time I'd ever seen the outside of the Compound in the daylight, and the first time I was on a bus heading southward away from the Labor Compound toward New City. This time, we turned right on the main road and navigated the opposite direction, due north, with the Labor Compound's massive wall on our right. I felt the eyes of the guards in the towers follow us as we drove past. I shuddered.

At last, we reached the Compound's northwest corner. Instead of turning right toward Old City, Zeek kept Willam pointed northward, down the long hill to sea level. Blocks and blocks of ruined homes and businesses filled both sides of the road. Unlike the ruins closer to town, no squatters lived here.

Directly north of the Labor Compound, we came to an IID roadblock, complete with sandbags and machine guns. The IID was the Imperial Intelligence Division, easily identified by their all-black uniforms. We waited as the agents examined our papers and inspected every inch of Willam, including the cabinets below the bed. An agent with a mirror on a stick checked the underside of the bed. Finally, we were allowed to pass through.

"That's new," Cheff said. "There was never a roadblock there before."

"It's part of the lockdown," Zeek said. "It's only been there a few days, maybe a week. And that was the easy inspection, going *out* of Fellstone City. They check twice as hard on the way in." He patted the special pony-carrying backpack. "The ponies can return to the dashboard now, Miss Buttons. I think they'll be safe for the rest of the trip."

"I was afraid the guards at the Iron Fortress would report us," Buttons said. "The ones we clobbered when we escaped. The ponies were worried."

"The ponies don't have to worry, Sis," Cheff said. "There's no way those two guards reported that they were bested by some kids."

Sable said quietly, "Meltern."

"That's right, Buttons," I said. "Meltern told us that the report stated fifty to one hundred armed men."

"Yeah," Mid said sullenly. "That's us. All one hundred of us."

"I'm sure you'll be fine, children," Zeek said. "If anyone was looking for you, I'd have heard by now. But keep your eyes open for IID agents or their Blueband snoops."

Once we were out of sight of the roadblock, Zeek showed us a small device, a little metal cylinder about the size of the palm of his hand with a bright red light on top. He flipped a switch and in a few seconds the red light turned to green. "Good! No bugs! I check every time—you never know."

Mid's eyes gleamed. "Wow! That's fantastic! Where'd you get that? Did you make it?"

"I didn't make it—that kind of stuff isn't my bailiwick. I got it from… well, let's say I got it from some friend of a mutual friend of ours, who happens to run a guest house in Old City."

"We know there are listening devices in the Labor Compound," Mid said. "But how could there be one in a moving vehicle, without wires?"

"Something new, I'm told," Zeek said. "It's called a 'wire recorder.' Can't say I understand it, but it records conversations. If we had one, an IID agent would pick it up when Willam is parked for the night."

"That's amazing!" Mid said. "I'd sure like to get my hands on one of those."

"I'll keep my eyes open," Zeek said, "and let you know if I find one." He turned halfway around in his seat. "Children," he said, "now that we're well away from the Labor Compound and Old City, and certified recorder-free, I can speak freely. Cheff was quite right. I am not only Zeek, Salvage Operator Extraordinaire, but also Zeek the intrepid FRM agent. And this is not only a work assignment, it's also your first official FRM mission. You did well not to blurt it out in my shack, though you had me worried briefly. Especially you, Miss Buttons. This detector only works on the wire recorders. It's useless against wired bugs."

Buttons looked up at him solemnly, eyes wide. "*You're* an FRM agent? A *real* FRM agent?"

Zeek laughed. "Yes, I am. But don't look so serious—I've been told that you are all sworn agents, too."

Cheff spoke up from the back seat. "Yes, sir, we are. After the— I'm sorry, sir, but I don't know how much I'm supposed to say."

"That's good, Cheff. Caution is always in order. I have been briefed on your last mission. Your *un*official mission. Not the details, of course, but the basics. I know that you and your... associates... rescued your uncle Karf from the Iron Fortress and took him back to Meltern's Guest House, all in one night." He shook his head. "Remarkable. It's never been done before. No one even imagined it was possible. I knew your uncle Karf. He was a fine man and a good agent." Buttons looked up sharply. "*Is* a fine man. I've been told he's alive and healing well. Sorry, young lady—I didn't mean to alarm you."

Buttons wiped a tear from her eye. "Can... can we see him?"

Zeek frowned. "Of course not! You know better than that! Besides, he's not in Fellstone City anymore, or so I've been told. But even if he were, to see him could cost both your lives and maybe more."

"Yes, sir," Buttons said. "I know. It's… well…" Her tears started again.

"There, now," Zeek said, and patted her tentatively on the knee. "It's hard, I know. These are hard times. We must be strong."

"Yes, sir," Buttons said again and wiped her eyes with the back of her hand. "I'll do my best, sir."

"Of course you will, Miss Buttons, of course you will." Zeek cleared his throat. "Now, speaking of hard times, I'm not sure you all realize how hard it's become since your, er, little 'field trip.'"

"Meltern told me a few things," Cheff said, "but not much. We are pretty isolated inside the Labor Compound."

"Well, I'll fill you in. The situation in Fellstone City is the reason for your first FRM assignment. You know the entire city has been under lockdown since the night of your raid on the Fortress."

We nodded—that much we knew.

"But you may not know the extent of the lockdown. Travel has been severely restricted. That's why Manyard checked us so carefully today. There'll be another check when we arrive at the shipwreck, and if they decide we've taken too long, they'll take Willam apart bolt by bolt and inspect everything.

"It's like that everywhere. All security personnel—soldiers, guards, even the Bluebands—are doing double duty. Rewards have been posted for any sort of information and greedy tipsters have caused the false arrest of parents, children, relatives, neighbors, and, naturally, the tipsters' personal enemies. You get the picture.

"Both market districts, Old City and New City, are restricted to three hours of operation per day. Fights have broken out due to the long lines and hoarding. There have even been a few people killed in Old City market, over a bag of potatoes." He sighed and shook his head. "I'm afraid this lockdown is bringing out the worst in our people.

"There's more: Since the potato shooting, the lockdown has become more severe. Ships are being held in the bay for inspection, not allowed to dock, so food supplies are scarce. There have been looting and vandalism, especially in New City. The guards there have orders to shoot looters on sight and have done so. Old City residents who work in New City have been compelled to stay in New City, leaving their families in Old City to fend for themselves. There's a strict curfew. Violators can expect severe beatings at best, but more likely they'll be shot. A week ago, the Emperor ordered a complete blockade of Fellstone City and other major cities. It's a bad time for Fellstone City, my young friends."

Cheff looked horrified. "We caused all that? But... we were only trying to save my Uncle..."

"I know, lad, I know. And I'm not saying you shouldn't have, either. Don't worry, it isn't entirely your fault. The situation in Fellstone was ripe for some sort of crisis. Your little escapade was merely the trigger. It was bound to happen sooner or later. For that matter, it's happened many times before, here in Fellstone and in other places, too. It's just part of life under our Beloved Emperor.

"It does, however, emphasize one point that all of you *must* take to heart: FRM agents never, ever, act independently. We always act on orders that come from higher up. The word is that Madame Entigy—you know who she is?"

Mid said, "Meltern told us she's the head of the FRM. In fact, he said that it was Madame Entigy's idea to make us official FRM agents."

"That's right. Well, the word is that Madame Entigy has an entire department devoted to strategic planning. Before any assignment is given, they consider the effects of the operation on the whole continent of Andaran. There are agents everywhere, you know, in all the big cities. So—"

"So no more acting on our own," Cheff said. "Got it."

"Good. Now it's time for us to take a little break."

When we reached the bottom of the long hill, on the outskirts of Fel Village, Zeek turned right onto a dirt track. I wondered where we were going—there was certainly no shipwreck in this direction. The dirt track turned out to be the driveway of a small vegetable farm, invisible from the main road, hidden in a cluster of tall trees. He stopped Willam in front of the farmhouse and tooted Willam's whistle politely a few times. A Lildur woman came out to the porch, waved, then disappeared back inside. A tall, thin Lildur man appeared, buttoning his worn, gray shirt.

Zeek waved at the man and climbed down from Willam's cab. "Ho, Klesky, what's new? Got any scrap metal for me? You do? Well, you'll have to keep it for a little while longer—I'm on a job today. Maybe I can pick it up on the way home." He clapped Klesky on the back. "Good to see you, man. It's been a while. Say, would it be okay if I tanked up while I'm here? I have a ways to go yet."

Klesky nodded his assent and said something to Zeek in a voice too low for us to hear. Zeek nodded back and Klesky went back into the house. Zeek shouted to us, "Okay, children. Climb out. If anyone needs to use the necessary, it's out back. Otherwise, stay within sight of Willam, okay? Mid, can you and Lery give me a hand?"

We climbed down from Willam's cab and stretched our legs. I took a deep breath. The air smelled wonderful. It was great to be out of the sooty, smoky air of the Labor Compound. Pally jumped down from the truck bed and made the rounds of every tree and bush on the farm. Sable took Buttons by the hand to a small pasture where a little gray donkey was contentedly munching thistles. Starry and Moka seemed genuinely delighted to meet a fellow equine. They rubbed noses with the donkey, then helped Buttons pull up handfuls of green grass, which the donkey accepted politely before returning to his delicious thistles.

Cheff and I followed Mid and Lery to where Mr. Klesky was hooking up a hose to a hand pump. Without a word, Lery took the other end of the hose and climbed up into the engine compartment. Mid climbed up after him.

Lery looked around the engine, then hooked up the hose to a fitting on the top of the water tank. He waved at Zeek, who began working the pump handle. After a while, Cheff took over the pumping.

Meanwhile, Mid had opened the door of the firebox on Willam's vertical boiler, and was shoveling in some coal from the bin. I took a turn pumping.

Zeek wiped his forehead with his greasy handkerchief. "Well, you are certainly a handy bunch! I can see I made a good choice when I picked you."

Lery waved and shouted, "Full!" He disconnected the hose from Willam's tank and handed it down to me. I dragged the end back to the pump, where Cheff was disconnecting the other end. Together, Cheff and I coiled the hose neatly.

Mrs. Klesky came out carrying a tray of iced felmoss tea with three young girls in tow. The youngest girl clung tightly to her mother's dress. "Come on, children! Have some cold tea."

The ponies said goodbye to their new donkey friend and Sable and Buttons came over. We each accepted a frosty glass, cubes of ice tinkling a cheerful tune. I wondered how in Andaran Mrs. Klesky found ice cubes way out here on the farm, but I didn't ask.

Buttons took a tentative sip from her glass, then drank heartily. "It's great!"

Mrs. Klesky laughed. "Yes, I make it with honey from our own bees. Have been, ever since we found out about the—"

Mr. Klesky shook his head slightly.

Mrs. Klesky nodded almost imperceptibly. "What I mean to say is that this here felmoss tea is plenty sweet, which should please everyone, except maybe some *real* men I could mention."

Everyone laughed at Zeek, who said, "What Mrs. Klesky means is that it's perfectly safe for us to drink the iced tea—no need to worry about you-know-what." He drained half his glass in one big swallow. "Ahhh, Mother Klesky, that is perfection! Thank you so much!"

The oldest Klesky girl, about my age, stepped out from behind her mother carrying a sack. She deliberately selected a big, red apple for each of us. She gave me mine last. "I'm Aldina. I saved the biggest one for you," she said, then looked up at me. "I *like* you—you're *cute!*" She turned and ran into the house.

Everyone burst into laughter. I blushed so hard I thought my face was going to fall off.

Zeek said, "Well, go ahead, boy, take a bite. It's not every day one receives the Giant Apple of Cuteness!" Everyone laughed again, and I blushed even harder, though I wouldn't have thought it possible. The apple was crunchy and sweet. "It's delicious!" I said. "Tell Aldina 'thank you' for me."

Mrs. Klesky said, "That's about the freshest apple you'll ever eat. The girls picked them from that tree right over there while you were filling up… that." She stabbed a forefinger at Willam.

Mrs. Klesky said goodbye and went back into the house, followed by the two younger girls. Then Mr. Klesky came out again. Zeek said, "All right, children. Mount up! Time to roll."

We clambered back into Willam, happily munching our apples. Pally leaped back into the truck bed. Out the window, I saw Zeek and Mr. Klesky talking seriously. Mr. Klesky slipped a small envelope to Zeek so skillfully that I nearly missed it. Zeek, in turn, pressed a little bag into Mr. Klesky's hand. Mr. Klesky tried to refuse, but it's not easy to refuse Zeek Bonnovus, Salvage Operator Extraordinaire.

Zeek clapped him on the back so hard he almost fell over. "So long, Klesky. I'll see you another time. And say goodbye to that women's club of yours!" Zeek climbed up into the driver's seat and opened the steam valve. "Are you ready, Buttons?"

Buttons pushed the shifter into first gear, and off we went down the bumpy driveway back to the main road.

"…the guard stood facing us with his arms crossed, blocking our path."

— 9 —

FIRST OFFICIAL MISSION

ONLY A FEW miles farther north we slowed down to enter Fel Village, a sleepy little settlement built around a large marina full of fishing boats. The only other time I'd been here, we'd sneaked through town late at night and 'borrowed' a steam launch, after nearly being eaten by a gigantic dog named Porgo.

"No roadblock here," Buttons observed.

"Fel Village is too small for the Emperor to bother with," Zeek explained. "It's not exactly a hotbed of revolutionary activity." He laughed.

Willam was the only steam vehicle in sight. Barefoot children and skinny dogs played in the streets and on the docks. Only the main street sported cobblestones. The side streets were little more than dirt tracks. Rows of colorful fishing boats tied to the docks made bright rainbows on the bay. A few fishermen mended their nets in small groups, chatting and sipping cool drinks. Across from the docks, the marketplace was closing for the day. The sun would soon set behind the Theva Mountains west of Fellstone Bay.

Zeek slowed Willam to a stop and hopped out. "Stay put, children. You too, Pally. I'll be right back." He crossed the street and spoke briefly with a man at one of the market stalls. The man started slicing a loaf of bread.

Zeek came back and climbed into the driver's seat. "Wait until you taste this, children. Old Marky makes the best fish sandwiches you've ever had in your life. You'll see! I hope you like fish sandwiches, yes?"

Mid looked a little green—he wasn't a big fish fan—but the rest of us nodded. We hadn't had much lunch today—we'd been too busy getting ready for the trip.

After a few minutes, Old Marky, an aging Lora with a wooden leg, limped to my window, walking stick in one hand, and handed me a grease-stained sack. "Fresh off the boat," he said. "A beautiful Solva fish caught by Rombi this morning and slow-roasted over charcoal only an hour ago. Nothing like it!" Old Marky tossed some scraps into the truck bed for Pally, who snarfled them up eagerly.

"Thank you, sir. I'm sure we'll enjoy them." At the sound of my voice, a huge yellow dog darted out of the marketplace, jumped up, put his paws on the side of the truck right under my window, and barked furiously. It was Porgo! I was sure he recognized my scent.

I snatched the bag away from the window and tried to slide it closed, but it was stuck, and wouldn't budge. Porgo continued barking maniacally and snapping at me with his slavering jaws. In the back of the truck, Pally commenced barking furiously at Porgo.

"Down, Porgo, down boy!" Old Marky was trying in vain to get a grip on Porgo's collar. "Stop it! Stop it at once, I say." Porgo paid no attention to Old Marky. He kept barking and leaping up at me. In desperation, Old Marky whacked Porgo on the backside with his walking stick. "I said stop it, Porgo! That's no way to treat a customer. Get on home, go on, get!"

Porgo yelped, tucked his tail between his legs, and slunk off through the marketplace, whimpering.

Pally glowed with pride for having warded off the intruder.

Old Marky shook his head. "I'm sorry, Zeek, I don't know what got into him. Porgo belongs to Syrsa, the fisherman. Porgo won't get on Syrsa's boat, so he keeps me company all day while Syrsa is out fishing. He's usually friendly with everyone, especially customers. I can't imagine what that was all about. You ever been to Fel Village before, young feller?"

"No, sir," I lied, "never." I didn't like to lie, but in this case, it seemed prudent.

"How about any of the rest of you? No? Curious." He shook his head again. "Well, who can know what a dog has on his mind, eh? Dogs do get notiony sometimes. Enjoy your sandwiches, kids. So long, Zeek. See you next time." He gave us a wave, then limped back to his stall, his walking stick clattering on the cobblestones.

Zeek opened the steam valve and Willam the Wheezer groaned northward once more. When we were clear of Fel Village, Zeek turned to us. "Now, where was I? Let me see, now. I told you about the lockdown, right, and I was about to tell you… what was it? Oh, yes, I remember. How the lockdown is the reason behind your first official mission.

"You see, children, the report you brought us about the jexan was important, far more important than you might imagine. The FRM has been gathering information about jexan for years, with little success. We knew it was getting into the food supply, but we didn't know how, when, or where. We knew it was making the people of Fellstone complacent and, of course, we tried to analyze the food, but we never had any pure samples to work with.

"When you children told Meltern how the jexan was being added to ordinary items in our food supply, it was a major breakthrough. When Meltern learned that it was a white powder, he had his men gather samples of every kind of foodstuff he could think of made with anything white, like flour or sugar. He sent a courier north to Tumberland with those samples and instructions to have them analyzed in the FRM laboratory there. The lab was to send the results back to us by that same courier, which they did. The courier left Tumberland a few days later. Understand so far?"

Cheff asked, "Why has it taken so long for the courier to arrive? Did he run into trouble?"

"No," Zeek said, "but he's about to, and that's where you come in. We received a message from Madame Entigy herself about a week ago. The lab results regarding the jexan are significant, you see. They may even be crucial for changing Fellstone City's—never mind, you don't need to know about that part of things. Not yet, anyway. It's enough for you to know that the results are highly important."

Mid asked, "Why didn't the lab guys simply tell Madame Entigy?"

Zeek smiled. "Excellent question, young Mr. Persil. Always thinking, you are. That's what I like best about you—your analytical mind. The answer is that they did. The FRM scientists in Tumberland told Madame Entigy everything that was tellable. But, besides the tellable information, the lab is sending samples of experimental anti-jexan compounds for us to try out in Fellstone City. We can't make it here in Fellstone—we don't have the equipment. So the lab boys in Tumberland made us several batches of the stuff and sent it our way."

"So," Cheff asked, "what exactly is the problem?"

Sable said, "Lockdown."

"Exactly, Miss Sable," Zeek said. "The courier left Tumberland before the situation became so severe. He knows nothing about the heightened security. He's been coming this way on foot, completely incommunicado."

"Why on foot?" I asked.

"Inspections," Sable said.

"Right again," Zeek agreed. "If he came by ship, all his luggage would be inspected. Much too risky. Also, being on foot is a part of his cover. He walks everywhere. He's considered a top agent, one least likely to be exposed. His cover story is excellent. The problem is that he has no idea about the roadblocks."

"And he's about to walk right into one!" Buttons said.

"Exactly!" Zeek said. "Smart girl!"

The ponies looked at each other and shook their heads sadly. Buttons said, "The ponies think that's a Very Bad Thing."

"The ponies are right," Zeek said, "in more ways than one. The anti-jexan compounds are extremely important. If they're lost, it'll be a huge setback. We'll have to gather more jexan samples, send them to Tumberland, and start the process all over again."

"Which wouldn't be easy with the lockdown in effect," Cheff said.

"It would be impossible," Zeek said. "Anyway, if the courier is caught, it would be a complete disaster. But it gets worse. The courier is an old fellow named Fentor Rignish. He's an old Fessal, extremely old."

"A *Fessal* FRM agent?" Mid asked. "Seems unlikely to me."

"It's rare, I admit," Zeek said, "but it does happen."

Sable turned and pierced Mid with her brilliant green eyes. "Lery."

Mid flushed and dropped his gaze. "Sorry, Lery, no offense. I keep forgetting you're a Fessal. I always think of you as, well, as my brother."

Lery smiled happily. "No… offense taken… Brother Mid."

"Is being a Fessal what makes Fentor Rignish so special?" Cheff asked.

"Partly," Zeek said. "He's also the oldest living FRM agent on the east coast, maybe in all of Andaran. He's been with the FRM since he was a young man—a boy, really—since the FRM reorganized after The Fall."

"Wow!" Buttons said. "That's a long time ago."

"It is that," Zeek said, "but that's still not all. He's also well-loved by everyone in the FRM who's met him and plenty of others who are not FRM. He's an extraordinary agent, but also an extraordinary person."

"Why is that?" I asked. "Did you ever meet him?"

"I did, once," Zeek said. He frowned. "It's hard to explain. He's seen and done a great deal, but that's not it." He sighed. "You'll have to see for yourself when you meet him."

"We're going to meet Fentor Rignish?" Buttons said. "Hurray! The ponies are excited. When?"

"Soon," Zeek said. "But there's still more to the story. There's a second FRM agent shadowing him, probably close by. He'll need to be intercepted, too. Rignish will tell you how to find him. I don't know anything about him."

"Why a shadow?" I asked.

"Redundancy," Sable murmured.

"Right," Mid said. "Of course."

"What's redundancy?" Buttons asked.

Cheff said, "Redundancy is when you have more than one of something, so that if the first one fails, you still have a second chance."

"It's like the emergency brake in old Willam, here," Zeek said. "If the foot brake fails, I can pull this handle and the emergency brake will stop us. See?"

"I see," Buttons said. "So this second agent is the emergency brake for Fentor Rignish?"

"Correct!" Zeek said. "You've got the idea."

"Is it because he's so old?" Buttons asked.

"Partly that," Zeek said, "and partly because the mission is so important. The shadow agent has a duplicate set of anti-jexan compounds in case Rignish fails." He stroked his chin stubble. "It would be a bad thing indeed if Fentor Rignish is caught. He'd be killed for sure. If the Sephs made him talk, which is almost a certainty, a lot of other good agents would die, too, both in Fellstone and in Tumberland. I'm sure Rignish is prepared to die before he'd talk, but the Sephs rarely let that happen. They use mind control to make their subjects cooperate. And as a Fessal, Rignish is extra-susceptible to mind control. So we can't let Rignish be captured, no matter what. Understand?"

"Yes," Cheff said. "So what, exactly, is our mission?"

"I thought I'd already made that clear," Zeek said. "During the salvage operation, you're to slip away from the wrecking camp, intercept Fentor Rignish and his shadow, apprise them of the lockdown situation in Fellstone City, accept the anti-jexan compounds, and bring them to me. I'll take it from there."

We sat there, stunned. I took off my glasses and wiped them with my shirt tail. Buttons took the ponies from the dashboard and held them in her lap. Finally, Cheff said, "Uh, no, sir, Mr. Zeek. You hadn't actually made that clear. That, um, sounds like a big mission."

"Too big for you and your crew, Karfendek?" Zeek asked.

Cheff polled each one of us silently. "No, sir, Mr. Zeek. Not too big at all. I'm sure we'll manage just fine."

"Good," Zeek said. "I'd hate to think I overestimated you."

"Hang on," Mid said. "Wait one little moment. You're telling me that we have to"—he enumerated on his fingers—"sneak out of the salvage camp without being noticed, find this Fentor Rignish fellow out in the woods somewhere, convince him that we're FRM agents even though we're a bunch of kids, get him to turn the anti-jexan compounds over to us—"

"Shadow," Sable added.

"—find the shadow agent and do the same with him, then sneak the anti-jexan compounds back into the salvage camp?"

Zeek considered. "That sounds about right."

"Right in the middle of a stinking *lockdown*?" Mid added.

Zeek said, "Yes, I think you've got it. Madame Entigy seems to feel that since you all caused the lockdown, it should rightly fall to you to fix the consequences of it. Don't you agree?"

Mid buried his face in his hands. "Sure, right, of course. Seems fair to me. Wouldn't want to disappoint Madame Entigy, after all, would we?"

We rode in silence, trying to take it all in. After what seemed an eternity, Buttons lifted the ponies to her ear and listened intently. "The ponies say it's fair, Mr. Zeek."

Zeek tried in vain not to smile. "Oh, they do, do they? I'm glad to hear it. What else do they say?"

Buttons held Starry and Moka to her ear again. "The ponies say, 'Piece of cake!'"

— 10 —

THE SHIPWRECK

WE DROVE THE last leg of the trip in silence, along the miles-long Crescent Beach that led to Shipwreck Point and eventually to the Dagness Peninsula. Rampant, overgrown vegetation covered the countryside, with few signs of life. From time to time we passed little piles of ruins or someone standing by the side of the road holding up a plate of food for sale. I asked Zeek, "Who are they? Where do they live?"

"Away back in the bush in tiny little villages or even in isolated single houses." He shook his head sadly. "They're extremely poor, mostly Sevros. They live on whatever they can find in the wild—small animals, roots, berries, fish. When they get a little extra meat, they smoke it and sell it by the road. It's usually ainga lizard."

"What's an ainga lizard?" Buttons asked.

"It's a kind of big lizard," Cheff said. "They're vegetarian and basically harmless in spite of their scary appearance. I see them sometimes around the Labor Compound, but not often. They're pretty popular—the meat tastes good. Much better than, well, other meat."

"Yuck!" Buttons made a sour face. "Who wants to eat a lizard?"

Cheff grinned. "You seemed to like it well enough when we had it."

"When we—you mean you made me eat *lizard*? And you didn't even tell me?"

"Well, Sis, you were so fussy about the 'fence chicken' that it seemed best not to mention the ainga."

"What's fence chicken?" Zeek asked.

"When Buttons was little," Cheff explained, "she wouldn't eat rat meat. So Aunt Dee started calling it 'fence chicken.'"

Zeek chuckled. "I see. Fence chicken. Makes sense. Nom!" He licked his chops. "Fence chicken *good*!"

We all laughed, except Buttons, who looked like she was about to heave.

"Ainga lizard isn't too bad," Mid said. "I used to get it back in Settport when I wasn't eating fish. It does taste a little like chicken."

"There's another one!" Buttons pointed at a ragged Sevro woman standing by the roadway. She held a plate of smoked ainga high in one hand and the hand of a small girl in a tattered dress with the other.

Zeek brought Willam to a stop. The woman came up to my window, and I slid it open. "Smoke ainga. Ver' good. You like? Take, eat!" Without waiting for an answer, she pushed seven skewers loaded with chunks of ainga through the window into my lap.

Zeek gave me a handful of coins which I passed on to the woman. She stared at them, unbelieving, then her eyes welled with tears. "T'ank you, t'ank you." She held the little girl up to the window so we could see her. She was covered in dirt, her hair was matted, and two shiny trails ran from her nose. "Baby sick. Ver' sick. Money he'p, he'p ver' much!" She put the little girl down and headed into the tall brush. Before she disappeared, she turned, waved, and called once more, "T'ank you, good mans!"

I passed out the skewers, then nibbled at mine. Not too bad. Mid was right—it did taste like chicken, only a little gamier. Lery tucked into his as though he ate ainga lizard every day. Mid watched Lery, then sniffed his own skewer, shrugged, and took a bite. Cheff and Sable ate theirs without comment.

Buttons stared at hers. "The ponies don't like lizard meat," she said, then gulped.

"How do you know, Sis?" Cheff asked. "They haven't even tried it."

Zeek finished his and threw the empty skewer out his window. Without a word, he reached over and took Buttons' skewer and started munching on it. "Ainga *good*!"

"That poor woman," Buttons said, "and that poor baby!"

"Poor is right," Zeek said. "Our good Emperor Pallador's enlightenment programs don't extend too far outside the cities."

"Who are these people?" I asked. "And why do they live out here?"

"They've always lived here," Zeek said, "since The Fall, anyway. When Pallador emptied the countrysides and gathered the survivors of the war into the cities and nearby farms, somehow these people, or, rather, their ancestors, avoided being caught. They've been out here ever since. They'd rather be poor than live under Pallador's rule." He heaved a sigh. "I can't say as I blame them, but it's a hard life. No doctors, no teachers, no utilities, nothing. Sometimes, when they can get enough money, they'll send someone to a nearby farm or even a village to buy clothes or medicine or whatever. Yes, it's a hard life. But at least they're free. Who's to say it isn't worth it?"

"Freedom is relative," Sable murmured.

"Sable's right," Cheff said. "What kind of freedom do they have, exactly? What kind of life is their 'freedom' going to give that little girl? Freedom to starve? Freedom to die of illnesses easily cured in Fellstone City? Freedom to be ignorant and uneducated? Freedom to live at the mercy of roadside handouts? Is that kind of freedom truly freedom? Or is it merely another kind of oppression?"

We thought about this for a while, then Buttons frowned and said in a husky voice, "The ponies think that nobody should have to live like that."

"You're right, Miss Buttons," Zeek said gently. "No one should."

"I wouldn't have thought it possible," Mid said, "but it makes me appreciate living in the Labor Compound. We have it easy by comparison."

"What about you, Zeek?" I asked. "You're not a prisoner. Why do you live in the Labor Compound? Couldn't you find a pleasant house in Old City?"

"I suppose I could," Zeek said. "You have to consider: it's not always possible, or even desirable, to avoid all oppression. It's often a question of trading one kind of oppression for another. Living in the Labor Compound is unpleasant in some ways, but it saves me a good deal of expense because the house comes with the job. More important, the location inside the Labor Compound makes it possible for me to carry out FRM business inside the camp."

"What kind of FRM business, besides us?" Buttons asked.

Zeek narrowed his eyes. "*Secret* FRM business, Miss Buttons."

"Sorry," Buttons said. "I get it—if we need to know, you'll tell us."

"That's right, I will," Zeek said. "Being the salvage operator gives me the opportunity to do some good for people, like you kids. Plenty of the junk that comes through the scrapyard finds its way into private hands—the stuff Mid uses for his inventions, for example."

"I couldn't do it without you, Zeek!" Mid said.

"Here's another thought," Zeek continued. "If I lived out in the jungle like that lady and her baby, I'd be free of Pallador's direct oppression, but I wouldn't be of much use to the FRM, would I? So I choose to trade a certain amount of personal freedom for the freedom to work against Pallador and his Empire and to help my fellow citizens when I can."

"Like we did today," Buttons agreed. "It wasn't much for us, but I bet the money you gave that poor woman was a lot for her. I hope she can get some medicine for the baby."

"Zeek made a good point," Cheff said. "We couldn't be useful if we lived out in the woods. I don't care much for the quality of life in the Labor Compound, but I'm glad that we can be FRM agents and maybe help fix this world someday. Someday soon, I hope."

"Someday," Zeek agreed. "I don't know how soon. But someday, for sure."

As the sun was setting, we turned away from the beach and climbed a small hill. When we rounded the last curve before descending to the point, Zeek pulled Willam off the road into a little turn-out. We saw the entire salvage operation far below.

The wrecked ship was an old, medium-sized steam freighter with huge side-mounted paddle wheels almost as tall as the ship. It had broken into two pieces, more or less amidships. The bow section was high on the rocks near the tip of the point. The stern had drifted a little and become wedged into a sandy cove a few hundred yards to the south of the bow section.

Between the two sections, Emperor Pallador's Army Corps of Engineers had set up an enormous camp. It bustled with hundreds of people, workers of all sorts. Rows of canvas tents lined the edges. Dozens of electric lights illuminated the entire camp. A large, steam-powered electrical generator, mounted on the back of a steam truck, chuffed away near the main gate. The kitchen tent stood in the center, easily identifiable by its steaming outdoor kettles, ovens, and grills, and the twenty or thirty long mess tables surrounding it.

A tall wire fence encircled the entire camp, topped with razor wire to discourage looters. An armed guard stood sentry every fifty yards along the fence, all the way around to the waterline on both sides. A gate near the road big enough for trucks to go through, complete with a canvas guard shack and barrier arm, dominated the entrance.

"There you have it, boys and girls," Zeek said. "That's our home-sweet-home for the next few days. It's hard to believe now, but by evening on Day Six that ship will be completely gone, with hardly a trace left behind."

"Are you sure, Zeek?" Cheff asked. "It doesn't seem likely."

"I'm sure. This isn't the first shipwreck I've salvaged, you know. The last one was… let me think… well, it was a long time ago. Before you were born, even. It was much like this one: ship broken in half, dozens of salvage companies, hundreds of workers. For the first few days, our job, all the salvage companies, will be to go through our assigned portions of the ship, searching for usable fixtures, furniture, plumbing, instruments, machinery, and any cargo that might still be there. I'm not expecting much cargo. This ship was an ore carrier, but I'm afraid the ore it was carrying is at the bottom of the bay, and whatever wasn't sunk has been looted by now. But, one never knows about a shipwreck.

"When the salvage crews are done with the small stuff, the torch crews come in and cut the hull into pieces small enough for us to handle. We'll stack old Willam full of scrap several times each day and take it back to the salvage yard. I'll spend the next six months feeding that scrap into my smelter. It'll come out all clean and shiny, formed into neat little ingots, ready to be used again, enough to last the Labor Compound for months, maybe years, even.

"We'd best head on in. It looks like we'll get there just in time for supper. Anybody have to go? Now's the time—the camp latrines won't be pleasant."

We boys headed for the bushes in one direction, the girls in the other. Pally found a convenient clump of underbrush. A few minutes later, we piled into Willam and down the hill we went to the salvage camp.

At the front gate, the guards examined our paperwork carefully and waved us through. Guards bristling with weapons stood in groups. No doubt about it—security was going to be tight.

We stopped at a large tent with a dubious sign:

WELCOME TENT
ALL VISITORS MUST REGISTER
VIOLATORS WILL BE SHOT

"Be dignified and respectful, children," Zeek said. "This is routine, should only take a minute or two."

We followed Zeek to a table and stood quietly in line behind him. A clerk in army uniform scrutinized Zeek's papers, put a checkmark next to Zeek's name on a list, stamped his pass, and gave him an identification badge which Zeek pinned on the left side of his union suit. The clerk gave Zeek a red card with a number on it. "That's your tent assignment. Find the tent with the matching number. It's"—he stood up and looked around the camp, then pointed generally north—"over there somewhere. Park your truck in the lot by the mess tables."

The clerk repeated the procedure for each of us without comment, but when Buttons' turn came, he glanced up at her and stopped. "How old are you? You don't look old enough to be on a salvage crew."

"I've almost finished Basic School, sir," Buttons said. "But I'm an excellent worker. Mr. Zeek asked for me especially, sir."

The clerk looked up at Zeek. "It's true," Zeek said. "She's an excellent worker. She and her brother make a great team."

"You see, sir," Buttons said, "I'm small, so I can crawl into places where big men can't. That way, we can rescue even more things, things that would be lost otherwise." She batted her eyes at the clerk and put on her best cute face.

The clerk thought this over, then shrugged. "Fine, whatever. It's nothing to me, anyway. I don't get paid enough to care." He stamped her pass and gave her an ID badge. "Be sure you get your passes stamped every time you enter or leave the camp. Violations are severely punished." He waved us through and called, "Next!"

We moved off a few feet. Zeek bent down and helped Buttons pin on her ID badge. "That was good thinking, Miss Buttons.

Also, a great idea. I hadn't thought of it. I'll be sure to find some nice, tight places for you to get into."

"I can't wait to see that," Mid said under his breath, and we laughed.

"Let's get some chow!" Zeek said. "You kids get in the chow line and save me a space. I'll park Willam."

Cheff led the way to the mess tent. The main attraction was a buffet much like Pallador's Bounty had been at the Iron Fortress, but with far fewer choices. The serving trays were piled high and smelled amazing.

As we took our trays and silverware and joined the line, Cheff said quietly, "Easy on items made with white powder of any kind, especially the bread and mashed potatoes. You never know. The meat and vegetables should be fine."

"Hi, everyone!" blared an unmistakable voice. "Are you guys in line? I just finished. It was great! I wasn't expecting to find you all here—did you get a job with a salvage company, too?"

Tocette, a tall, big-boned Fessal girl, one of Brex's Blueband squad, waved at us. Unlike the rest of the Labor Compound Bluebands, Tocette was overweight, perpetually disheveled, and generally in need of some personal hygiene.

"Hi, Zeek!" Tocette brayed. "Are you guys working for Zeek this trip?"

"Hi, Tocette!" Cheff said. "We saw you and Brex at the bus stop, but we didn't imagine that you were coming here. And yes, Zeek is our boss for the next few days. I didn't know you two knew each other."

"Of course we do!" Zeek said. "We're old friends, aren't we, Tocette?"

She said enthusiastically, "We sure are, Boss."

"It's nice to see you again, Tocette," Zeek said, taking her hand and shaking it. "We've missed you down at the scrapyard. I enjoyed working with you last year. Have you known my new friends, here, for long?"

Cheff said, "We go to school together, but we only got to know the Beautiful and Intrepid Tocette a few weeks ago."

Tocette blushed and tried in vain to smooth her hair and straighten her stained clothing. "Aw, Cheff…"

Zeek asked her, "Who are you working for on this trip?"

Tocette's brow furrowed. "Um… I'm not too sure. It's a woman from the Toddary District, I think. Brex takes care of all that kind of stuff."

"Hmm," Zeek said, "the Toddary District, eh? Must be Whipple."

"Oh. That sounds right, I think," Tocette said. "I'm not really sure. She picked us up at the bus stop in her truck. It's red. And shiny."

"Yes, Whipple's truck is red," Zeek said. "I wonder how she got a troop of Bluebands as helpers? Well, good for you, Tocette. She's a good woman. I'm sure she'll treat you right."

"Oh. I hope so. Well, I guess I'll be seeing you around the camp. So long, Zeek!" She walloped Cheff on the back, then turned and chatted briefly with Sable and Buttons. She seemed genuinely delighted to see Starry and Moka again and gave each of them a pat on the head. "Time for supper! It's going to be fantastic!" She waved goodbye and wandered off.

Zeek asked Cheff, "Is Tocette a friend of yours?"

"Not exactly," Cheff said. "We go to school with her. She's a Blueband. A few weeks ago, she 'chaperoned' us on our field trip to the Iron Fortress. That was the night before—you know."

"She… threw up," Lery said. "A lot."

Cheff laughed. "She did that, all right. Got a little too much of Pallador's Bounty. In fact, that was how we discovered the, uh, in the food, you see."

"Ah," Zeek said. "I understand. Will she be a problem?"

"No," Mid said. "Tocette is basically harmless. The problem is that Tocette's here with her Blueband leader, Miss Averith Brex, and she *is* a problem—a serious one."

"Brex doesn't like us much," Cheff said. "She suspects that we're up to something and she's determined to find out what it is."

"Also," Mid said, "Cheff and Sable had a run-in with Brex on that same field trip. She was humiliated and wants to see them punished. My guess is that when she finds out we're here—and she will, Tocette will see to that—she'll be all over us, looking for an excuse to make trouble."

"Well," Zeek said, "that is unfortunate. I know Whipple pretty well. Maybe I can work out something with her to keep Brex and her people out of our hair. I'll see what I can do."

Mid shook his head. "This keeps on getting better and better, doesn't it?"

Cheff punched Mid's shoulder. "Don't fret, Old Son. We'll find a way. We always do. One thing at a time. For now, let's get some chow and a good night's sleep."

*"The stern had drifted a few hundred yards to the
south of the bow."*

— 11 —

THE SALVAGE CAMP

WE ENJOYED OUR supper—Tocette was right, it was fantastic. The food was wholesome and abundant. If there was any jexan in it, there wasn't enough to make us sick or dizzy. We saw no sign of Tocette, Brex, or her crew. I guessed they'd eaten earlier.

Afterward, Zeek found our tent assignment. We had two tents next to each other, on the north side of the camp. Each tent had four camp cots. Zeek took in the situation, then announced, "Okay, oldest boys with me: Cheff, Lery, and Mid. Books, you don't mind bunking with the girls, do you?"

"No, sir," I said. "If they don't mind, I don't mind."

Buttons grinned. "I don't mind. The ponies don't mind either. We'll have loads of fun! How about you, Sable?"

Sable looked at me, her green eyes almost glowing in the dark. "All good."

"Fine, fine," Zeek said. "That's settled, then. Let's get some sleep. Work starts early in the morning."

He and the other boys disappeared into their tent. Sable glanced at me and disappeared into ours. I hesitated, but Buttons said, "C'mon, Books! What are you waiting for? We're gonna have some fun!"

The only fun we had, though, was wrapping up in our blankets and going to bed. I was asleep in a heartbeat—it had been a long day.

The next morning, I woke up shivering. Even though it was early autumn, mornings were cold by the bay. I wrapped my blanket around my shoulders and went out to the latrines.

By the time I got back, Zeek had built a small campfire in front of our tents and was brewing a pot of felmoss tea. "There you are," he said. "Just in time! Pull up a rock and have a cup."

I sat on a rock and sipped the bitter brew as I struggled to wake up all the way. There's nothing like felmoss tea to help get one going in the morning, but I wished I had some sugar. I thought of the honeyed iced tea Mrs. Klesky served us yesterday—sweet!

Zeek took a small metal flask from his hip pocket and poured a healthy dose of brown liquid into his cup. "There we are," he said. "Felmoss Plus." He laughed and took a huge swig from the mug. "Ahh, that's good!" He sighed contentedly. "Now gather around, children. I have something to tell you."

We scooted in close.

"I have our assignment for the day. We are going to go through the crew quarters in the stern section of the ship, sections A through F. Other crews will scavenge the other sections. You'll be looking for anything useful: plumbing, wiring, speakers, valves, gauges, anything at all, even the crew's personal effects. Got it?"

We got it.

"Except you won't," Zeek said. "I've arranged with another operator, also an FRM agent, to borrow half of his workers for the next few days. He was notified in advance and brought extra crew. They'll be doing your jobs for you on the ship. Meanwhile, you'll sneak out of the camp and execute your FRM mission. Understand?"

We understood.

"There's something I didn't tell you yesterday," Zeek continued. "The old Fessal you're going to meet is a pack peddler."

"What's a pack peddler?" Buttons asked.

"What's a pack peddler?" Zeek echoed. "Well might you ask!"

"I never heard of one before," Buttons said. She checked with Starry and Moka. "The ponies never heard of one, either."

"And with good reason," Zeek said. "There aren't many left these days. For all I know, Fentor Rignish may be the last pack peddler in all of Andaran. But when I was a little boy, long ago, there were still many pack peddlers.

"Nowadays, if you need something for the house, you go to the market, right? Well, *you* don't—you have to go to the vendors in the Labor Compound. But you've seen the market in Old City?"

"Sure," Buttons said. "Cheff bought us treats there."

"Right," Zeek said. "But for many of us, growing up in the hinterlands in the decades after The Fall, or people like that woman who sold us the ainga meat, there weren't any markets. I grew up in a small town way up in the Tumber Range. The pack peddlers came two or three times a year. They brought us things that we couldn't make ourselves: tools, clothes, needles, thread, rugs, kitchenware, toys, even musical instruments.

"The arrival of a pack peddler was a holiday for us, an exciting occasion. Work stopped. The women argued over whose house the pack peddler would stay in. The men opened kegs of beer and broke out the spirits." He patted the little flask keeping him warm at his hip. "It was quite the occasion. The pack peddler would open his big bundle right on our cabin floor. We loved to see it, for it was seldom that we saw new things. What a sight it was for us kids in those days!" He sighed wistfully.

"It was hard to be a pack peddler. The packs were heavy, and the mountains were steep. The pack peddlers carried their huge bundles on their backs, though a few of the more successful ones had donkeys or even horses. One had a cart... later he built a store in Toof-Toof and became a wealthy merchant.

"It was dangerous, too. They traveled alone and sometimes carried a great deal of cash. Some of them were robbed and a few were murdered. But mostly, they were welcomed warmly by nearly everyone." Zeek sighed again. "Those were the days! It was a wonderful thing for one man to bring such happiness and joy to so many. Conditions were hard, back then, much harder than today, and the pack peddlers were one of few bright spots in our lives."

"That sounds wonderful," Buttons said. "And we're going to meet one?"

"Yes, you are," Zeek said. "Perhaps the last one. Fentor Rignish has been a pack peddler since before I was born. He's traveled all over the eastern part of Andaran and maybe even the west, I don't know." Zeek leaned in close. "It's the perfect cover for an FRM agent. It's not merely his cover—it's his job and has been all his life. He has an imperial permit to travel almost everywhere. He knows everyone. He hears all the gossip, all the news. He's been carrying FRM messages up and down the East Coast for decades and has never been suspected. He's quite old now. It would be a shame if he ran into an ambush. And it's your mission to keep him safe."

Three stout young Lora men approached our fire. "Are you Zeek Bonnovus?" the tallest one asked.

"Yes," Zeek said. "Are you my helpers for the day?"

"We are," he answered, "and for as many days as you need us. No worries, all the details are taken care of."

"Good," Zeek said. "The three of you are replacing the six of them. You'll have to work twice as fast!"

The Lora laughed and said, "No worries, Boss. We're fast, you'll see."

"Well, then," Zeek said, "let's you and us get ourselves on the outside of some breakfast and get this day moving."

We trudged to the mess tent and filled up on eggs, smoked meats, and a delectable assortment of fresh fruits.

"Eat hearty," Zeek told us. "You never know when you'll get your next meal."

When we were finished, Zeek patted his bulging belly and belched discreetly. "Okay, children, your big moment has come. I'm going to take these three strapping young men to our salvage assignment while you go back to our tents. Grab your bags, make sure you aren't being watched, then one by one slip north out of the camp into the woods. Our tent is halfway between two of the sentries, so if you keep your heads down, you'll have no trouble getting out. When you've all gotten safely away, follow the shoreline north. Old Rignish is supposed to cross the bay in a small boat a little north of here, either today or tomorrow. Locate him, get the anti-jexan compounds, then find his shadow agent. Rignish will be able to tell you where the shadow agent is. Got it?"

We exchanged a glance, then Cheff said, "Got it, sir. We'll do our best."

We sat around the long wooden table, drinking one last cup of felmoss tea. Cheff casually stood up, stretched, and looked all around. Satisfied that no one was paying any attention, he said, "Okay, Mid, you first. Act like you're heading for the latrines, but keep going to our tents, and from there into the woods. Wait for the rest of us there."

Without another word, Mid rose and stretched as Cheff had, then ambled off toward the latrines.

Cheff said, "Okay, Lery, your turn."

A few seconds later, Lery, too, had disappeared.

"Now you, Books," Cheff said.

My heart fluttered in my chest like a butterfly's wings. Were we going to simply walk out of the salvage camp into the woods? I could hardly believe it. But I rose and stretched like the others had, then, trying to look as casual as I could, I started for our tent. My heart had stopped fluttering—now it was trying to hammer its way right out of my rib cage. I strolled past the latrines, eyes straight ahead, ducked into our tent, picked up my gear bag, went out again under the back wall of the tent, and crouched all the way to the north edge of the camp. I glanced at the sentries in both directions, but they were staring straight ahead, oblivious. Perhaps, like the soldier who checked us in, they weren't paid enough to care. I ducked under the wire fence into the woods, where I joined Mid and Lery. We watched through the trees as Cheff sent Sable and Buttons our way. Last, Cheff followed them.

When we were all together again, Cheff laughed. "I'm always amazed at what one can get away with if they act as though everything is normal."

"It's true," Mid said. "I saw Cheff change his pants in the middle of the schoolyard once, and nobody even noticed."

"Why'd he have to do that?" I asked.

Cheff glared at me. "Never mind. The point is, I simply acted as though it were perfectly normal. Piece of cake."

Buttons giggled. "The ponies approve," she said.

"Great!" Cheff said. "Let's get out of here before some busybody guard decides to poke his nose into our business."

He turned and strode northward through the forest. The rest of us fell in behind him.

— 12 —

NORTHWARD ALONG THE COAST

WE HIKED SINGLE-FILE through the forest near the shore for maybe a half-hour, then Cheff called for a break. "I think we're far enough from the salvage camp that we don't have to worry about being detected. Let's spread out and expand our search area. Instead of going single-file, we'll make a horizontal sweep chain.

"I'll take the position on the left, near the edge of the forest, where I have a clear view of the beach. Mid, you'll be on my right, Lery will be on your right, then Books, then Buttons, then Sable on the far right, deep into the woods. We'll stay within sight of each other, but only just barely. Got it?"

"Won't that slow us down?" Mid asked.

"A little, perhaps," Cheff said, "but not nearly as much as if we miss Rignish and have to repeat our search. Besides, we'll cover a lot more ground."

"Also," I said, "if we go slower, we'll conserve our strength and last longer."

"True," Cheff said. "We have no idea exactly where the old fellow crossed the bay, or when. Assuming he's already across, that is. It could be a long day."

"What are we looking for?" Buttons asked.

"Any sign of someone passing through the area," Cheff said. "If he crossed the bay, he must have a boat. He would have had to hide the boat somewhere. So that's one thing."

"Footprints," Sable said.

"Right," Cheff said, "or any other sign."

"Such as?" Mid asked.

"Flattened grass, broken branches or twigs, bits of clothing in the brush," Cheff said.

"If he ate something, he might have dropped bits of it," Buttons said.

"Good, Sis," Cheff said. "That's using your head."

Lery said, "If… he's been here… more… more than a day, he might have made… a fire."

"Great!" Cheff said. "What a great team you are! You all seem to have the right idea. Keep your eyes open and see what you can see. Ready? Okay, spread out!"

We spread out as Cheff had directed until we could barely see each other. When we were all in position, Sable gave a thumbs-up and we passed it down the line to Cheff, who returned it and called, "Move out!"

It was slow going. The thick vegetation near the shore made hiking difficult, though the shade was cool and pleasant. The dense underbrush rendered some spots impassable and had to be bypassed. We navigated rocks, fallen trees and branches, and sometimes even holes. Nevertheless, as Cheff had said, we covered a great deal of ground. We searched without result until the sun was high overhead, then Cheff called a stop for lunch. Sable came in from the extreme right, bringing everyone else along with her.

Cheff passed some biscuits around. "I nabbed these from the breakfast buffet. It's not much, but it's what there is."

"Not exactly… Friend Cheff," Lery said, smiling. He picked a spot near the edge of the woods, but not visible from the beach, and cleared a small bit of ground. Next, he gathered a few twigs, then took some dry tinder out of his day pack. He quickly had a small fire going.

"Dry twigs," Sable said. "No smoke."

"Right," Cheff said. "Good work, Lery. Everybody grab some dry sticks."

While we were gathering, Lery took a funny metal gadget from his pack. It unfolded into a clever little grill, which he placed over the fire. Next out of his pack came a small teapot, which he filled from his canteen and put on the little grill to boil. He added some dried leaves to the boiling water. "Felmoss tea," Lery said. "I got some… from Zeek."

We watched, fascinated. Cheff said, "Well done, Lery! I had no idea you came equipped for camp cooking."

Lery smiled proudly. "The right tools… for the right job." We laughed, and he continued, "I got… got these when… I was… working for… Mr. Meltern. He had me work… in the kitchen… and I learned… some stuff. When I… left, and came to… to Mid's house… Mr. Meltern let me… 'borrow' a few things."

"And you never said a word to me about it," Mid said. "You're amazing, Lery!"

Lery, still smiling, took some dried meat from his pack and passed it around. We took our camp cups from our respective bags and Lery poured the tea.

What started with a single dried biscuit turned into a fine lunch with meat and hot felmoss tea. It was quite the treat! We could have gone all day on the biscuit alone—we were used to being hungry, a normal part of life in the Fellstone Labor Compound—but having some extra hiking fuel would make the whole day go better.

By the time we finished, the little fire had died down. Lery covered the coals with sand from the beach, folded and stowed his little grill, and tied his pack shut.

Cheff patted Lery on the shoulder. "Thank you, Lery. That was a wonderful snack!"

"Glad you… liked it, Friend Cheff," Lery said. "More later."

"There's more?" I asked. "Like what?"

"Surprise," Lery said. "You'll have to… to wait." He chuckled and moved away to take his search position again.

When we were all in place, Sable gave the thumbs-up, and we were moving once more. The afternoon wore on, insects buzzing, our sweat dripping, and our feet getting sore.

About an hour after our midday break, Mid called out, "Boat!"

Cheff signaled a halt and went over to Mid's position to investigate. "Come on over, everyone, but be careful not to walk over his trail!"

A battered wooden one-man rowboat, painted a dull greenish-gray, lay concealed beneath a layer of brush and leaves, turned upside down over a pair of oars.

"How do we know if it's his, Cheff?" Buttons asked.

"We don't, for sure, but it's all we've got so far."

Sable knelt and reached under the little boat. "Oars. Wet."

We examined the paddle ends.

Cheff said, "Sure enough, they're still damp. Good spotting, Sable. These have been used in the last day or so." He replaced the oars and stood. "I think we must assume, for the time being, that this is Fentor Rignish's boat. Everyone agree?"

We agreed.

"Then our next step is to see if we can find his trail. The ground here is pretty rocky—I don't see any footprints. Let's spread out again and turn inland, see if we can spot anything. If you do see something, be careful not to trample it."

We fanned out, then started slowly eastward, away from the beach. A few minutes later, Sable sang out, "Trail."

Sure enough, a single set of footprints wound through the underbrush.

"Right," Cheff said. "Single file, everyone. Follow Sable."

Sable advanced, crouching low, for over an hour, stopping frequently to examine a bent blade of grass or a broken twig.

Finally, Buttons called out, "Look! Over there, by that tree!"

A small Fessal man leaned against a tree trunk. By his side, a bundle almost as big as the man himself was tied up with rope.

"That must be Rignish," Mid said. "Look at that pack. It's huge!"

We approached slowly, not wanting to startle the old man, but he didn't stir. We stood in a circle and watched him for a while, then Buttons asked, "Do you think he's… dead?"

"I don't know," Cheff said. "I can't tell if he's breathing. Mid, poke him and see if he wakes up."

Mid took a step backward. "I'm not going to poke him. You poke him yourself."

Cheff sighed and picked up a little stick, then edged closer to the old man. Tentatively, he reached out with the stick and touched the man on his shoulder. Nothing happened.

"Harder," Mid said.

Cheff poked a little harder. Still nothing.

"*Harder!*" Mid said again.

"I don't know," Cheff said. "I'm not sure that's such a good idea."

"Why not?" asked Mid. "If he's dead, he won't care."

"I… well… I don't want to poke a dead guy," Cheff said, then looked embarrassed.

Sable covered her mouth with her hand.

"Boys are so silly!" Buttons said. She walked right up to the old man, picked up his hand, and patted it. "Excuse me, sir, excuse me. Are you dead?"

The old man woke up with a start. Buttons screamed a tiny little scream and jumped back.

The old man looked all around, tried in vain to struggle to his feet, then sagged back to the ground. "Where am I? Who are you?"

Buttons approached him again and knelt by his side. She took his wrinkled hand in hers again. "I'm sorry I startled you, sir. My name is Buttons, and these are my friends. We're looking for Mr. Fentor Rignish. Are you him, sir?"

"Well, of course I'm him. Who else would I be? I've been Fentor Rignish all my life. Now, you tell *me*—who wants to know?"

Cheff knelt next to Buttons. "My name is Cheff, Cheff Karfendek. We've been sent by a friend of yours to give you a message. A friend who lives in Old Fellstone City. He runs a guest house there."

"A guest house? I've been to hundreds of guest houses. I'm a pack peddler, you know." He patted the enormous pack by his side. "Have been, for—" he took off his hat and scratched his head—"well, a long time. It's my job. I have a license from Emperor Pallador himself. It's right here, somewhere." He patted his clothes and looked in his pockets.

Cheff was smiling now. "It's okay, Mr. Rignish. We believe you. We don't need to see your license."

"You don't? Then what *do* you want, young feller? Get to the point! I haven't got all day, you know. Got places to go! I'm a busy man. I'm supposed to be in Fellstone by… Say, sonny, what day is this, anyway?"

"It's Second Day," Cheff said, "and it's early afternoon."

"Second Day!" the old man said and tried again to struggle to his feet. "I'm going to be late! I have to get moving. Here, sonny, help me up."

Cheff and Lery each took an elbow and gently raised the old man to his feet. "There you are, sir," Cheff said. "Can you stand up on your own, now, if we let go?"

"Why, of course I can stand up by myself! Why shouldn't I be able to? Let me go!"

Cheff and Lery let go of his elbows, and Rignish took a tentative step forward. He yelped, clutched his side, and collapsed by the tree again.

Buttons rushed to him. "What's the matter, Mr. Rignish? Are you hurt?"

Sable was already examining his wound. "Hurt," she whispered. "Bad."

"How bad?" Cheff asked.

Sable gently probed the wound and Fentor Rignish yelped again, louder this time. "Very bad."

"What happened, Mr. Rignish?" Cheff asked. "How did you hurt yourself?"

"Aw, it was silly. I feel like an old fool! I was on the other side of the bay, by the Great Stone of Fel, getting ready to cross. Before I launched the boat, I thought I'd check to see if there were any ships coming this way. I climbed partway up the Stone to get a better look, and my foot slipped. I fell and landed sideways on a jagged rock. Banged myself up pretty bad, I guess, but I didn't let that stop me. What do I care about a bruise, even a bad bruise? I got the boat across the bay all right, but it was dark when I got here. I must have passed out on the beach, you see, because when I woke up again it was morning. Yesterday morning? I'm not too sure. I dragged the boat into the forest and hid it."

"Yes, sir," Mid said. "We found it. It was hidden well."

Fentor Rignish snorted. "Nonsense! If it were hidden well, you never would have found it! I'm losing my touch. Getting old, I suppose. Would never have happened a few years ago. Anyway, I passed out again, I think. I don't know for how long. When I woke up, it was still before noon, so I hiked until I came to this tree. But I was so tired I thought I'd close my eyes for a little while." He closed his eyes. "So… tired…"

"I think he passed out again," I said.

Sable pulled his lips open. His gums were gray. "Bleeding inside."

"Can we help him?" Cheff asked.

"No." Sable said. "Too late."

"Oh, no," Buttons wailed. "You mean he's gonna… gonna…?" Tears flowed down her cheeks. She put her arms around Cheff and buried her face in his vest.

"We could try to take him to the hospital in New City," Cheff said, "but I think he's too weak to make it far."

"Concur," Sable said.

"Even if he could make it," Mid said, "they'd figure out he's an agent, and kill him."

"I could… could… carry him," Lery said.

Sable shook her head. "Would kill him."

Buttons sobbed, "What *can* we do then? We have to do *something*!"

"I'm sorry, Sis." Cheff stroked her hair. I don't think there's much we *can* do.

"No!" She stamped her foot. "He *can't* die! I won't let him! If he dies, we'll have to bury him and the ponies *hate* digging! We've got to *do* something, Cheff!"

"Buttons." Sable gently pried her away from her brother. "Comfortable. Help."

"Good idea, Sable," Cheff said. "If we can't do anything else, we can at least try to make him a little more comfortable. Buttons, why don't you help Lery make him some tea or maybe some broth?"

"Okay, Cheff." Buttons sniffled and wiped her face. Then she and Lery got busy making a small fire and heating some water with a few chunks of dried beef in it.

"Meanwhile," Cheff said to no one in particular, "we'll wait for him to wake up again. Maybe he'll tell us about his shadow agent."

We settled down in a circle around Mr. Fentor Rignish, to see what his next waking would bring.

— 13 —

FENTOR RIGNISH

LERY MADE A second small fire next to the first one and brewed a pot of felmoss tea. He passed out another round of biscuits and dried meat. No one felt much like talking, so we nibbled and sipped and waited.

An hour or so later, mid-afternoon, Fentor Rignish woke with a start. "Where am I? Who are you people? What am I doing here?"

Cheff and I knelt on one side of him, Sable on the other. Sable picked up one of his gnarled hands and held it in hers.

Buttons filled her tea mug from the kettle and offered it to him. He accepted it and took a big swallow. "Thank you, young lady. That's just the thing for a cool autumn afternoon." He turned to Cheff. "Now, then, who are you people and why are you here?"

"It's me, Cheff Karfendek, sir. Don't you remember? We were talking, then you passed out."

"Karfendek?" the old man asked. "I knew a Karfendek once, years ago. Lived in the Toddary district. A good man. A Lora, too—looked something like you, as I recall. Are you his kid?"

"I think I might be, sir," Cheff said. "We lived in the Toddary District when I was little."

"Well, good for you," Rignish said. He shifted his weight and groaned, then coughed violently. He pulled a handkerchief out of his pocket and wiped his face and his sweaty forehead. "Now, young Karfendek, if you don't mind, how about telling me what you're doing out here in the woods?"

"Well, sir," Cheff said, "it's like this: my friends and I were sent to find you. We have a message for you from someone you know, Mr. Meltern. A secret message, sir, if you get my meaning."

The old man's bushy eyebrows arched. "Meltern? Of Meltern's Guest House? In Old Fellstone City?"

"That's the one," Cheff said.

"But he's… he's an… but then you must be, too…"

Cheff lowered his voice. "Agents, sir. FRM agents, like you. We all are."

Fentor Rignish looked us over carefully. "But… you're all so young! Is the FRM that desperate for recruits these days? Why, the one who brought me the tea is only a little girl!"

Cheff said, "Not desperate, sir. Special circumstances. It's a long story."

Rignish frowned. "I don't suppose it had anything to do with a story I heard recently concerning another Karfendek and the Iron Fortress?"

Cheff grinned. "Well, sir—"

"Don't tell me, sonny. I don't need to know. Best not to speak of it. But I'm beginning to get the idea." He put his handkerchief over his mouth and coughed, and this time it came away bloody. "Sorry, sonny. I seem to have hurt myself somewhere along the way." He examined the handkerchief, then folded it so the blood didn't show. "Better give me that message quick, sonny. I'm not feeling so good."

"It's this, sir: all of Fellstone is under lockdown. There's no chance for you to get into Fellstone City without getting caught. You're to give me the, um, research materials, and return to Tumberland."

Rignish coughed again. There was even more blood this time. "Is that all?"

"Almost," Cheff said. "You're also to tell us where to find your shadow agent, and we're to give him the same message."

"I see. And I'm supposed to believe you? With no proof?" Another coughing fit gripped him. Cheff and Sable helped him to lean forward and clear his lungs.

"There wasn't much time to figure out proof, sir," Cheff said. "We only found out about this mission yesterday."

"If Fellstone City is locked down, as you say, then how did you get out of town?"

"We got hired for a salvage operation out on Shipwreck Point. We're supposed to be there now. We're working for a man named Zeek Bonnovus. Maybe you know him, too? I hear he frequents Meltern's Guest House."

Fentor Rignish laughed, but it turned into another coughing fit. "Yes," he said when he could speak again, "yes, I know Zeek. I met him once, long ago. Is he still driving that old truck of his? What was it he called it? Wilbert the Whiner, I think it was." He looked cannily at Cheff.

"I think you mean Willam the Wheezer, sir," Cheff said.

"Of course, of course," Rignish said. "Okay, young man. It's not exactly proof, but you seem to have your facts straight, anyway." He coughed some more. Cheff and Sable helped him lean forward again.

Cheff said, "If it would help, sir, we know another name that not many people know."

"Oh? And what might that be?"

Cheff whispered, "Madame Entigy."

"Quiet!" the old man snapped. "That name should never pass your lips unnecessarily."

"Yes, sir," Cheff said. "Sorry, sir."

"No harm done, sonny. In fact, come to think of it, maybe it *was* necessary in this case. All right, I'll accept that you're who you say you are." He took a long look at Lery. "You FRM, too?"

"Yes… I am… sir."

"Good on you! I thought I was the only Fessal in the FRM. I wish there were more. Now, pay attention, children, this is important."

He patted the huge peddler's pack at his side. "You'll find what you're looking for in this pack. Don't open it now—take the whole thing back to Zeek. He'll know what to do."

"Won't you need the rest of the stuff back in Tumberland?" Mid asked.

Rignish looked sadly at Mid. "No, son. I'm not going back to Tumberland. I don't think I'm going anywhere. Looks like this is the end of the trail for me."

Mid said, "Don't talk like that, sir. We'll fetch Zeek and his truck and get you out of here. We'll have you patched up in no time."

Rignish shook his head slowly. "Not this time, son. I'm hurt bad, down deep inside. I can feel it. Anyway, even if I survived the trip, where would I go? Can't go to Fellstone, if it's locked down. And if I could, they'd kill me anyhow, or worse."

Mid clenched his fists so hard his knuckles turned white. "But, Mr. Rignish—"

"Mid," Sable said quietly.

"What?" Mid shouted.

Sable shook her head. "No, Mid."

Mid glared at her, jammed his fists into his pockets, and turned away.

"It's all right, young feller. We all have to go sometime. I've had a long and beautiful life." He coughed again in long, wracking spasms. When it was over, he could barely speak. "There's plenty in that pack you can use, I'm sure. Help yourselves. But take it to Zeek first."

"I'm sorry, sir," Cheff said, "but there's one more thing. We're supposed to ask you about your shadow agent."

"Oh, yes, my infernal shadow. It's because I'm old, you see, they don't trust me on my own anymore." He chuckled and coughed into his handkerchief again. "Looks like they were right, too. However, I haven't seen my shadow since before I crossed the bay. The shadow was supposed to cross right after me, but I haven't seen hide nor hair since." He coughed again, weakly. "Figures. There's never a shadow agent around when you need one. Don't worry. Have a look around. Can't be too far from here. Probably trying to figure out where I've gotten to. Get the shadow's pack, too, don't forget. Now… gotta rest."

Cheff and Sable helped him lean back against his tree trunk and made him comfortable. Buttons brought him another cup of tea. "Ah… felmoss tea… one of life's great pleasures." He took a sip and sighed contentedly. "Now I need to close my eyes, just for a minute…" He closed his eyes, but they snapped open again. "I'm sure glad you children are here. Very glad…" He closed his eyes again and was asleep instantly.

"Is… is he…?" Buttons asked.

"Not yet," Cheff answered, "but—"

"Soon," Sable intoned.

Buttons sat down by the fire, her lips set into a grim line, her ponies clutched in a white-knuckled grip. Lery brewed another pot of tea and we warmed ourselves by the little fire for a while.

Sable remained with Fentor Rignish, holding his hand in hers. After a while, she carefully placed his hand in his lap and stood up. Cheff looked up at her and she shook her head.

Cheff said gently, "Okay, gang. Mr. Rignish is gone. We need to bury him and mark the place. I'm sure Zeek, or someone, will come to get him later and take him to a proper resting place. Lery, let's have that camp shovel from your tool bag. It's getting late, and we still have a shadow agent to find." He looked around. "I guess we'll put him right here, by his tree. We can carve a marker on the tree for now."

Lery took the camp shovel from his pack, but when Cheff reached for it, Lery shook his head and began digging. He dug quickly and efficiently with the little folding shovel, and in a quarter of an hour, the grave was nearly ready.

"It should be deeper," Mid said.

"It should," Cheff agreed, "but this will have to do for now. It'll keep the wild animals from bothering him, anyway."

We found an old blanket in his pack and carefully wrapped him in it, then gently lowered him into the grave and arranged him in a dignified way. Lery was about to start filling in, but Buttons said, "Wait." She gathered a small bunch of flowers which she placed on the blanket. "Okay," she said, then walked off a dozen paces so she didn't have to watch. When she thought no one was looking, she made each of the ponies wave goodbye.

When Lery was done, Mid asked Cheff, "Should we say something?"

"I don't know what it would be," Cheff said. Buttons gave him a look. "But I'll try," he added hastily.

We stood solemnly around the grave. Buttons reached out and put her hand in mine. This wasn't our first death, not for any of us. Everyone in the Fellstone Labor Compound had lost someone dear to them. Most of us had lost loved ones, including our fathers. But this was different, somehow. This time it was *our* loss, the six of us together, and ours alone.

Cheff cleared his throat and said huskily, "Goodbye, Fentor Rignish. We didn't know you very well. We wish we'd had time to know you better. From what we've heard, you were a good man and an outstanding agent. We'll all do our best to follow your example. For now, rest easy. We'll be back to get you and take you home when the mission's over. The mission must come first—we know you'll understand."

Cheff took a deep breath, then walked over and picked up Mr. Rignish's peddler's pack. "Oof! That's heavy. How did that little man manage to pack this thing?"

"Practice," Sable murmured.

"Many years of practice, I expect," Mid said.

"Right." Cheff staggered forward a few steps.

Lery came up behind him and took the pack. He slung it over his shoulder with one hand, effortlessly.

"Right," Cheff said again. "Thanks, Lery. Let's take it back to Rignish's little boat, and hide it underneath. We'll pick it up again after we find the shadow agent. We have to get moving—it's getting late in the day."

"Okay… Friend Cheff." Lery started back the way we came, and the rest of us fell in behind.

"'I'm sure glad you children are here. Very glad…'
He closed his eyes again…"

— 14 —

THE SHADOW AGENT

WE TRUDGED BACK to where Fentor Rignish's little boat was only partially concealed. Cheff and Mid lifted the boat while Lery placed the peddler's pack beneath it.

"Let's camouflage it," Cheff said, so we gathered branches and handfuls of leaves and grass and covered it as best we could.

"Aren't you worried someone might find it anyway?" Mid asked.

"A little," Cheff said, "but they'd have to be looking for it. It seems unlikely that someone's going to stumble over it way out here in the wilderness. It's a chance I'm willing to take."

"Maybe we should find the compounds and take those with us," Mid said.

"Maybe," Cheff said, "but maybe not. If we get caught trying to find the shadow agent, they'll be confiscated."

"So," Mid said, "it's a risk either way."

"Right," Cheff said. "I'd rather take a chance on hiding it. It would take time to find the compounds in that pack, and we're running out of daylight."

"True," Mid said. "Also, carrying that heavy pack would slow us down."

"Agreed," Cheff said. "Okay, everyone. Let's get back into our search pattern and head north again. Same formation as before. If what Mr. Rignish said was accurate, we should find the shadow before long."

Cheff went back to the edge of the forest by the beach and the rest of us fell into line. Once more, Sable gave the thumbs up and we started northward.

Our end-of-day exhaustion plus heat and humidity and the buzzing insects made it harder to concentrate than it had been in the morning. Little rivulets of sweat ran down our foreheads into our eyes. On top of all this, we had the shock and grief of Mr. Rignish's passing. From time to time, Cheff called out for us to concentrate, to focus, to stay aware, to pay attention. I was drooping, and I'm sure the others were, too.

We searched for another hour, maybe a little more, then Sable called a stop. The word came down the chain, and we crept to her position. She was crouched behind a small thicket of pimmo berries. She put her finger to her lips and pointed across a small clearing.

On the edge of a pond, with no apparent attempt to conceal it, was a bright-red two-man tent, the kind rich people take on camping holidays. In front, a huge fire blazed brightly. Over the fire, hanging from a makeshift tripod, a rather large pot of something steamed. The smoke from the fire billowed high into the nearly cloudless sky.

We stared at the spectacle for some time, speechless.

At length, Mid asked, "That can't be the shadow agent's camp, can it?"

"I don't know," Cheff said. "There's obviously no attempt to be subtle or concealed."

"It looks like tourist gear," Mid said. "You know—campers."

"Not from Fellstone City," Cheff said. "Not in the middle of a lockdown."

"Settport, maybe?" I asked. "Some rich folks on vacation?"

"Unlikely," Sable murmured.

"Right," Cheff said, "that would be unlikely. Probably not a tourist. But what, then?"

We watched in silence for a while, then Lery said, "Look!"

A girl, dressed in some sort of tan uniform, came out of the tent and stood by the fire. She took a deep breath, stretched, and yawned noisily. She lifted the lid of the cooking pot and tasted the contents with a large wooden spoon. She smacked her lips, satisfied, and filled a small bowl.

Mid scratched his head. "I don't get it. How could she possibly be the shadow agent? She's a girl, for one thing."

Buttons socked Mid solidly in the ribs. "So what if she is?"

"Oof! Sorry, Buttons. I didn't mean FRM agents can't be girls. It's just that I was expecting someone older, someone experienced, like Mr. Rignish."

"She isn't much like Mr. Rignish," Buttons said, "that's for sure! Right, Cheff? Cheff?"

"Right," Cheff said. "She's… *beautiful*!"

Mid's jaw dropped. "What are you talking about, Cheff? She's obviously an idiot."

"A *beautiful* idiot," Cheff mumbled.

Lery snickered.

Buttons smacked her forehead with her palm. "Snap out of it, Cheff. We have to figure out if she's the shadow agent or not."

"Preferably before it gets dark, Old Man," Mid said. He pounded Cheff's shoulder. "Cheff!"

"What?" Cheff asked dreamily, then shook himself. "Right, of course we do. I'll go ask her." He stood up and started to walk right out into the clearing.

Sable grabbed him by the belt and pulled him back down into the thicket. "You stay. I'll go."

"But—"

Sable cut him off with a piercing glance, then sneaked along the edge of the clearing. In a heartbeat, Sable was out of sight. We waited, watching the young woman daintily sip spoonfuls of her stew, or soup, or whatever it was.

After a few minutes, Lery pointed to the campsite. Sable came out of the tree line behind the red tent. She padded silently to where the girl was eating, but the girl must have heard something, because she turned toward Sable, leaped to her feet, and started winding up for a scream. Sable clapped one hand over her mouth, put her other arm around her neck, and dragged the girl into the woods.

Mid raised his eyebrows. "I guess that's one way to open a conversation. I'd love to hear the rest of it."

"Me, too," Cheff said. "Let's go!"

We followed Cheff around the edge of the clearing until we found Sable, still restraining the girl in a chokehold. The girl thrashed about furiously, struggling against Sable's grip. When she caught sight of the rest of us, she struggled even harder.

Cheff approached and knelt beside the pair. He stared into the girl's eyes.

"Cheff!" Sable said.

"Right, sorry. By your leave, Miss, if you'll promise to stop struggling and to be quiet, my friend will ease her grip on your neck."

The girl glared at him, then nodded.

Sable relaxed her hold sufficiently for the girl to catch her breath.

"Who are you? What is the meaning of this? How dare you put your filthy hands—"

Sable tightened her grip again.

"Hey!" Cheff said, "Easy! You'll hurt her."

Mid took Cheff by the arm and led him a dozen paces away. "I think you should stay over here for now, Old Man."

Cheff frowned and folded his arms across his chest, but he stayed put.

Mid came back to the girl and laughed. "If that's your idea of quiet, we'll have to tie you up and gag you. Is that what you want?"

The girl shook her head.

"All right, then. Let's try again."

Sable relaxed her grip. The girl opened her mouth, thought the better of it, and grew still.

"Good," Mid said. "That's a start. Now, would you care to tell us who you are and what you're doing here?"

"I most certainly would not!" the girl hissed. "I object to being handled in such a manner. I insist that you let me go at once. Or else!"

Buttons giggled. "The ponies want to know, or else what? Whatcha gonna do about it, huh?"

"Buttons, please." Mid sighed. "Look, Miss Whoever-you-are, I don't think you're getting the idea. We belong out here, the six of us. It's our job to be out here. We're *supposed* to be out here, see? You, on the other hand, with your red tent and smoky fire and elaborate camp, most certainly do *not* belong out here. So we have to ask ourselves, who is this person and what is her business here? Is she a civilian?"

"An exceptionally *dumb* civilian," Buttons piped up helpfully.

"Buttons, *please.*" Mid continued, "If this person is a civilian, she's in a lot of trouble. Violation of the lockdown carries a death penalty. If she's not a civilian, then she's in someone's service. Pallador's? A Blueband, perhaps? Maybe, maybe not. That doesn't look like a Blueband uniform you have on, but it's some kind of uniform, certainly."

"This is *not* a uniform, it's a—"

Mid held up a hand for silence. "*Our problem,* Miss, is that we can't afford to take chances. Our… task… out here in the woods is of a critical nature, to say the least. I'm pretty sure our superiors would concur that a single civilian casualty is an acceptable rate of collateral damage."

"Well said," Sable murmured.

Mid took a long, deep breath. "I suppose it's all right for me to reveal one feature of our task: we're looking for someone. If you can prove you're the one we're looking for, we'll be happy to tell you who we are and what we're doing here. If you can't, well... then I'm afraid we'll have to make sure you can never tell anyone about us. You've seen our faces, you see. We'll have to have our friend, here"—he pointed at Lery with his thumb—"*take care of you*."

Lery stepped forward, loomed over the girl, cracked his knuckles, and grinned.

The girl edged away from Lery.

"It's nothing personal, Miss," Mid said. "You were in the wrong place at the wrong time. We simply can't afford to let you go. Understand?"

I thought she was going to start struggling again, but instead, she said coldly, "Would you please tell the dark one to help me sit up?"

Sable helped the girl to a sitting position. "My name is Carra Trenta Wolcutt, of the Tumberland Wolcutts. I don't suppose any of *you* have ever heard of me or my family." She turned her nose up. "It certainly doesn't seem likely."

Cheff, who had been working his way closer, said "Hello, Miss Wolcutt! I'm Cheff, Cheff Karfendek." Cheff's dreamy look had returned. He stuck out his hand. "I'm pleased to meet you! I'm a Lora, like you!"

"Oh, *brother*!" Buttons said.

"I noticed," the girl said, her voice dripping with disdain.

"And this is my baby sister, But—"

Mid gently pushed Cheff back. "Easy, Cheff. How about you go back to your spot over there and play it cool and we'll handle this one, okay?"

Cheff looked puzzled, but said, "Well, okay, Mid, if that's the way you want it."

"Thank you, Cheff. It is the way I want it, for now. Take a little break. Go back to your waiting place. Humor me."

"Right. By the way, that was a great speech you gave—all those fancy words!" He sauntered back to his designated waiting place, then waved at Mid. "Okay, I'm here! Right where you said. Carry on!"

"That's fine, Cheff, just fine." Mid waved back. "Now then, Miss Wolcutt, suppose you tell me what a girl from Tumberland is doing all the way down here in the wilds of Fellstone, hmm?"

"I'm not a *girl*," Carra snapped.

"She sure looks like a girl to me," Cheff called from his retreat. "A *lovely* girl."

"Cheff, for Andaran's sake!"

"Sorry, Mid."

Buttons held the ponies up and looked them in the eye. "The ponies say that she certainly isn't a very *nice* girl. Not too smart, either."

Carra Trenta Wolcott stared at Buttons.

Mid continued, "Well, Miss Wolcutt? What about it?"

"I... I... can't tell you," Carra said. "I'm sorry, I just can't."

"That's awkward," Mid said. He turned to us. "Now what?"

Sable said, "Tell her."

"What? Tell her what? Who we are?" Mid asked.

"Tell her," Sable repeated.

"Well, okay. If she's the wrong person, we can always..."

Lery loomed again. Carra leaned away from him. "Make him stop," she said.

"All right, Miss Wolcutt," Mid said, "it's like this: the six of us received orders to find a certain pack peddler and warn him that Fellstone City is under a strict lockdown and that it's not safe for him to go there. Instead, he was to deliver his... shipment... to us and return to Tumberland. We found him a couple of hours ago and delivered the message."

Carra's eyes grew wide, but she kept quiet.

"We were also directed to find a second person, someone who was watching over the old man, and give them the same message. If you can demonstrate to our satisfaction that you are that second person, then all is well. If not…"

Carra started to laugh. She laughed so hard that tears ran down her face, and she couldn't catch her breath. She gasped for air, wiped her eyes, then laughed even harder.

The six of us watched her, unamused.

"*You?*" she said between gasps, "The six of *you* are FRM agents? A skinny Lildur kid with glasses—

I pushed my glasses up on my nose.

"—a fat Troh—"

"Hey!" Mid patted his belly.

"—a spider-legged Kreff girl—

Sable smiled, showing her fangs.

"—a shaggy Lora kid and his insane brat sister with her talking ponies—

Buttons raised her eyebrows and gaped at the ponies, who gaped right back at her.

"—and whatever *that* is, with some kind of plumbing tool hanging on his belt? You've *got* to be kidding me!" She dissolved into laughter again.

"This is hopeless," Mid said. "Lery, take care of her, and we'll go through her things. It'll be dark soon. We need to get moving."

Lery grinned, showing all his jagged Fessal teeth, and came forward once more, unhooking the giant pipe wrench from his belt.

"No! Wait!" Carra said. "Please. I'll tell you everything." She wiped her face on her sleeve. "I just can't believe that *you*—" She finally caught Mid's expression and stopped abruptly.

"Well, we are, Miss High-and-Mighty Carra Trenta Wolcutt of the Tumberland Wolcutts!" Buttons said. "And you'd better get used to it if you know what's good for you. Besides, you're hardly one to talk about who's a *real* agent—camped out in this clearing for all the world to see, as though you owned the place. Your campfire smoke can be seen for miles. The ponies and I are city girls, and we know better than that." She held Starry and Moka up so they could glower at Carra. "The ponies disapprove—and so do I."

Carra stared at Buttons and the ponies. "The *ponies* disapprove—what, are you all *mad*?"

"Well," I said off-handedly, "We're not exactly happy about it."

Buttons giggled, Lery grinned. Even Sable smiled a little.

"Buttons is right about that smoke," I said, "And we're not the only ones who will notice. You've built a regular signal beacon. The sooner we get away from here, the better."

"True," Sable said. "Time to go."

"Very well," Mid said. "Let's conclude our business. It's quite simple: you're to give us the special materials you're carrying, then turn around and head back to Tumberland. We'll escort you back to your boat and help you get launched. Agreed?"

"I'm sorry, no. It's not at all that simple. What's your name, kid?"

Mid frowned at 'kid,' but answered, "Mid."

"You see, Mid, I *am* an FRM agent, as you have obviously guessed. A *proper* FRM agent, I might add. In addition to my mission to shadow that *atrocious* old man, I have an mission of my own. I'm to make contact with a certain Mr. Meltern, who is to provide me with a quantity of an herb native to this region, name-ly, rovaldia. I'm to deliver the rovaldia to the FRM laboratory in Tumberland. So, unless you happen to have a rather large quan-tity of rovaldia with you, I'm afraid I'm going to have to continue on to Fellstone City, in spite of your possibly well meant, but se-verely misguided, instructions." She crossed her arms and looked smug. "Well, do you, kid?"

"Of course we don't!" Mid said. "Huh. This certainly complicates things. Wait here. Lery, watch her."

Lery came over and sat down right in front of Carra. "Okay," he said. "I'm watching."

The rest of us went to where Cheff was waiting. Mid took Cheff by the shoulders and shook him. "Snap out of it, Cheff. We've got troubles."

"She is *beautiful,* isn't she?" Cheff asked.

Buttons kicked Cheff in the shin as hard as she could.

"Ow!" Cheff yelled, hopping around on one foot. "What did you do that for?"

"Sorry, Cheff," Buttons said. "Forget about that girl. We have an important decision to make."

"Well, all right," Cheff said, "but you didn't have to kick me. You could have said so." He rubbed his shinbone, wincing. "What's the trouble?"

Mid said, "That girl, Carra, has to take a load of something called rovaldia back to Tumberland. We can't just send her home."

"Rovaldia?" Cheff asked. "Where are we going to get rovaldia? It doesn't grow up north here, or even around Fellstone City. As far as I know, it only grows in The Fel, in the wetlands."

"She's demanding to meet Meltern," Mid said, "but Zeek said we're supposed to send her home."

I glanced over at Carra. Lery was sitting right in front of her, staring at her. Carra's fists were clenched, but she showed no signs of imminent bolting.

"It's too far to walk to Meltern's Guest House from here," Mid said. "It would take days, and we'd be missed."

"How about this," Cheff asked, "we take her back to the salvage camp and explain the situation to Zeek? If he decides she needs to see Meltern, he can take her in Willam."

"That sounds right to me," I said.

"Me, too," Mid said.

"Good," Sable said.

"The ponies approve," Buttons said.

"Fine," Cheff said. "It's settled. Let's see if we can get Carra on board. Mid, you'd better handle the conversation. Something about her makes my head go funny."

Buttons looked disgusted. "Yeah, real funny. Downright hilarious."

"How are we going to get Carra to agree?" I asked.

"I have an idea," Mid said. "Follow my lead."

We returned to Carra and Lery, except for Cheff, who remained at a distance.

"On the edge of a pond, with no apparent attempt to conceal it, was a bright-red two-man tent…"

— 15 —

CARRA TRENTA WOLCUTT

M ID WALKED UP to her. "Well, Miss Carra Trenta Wolcutt," he said, "your fate has been decided."

"Oh?" She arched her eyebrows and studied her fingernails. "I can *hardly* wait."

"We're going to give you a choice."

"*How* exciting." She discovered a speck of dirt under the third finger of her left hand and flicked it out with the forefinger of her right hand.

"Either," Mid said, "you give us your solemn word as an FRM agent that you will cooperate with us and follow our orders to the letter…"

"Or?"

"Or Lery, here, will dig you a grave and you can stay here in this forest. Forever."

"You wouldn't *dare*."

"Already… dug one… grave today," Lery said.

"I don't believe you," Carra said, but she looked worried.

"You'd *better* believe it," Buttons said. "How do you think Lery got so dirty?"

"This is ridiculous!" Carra protested.

"Okay," Mid said, "have it your way. Books, tie her up. Lery?"

Lery hung his pipe wrench back on his belt, took his folding camp shovel from his tool bag, moved a few feet off, and began digging.

"You wouldn't dare! I'm Carra Trenta Wolcutt, of the Tumberland Wolcutts!"

Mid helped me tie her hands and feet with some short lengths of cord from his tech bag. He kicked some dirt with his shoe. "Yeah, you mentioned that before. Doesn't mean anything to me. I'm from Settport. Mean anything to you, Lery?"

"Nope."

"Sable?"

Sable shook her head.

"How about you, Books?"

"I've heard of the Wolcutts," I said, trying to make my voice gruff, "but never of this one. The Wolcutts are a big name up in Tumberland. Forestry operations—logging, lumber mills, trucking, that sort of thing. Inordinately rich. Of course, anyone could *claim* to be a Wolcutt. Doesn't make them one."

"Anyway," Mid said, "it doesn't matter much, one way or the other, out here in the woods."

"Of course I'm a Wolcutt! Who are you to question me, you little Lildur runt! I'll have you know the Wolcutts are the oldest family in Tumberland!"

At 'Lildur runt,' Lery began digging harder.

"Oh, now, that's just not nice!" Buttons said. "Is it, Starry?" Starry didn't think so, either. Buttons hefted Starry, feeling the weight of the ball bearings and scrap iron she was stuffed with, then slapped Starry against her palm a few times. "Can I hit her, Mid? Starry wants to give her a good smack. Starry thinks Miss Fancy-pants-rich-Tumberland-girl should use better manners."

"Get away from me, brat!" Carra edged away from Buttons.

"Easy, Buttons," Mid said. "Wait until Lery's finished. Then you can do as you please."

Carra looked at each of us. A dozen yards away, Cheff's face was grim. Mid looked plain disgusted. Buttons scowled and slapped Starry against her palm. I did my best to look disgusted, too. Sable grinned and showed the points of her brilliant white Kreff fangs.

Carra shuddered. "You're serious, aren't you?"

No one answered.

"Why don't you take my bag and let me go?"

Mid shrugged. "And risk you getting the rest of us killed? Not a chance."

"I'll go straight back to Tumberland, I promise."

"No good," Mid said. He pointed at Carra's bright red tent in the clearing. "You're obviously some kind of moron. It's a wonder you weren't caught already. I'm afraid we can't risk it."

"But what about the other agent, the one I'm shadowing?"

"What about him?" Mid asked.

"Who's going to look after him?"

"He's dead," Buttons said. "That's the other grave we dug."

"Dead! You *killed* that old man? I don't believe you."

Mid whirled on her. "No, you fool. We didn't kill him—*you* did! He fell off a rock while you were 'caring' for him and died from bleeding inside. Some shadow agent you are."

"Fentor's dead?" Carra was stunned, but recovered quickly. "Well. He was much too old to be an FRM agent, anyway."

"That does it!" Buttons stalked over to where Carra was sitting and drew her arm back, Starry in her hand. "You're just plain *nasty*!"

"Hold it, Buttons," Mid said, grabbing her wrist.

"Aw, Mid, she—"

"Hold it, I said. Okay?"

Buttons kicked some dirt onto Carra. "Okay, Mid. You're the boss."

Lery called, "Mid! The grave is… about… ready."

Sable and Mid took the frantically struggling Carra by the elbows, lifted her to her feet, and dragged her over to the freshly dug grave. Cheff remained at a distance. Lery hefted the folding shovel.

"Wait! Stop!" Carra's voice was shrill.

"What is it now?" Mid asked.

"I agree. I'll agree to anything you say! Please don't kill me."

"You had your chance," Mid growled.

"And after what you did to that poor old man," Buttons said, "it serves you right!"

Carra fell to her knees. "I'm sorry. I never meant for him to be hurt. I watched him all the way from Tumberland. I lost track of him yesterday, right before he crossed the water. It was only for a few minutes! The next thing I knew, he was halfway across the bay. I followed him as quickly as I could, but the current was strong and I drifted northward out of the bay. I'm so *sorry*! I was sure I'd find him on this side, but I searched all day and most of the night, and I couldn't. So I made camp. I thought maybe he'd see the smoke and find me!" She started to cry. "That poor man," she sobbed. "I can't believe he's dead."

"He's dead," Mid said coldly. "We watched him die."

"I'm… I'm glad you were with him. I'm glad he didn't die alone."

"All right, enough!" Mid said. "Let's get this over with and get back to work."

Lery raised his camp shovel.

Carra squinched her eyes shut.

"Rovaldia," Sable murmured.

"Wait a minute, Lery," Buttons said.

Lery lowered the shovel.

"What is it, Buttons?" Mid asked.

"Sable's right. What about the rovaldia? She said she had to take some back to the Tumberland lab. It might be important."

Mid stroked his chin. "Yes, that's right. Tell us about it, Miss Carra Trenta Wolcutt. What do they want rovaldia for?"

"I… I don't know, exactly. It has something to do with the antidote for jexan. They said it was pretty urgent."

Mid consulted with Cheff. The two put their heads together and whispered. Then Mid came back to Carra, still kneeling at the head of the grave. "We agree that the rovaldia mission may be important."

"Oh, it is, it is!"

"Quiet, please. We're willing to spare you on one condition."

"Yes, anything."

"It's the same condition as before. You give your word as an FRM agent to cooperate with us and follow our orders to the letter. In exchange, we'll see to it that you get to Meltern, our leader. He'll decide what to do about you and the rovaldia."

Carra hesitated.

"Last chance," Mid said. "Take it or leave it. I'm sure we can work out the rovaldia issue without you if we have to."

Carra took a deep breath. "I promise, on my honor as an FRM agent, to cooperate fully with you six and follow your orders to the letter."

Lery stuck his face into hers. "And… and you'd better… apologize… to Books and… Buttons."

At once, Carra said, "Books, Buttons, I apologize for calling you a runt and a brat. I was upset. I hope you'll forgive me. Please."

I shrugged. "Sure, whatever."

"Fat chance," Buttons said and kicked more of the rich, brown forest dirt in Carra's direction. She turned and ambled over to Cheff, still smacking Starry pointedly against her palm.

Mid untied Carra's hands and feet. "You'd best pack up your camp as quickly as possible."

"Leave it," Cheff called.

"Evidence," Sable murmured.

"She's right, Cheff," Mid said. "Wouldn't do to have somebody run across it and follow us. For that matter, where is your boat?"

"I left it on the beach."

"You *what*?" Mid yelled. "You *are* some rare kind of fool, aren't you?"

"Easy, Mid," Cheff said. "We'll go back that way and hide it."

"If someone hasn't found it already," Mid said.

We checked the clearing for signs of anyone, then Carra dashed out and packed up her tent and cooking gear, smothered her fire with dirt, strapped on her pack, and rejoined us in the forest. No one offered to help her carry her pack, though it was nearly as big as Fentor Rignish's.

"Okay," Mid said. "Which way's your boat?"

Carra looked perplexed.

"Unbelievable." Mid shook his head. "Sable, if you please?"

Sable crouched and started looking for sign. In short order, she picked up Carra's trail, and we followed it back through the forest toward the bay.

When we got to the beach, we paused at the edge of the woods. Sure enough, like a brilliant, shining star right in the middle of the sand, there was Carra's little canvas canoe, painted bright yellow.

"You didn't even *try* to hide it?" Mid asked. "I don't get it."

Sable looked up and down the beach. "Clear," she said.

"Okay," Mid said to Carra. "Go."

Carra ran out and retrieved the canoe. We dragged it into the dense forest, then camouflaged it as we had Mr. Rignish's little boat. Lery took his knife and skinned a strip of bark off a nearby tree, so we could find it again.

"Okay, Sable," Mid said, "can you lead us back to Mr. Rignish's boat? It'll be dark soon."

The stars were already coming out overhead. Across the channel, the Fellstone Light's beacon had come on for the night.

Sable jogged south through the forest at a brisk pace. There was no need to go slowly now—our search was over. Sable led us directly to Mr. Rignish's little craft. Lery fished out the peddler's pack and slung it over his shoulder. Carra looked solemn but didn't comment.

We followed Sable to the salvage camp, where we waited in the woods until it was completely dark. Then Cheff, Buttons, Mid, and I made our way to my tent. Zeek wasn't around—I hoped he was getting us some extra food from the chow line.

"Let me borrow your ID badge, Buttons," Mid said.

Buttons unpinned her badge and gave it to him.

"Stay right here. I'll be back shortly." Mid vanished into the darkness.

A few minutes later, he returned with Carra, Sable, and Lery. Carra was wearing Buttons' ID badge.

"No problems," Mid said. "We didn't even see a guard—they must be eating. It looks like the mess tent is still serving supper. Lery, how about you, Buttons, and Sable hit the chow line, and bring back enough for the rest of us? Miss Tumberland, here, and I are going to go through her pack and Mr. Rignish's and locate the you-know-what. Um, Cheff, could Books and I have a word with you in private?"

"Of course. Let's step outside."

Mid scanned the area to make certain that no one was within earshot, then asked Cheff, "Are you going to be okay with that girl? What about the way she makes you feel funny inside?"

"I… I don't know, Old Son. I've never felt like this before. My brain tells me that she's stupid and mean and incompetent, but then I take one look at her and I forget all about that. All I can think of is how beautiful she is."

"You've lived in the Labor Compound too long, Old Man. You need to get out more. It doesn't matter how beautiful she is—the mission has to come first."

Cheff hung his head. "I know, I know. What am I going to do?"

"You're going to keep in mind that all of Andaran is hanging on what we do in the next few days. It's a matter of life and death for thousands, maybe millions."

I added, "People have *already* died for this mission, Cheff."

Cheff stood up straight and set his jaw. "You're right, of course, both of you. I need to keep myself focused and my mind on the mission. I'll leave Carra up to you, okay?"

"Okay, Cheff. But if you still have a problem, promise you'll tell me right away. Not that everyone can't tell." Mid grinned.

"I promise, Old Son."

I said, "How about Cheff and I go to the mess area and join up with the others? You can deal with Carra by yourself, can't you?"

"Sure," Mid said, "go ahead."

"Come on, Cheff, let's go," I said.

We had no sooner found Lery, Buttons, and Sable in the chow line than Miss Averith Brex made an appearance, complete with her report book tucked under her left arm. "There you are, vermin! Where have you been all day? I've been watching for you, but haven't seen a sign of you or your pathetic friends."

"Why, good evening, Miss Brex," Cheff said. "I hope you enjoyed your evening repast."

"Knock it off, Karfendek!" Brex snapped. "I'm waiting."

"We've been salvaging with Zeek, of course," Cheff said. "Down deep in the innards of that unfortunate wrecked ship."

"That's right," Buttons said. "I got to crawl through some air ducts because I'm the littlest." She put on her cute face and batted her eyes at Brex. "That's why I'm so dirty."

"Brat!" Brex spat. "Bow or stern?"

I closed my eyes and tried to remember which part Zeek had said our assignment was in. "Stern, of course. That's Zeek's assignment. Sections A through F."

Brex glared at me. "I'll verify that. Where's Persil?"

"Back at our tent," Cheff said. "He's cleaning up our tools and putting them away for the night."

"Hmph. I'll pay him a visit, too, I think." She stalked off toward the tents.

I whispered to Cheff, "I hope Mid has Carra out of sight."

"Yeah," Cheff said, "that could be awkward. Buttons, maybe you ought to run back and warn them."

"Right," Buttons said, and was gone.

"Come on," Cheff said, "let's make a big show of being present for supper. That's probably the most helpful thing we can do right now."

We got our food and found Zeek sitting at a table with some of the other salvage operators and the three young men we'd met briefly that morning.

He waved cheerfully. "Hi, kids! How's it going?"

"Great!" Cheff said. "We got all the materials in the truck. Mid's cleaning up the tools, back in the tent."

"Of course, of course." He turned to his colleagues. "How do you like that, huh? Don't I have some great workers?" He took his little flask from his hip and poured a generous measure into each of the other salvage operators' cups. "There you are! Nothing like a little nip to ward off the night chill, especially so close to the bay. Isn't that right?" He leaned over and said in Cheff's ear, "Finish quickly and get back to the tent. I'll be there as soon as I can."

We finished, then hit the chow line again. Cheff said to one of the food workers, "Say, a couple of our crew are stuck cleaning tools. Is it okay if we take some chow back to them?"

"Sure, kid," one of the workers said. "Help yourself. Here, take some extra bowls. You can drop them off at breakfast, okay?"

"Great! Thanks, much appreciated!"

We each loaded a bowl to its brim, then dashed back to the tents.

Operation Lockdown

— 16 —
CARRA MEETS ZEEK

WHEN WE GOT back to my tent, Brex was already there. She stood inside the doorway, looking the situation over.

"Excuse me, please, Miss Brex," I said, as I edged past her. I handed a bowl of food to Buttons. Carra was nowhere in sight. Buttons sat on the edge of one of the camp beds, swinging her legs.

"Hello… Miss Brex," Lery said, as he came in and handed his bowl to Mid.

Sable came through next, carrying her bowl, but didn't speak to Brex.

Brex looked Sable over, head to toe. "Who's your bowl for, Spiderlegs?"

"Lunch," Sable murmured. "Tomorrow."

Cheff handed his bowl to Sable. "Could you pack mine up for me, too, please? Zeek says we'll be gone all day tomorrow and we need to pack our lunch with us. I think he's going to have us run a load of scrap to his salvage yard in the Labor Compound."

Brex narrowed her eyes. "And I suppose it'll take all six of you to do that?"

"Zeek says it will," Cheff said pleasantly. "I'm not sure why. Maybe there's some additional work to be done there. Anyway, Zeek's the boss. If he says go, we go."

"Hmmph!" Brex said. "A likely story. I have a feeling you all are up to something, and I'm going find out what."

"Zeek," Sable said.

"What about him?" Brex snapped.

"Sable means," Cheff said, "that if you want to know what we're all up to, you should ask Zeek. We don't have any secrets. I'm sure he'll be happy to explain everything to you."

"That's right, Miss Brex," Mid said. "We understand that your load of responsibility is much greater than normal during the lockdown, and we're happy to cooperate in any way we can." He flashed her a grin.

Buttons batted her eyes at Brex. "The ponies say that they'll help, too."

Tocette burst into the tent, bumping Brex into Sable and nearly knocking the bowl of food out of Sable's hands. "Hi, everyone! What a great day, wasn't it? I hope you guys had as much fun as we did. We were working in the bow section. Were you guys in the stern? I didn't see you all day. I'll bet that's why. Whatcha doin', Cheff?"

Cheff waved. "Hello, Beautiful and Intrepid Tocette! Yup, we were in the stern. That's where Zeek's assignment is."

"Oh." Tocette failed to notice that Miss Averith Brex was glaring at her with a glare that might have killed a small mammal or maybe even a medium-sized one. "You guys sure got a good job! Zeek's a good boss. Sometimes, before I joined the Bluebands, I used to do odd jobs for him at his salvage yard. I loved riding in Willam the Wheezer. Zeek used to let me work the shifter."

Buttons ceremoniously shook Tocette's hand. "Zeek taught me to work the shifter on the way here. You know what that makes us? Shifter sisters!"

"Oh. Shifter sisters?" A grin slowly spread over Tocette's face. "I suppose it does. I like it. I never had a shifter sister before." She took Buttons' little hand in her filthy giant paw and danced a little jig. "Shifter sister, shifter sister, Buttons and I are shifter sisters."

"Ehem!" Brex said. "Stop that at once, Cadet Crindel. What sort of way is that for a Blueband Cadet to act?"

Tocette stopped abruptly. "Sorry, Miss Brex. I guess I got carried away."

"Indeed. Did you come here for a reason, Cadet?"

"Yes, Miss Brex, I certainly did. A good reason."

Brex waited, then said, "Cadet!"

"Yes, Miss Brex?"

"Will you tell me, please?"

"Of course, Miss Brex, certainly." Tocette frowned. "Um… tell you what, exactly, Miss Brex?"

"Tell. Me. Why. You. Came. Here." With each word, Brex slapped her report book against her palm.

"Oh. Captain Kellery said to tell you that there's going to be a meeting of all the Blueband squad leaders in the salvage camp."

"Did he tell you where and when this meeting was to be?"

"Oh. Yes, Miss Brex, he did that."

Brex waited again, then shouted, "Cadet Crindel!"

"Yes, Miss Br—oh, er, it's going to be at one of the mess tables, right away."

"Right away? How long ago did he tell you that."

"Um… I'm not sure, Miss Brex. It took me a while to find you."

"Moron! You should have said so immediately!"

"Yes, Miss Brex. Sorry, Miss Brex."

"Oh, shut up, Cadet Idiot. Let's go!" She spun and marched out of the tent, Tocette right behind her.

When she was gone, we laughed until we cried. Even Sable allowed herself a small smile.

"Oh, man," Cheff said, "you have to love that girl!"

"Bounty," Sable murmured.

"Of course!" Cheff said in an undertone. "She came from the mess tent. I'll bet she's chock-full of jexan."

"The ponies say she was acting exactly like she did at the—you know," Buttons said, then in a whisper, "the Iron Fortress."

"Well, I'm sure glad she's on Brex's side, not ours," Mid said.

"What did you do with our new friend?" I asked Mid.

"Oh, right. I nearly forgot." He poked his head out of the tent flap to make sure no one was around, then went to the back of the tent and lifted the bottom of the canvas wall.

Carra Trenta Wolcutt wriggled into the tent, stood up, and brushed the dirt off her clothes. "All clear?"

Cheff gazed at Carra. "Mmmhmm, it sure is, lovely Carra."

"Oh, brother, he's at it again!" Buttons went over to him and led him to the front of the tent.

Mid said quietly, "You'd better stay near the door, Cheff."

Cheff shook his head to clear it. "She's so… I don't know. She just *is*."

"I thought you said you weren't going to be having any more trouble with that?"

"I didn't think I was." He scratched his head. "It's funny, Old Son. My brain says one thing, but—"

"Right," Mid said. "I get it. Stay there. Did you find the—"

"Hello, children!" Zeek came in through the flap, and suddenly the tent was crowded. "I'm sorry I took so long—I had to put in an appearance with the other salvage operators. Among other things, I had a word with Whipple to make sure that our assignment will continue to be in the stern section all week and that she'll keep Blueband Captain Kellery and his troops in the bow. So that's one less thing to worry about." He cleared a seat for himself on the camp cot closest to the door, next to where Cheff was standing. "So, children, tell me all about it. How did the mission go? Did you find—" He spotted Carra near the back wall. "Who in Andaran is that?"

"That," Cheff said, "is Miss Carra Trenta Wolcutt of the Tumberland Wolcutts. She's also Fentor Rignish's shadow agent."

"I see." Zeek stroked his stubbly chin. "And she's here, why? I'm sure that wasn't part of the plan. You were supposed to warn her off, get the research materials, and send her home."

"I'm sorry, Zeek, but there were complications." Cheff filled Zeek in on the events of the day, Fentor Rignish's untimely death, our agreement with Carra, and the need for rovaldia in Tumberland.

Zeek took his battered hat from his head and ran his fingers through his hair. "So, old Rignish is gone. I can't say I'm surprised—the amazing thing is that he lasted this long. He is—*was*—quite a man, and a fine agent. He will be missed." He stared at the floor, then said, "Another time, in another place, remind me to tell you some stories about Rignish. He had an amazing life. I knew him a little bit—once we had a mission, of sorts, together. I've never met anyone like him."

"He remembered you," Cheff said.

"He said you were a friend," Mid said.

"Did he, now? Well, that's fine, fine." Zeek took a deep breath. "I'm glad to hear it." He looked around the tent. "Did you get the, um, package from him?"

"Yes, sir," Cheff said. "Before he died, he gave us his pack. Said we could likely use the contents, considering the shape we're in."

Zeek laughed. "That's Fentor Rignish, all right. And I'm sure you can, boy. Where is it?"

Mid patted Buttons' cot, on which he was sitting. "Under here." He pointed at my cot. "Carra's is under there. Brex never noticed."

"Good, well done, Mid. And the research materials?"

"We got Mr. Rignish's, and Carra's, too," Mid said. "They're both in my tech bag. We thought about hiding them, but it seemed prudent to keep them close."

"Also well done. Here, give them to me. After a while, I'll put them and Fentor's pack in a safe place where no one will ever find them. Willam has many, many secrets, you know." He winked at us. "Well, children, I must say that you've exceeded my expectations, especially in view of the added complications. I'll admit I had my doubts about you children at first, but it's becoming quite clear why Madame Entigy has such faith in you.

"As for you, Miss Wolcutt, I expect you to keep your word of honor to Cheff and the others. I'll decide what to do with you in the morning. For now, you can bunk here with the other girls and Books. You'd best wear Buttons' ID tag for the night. Buttons can always say she lost hers."

Buttons put on her innocent face and gazed up at Zeek. "I sure can, Mr. Zeek. And I *know* people would believe me. I'd be *so* sincerely sorry."

Zeek chuckled. "I'm sure you would."

"One more thing, sir," Mid said. "When Brex was here snooping around before you came back, we told her that you have plans to take us back to the salvage yard tomorrow, to help you unload. We saw that Willam was full, and thought that might put her off the scent for a day, whether we actually go or not."

"We guessed," Cheff said, "that Meltern might want a word with our new friend."

"Good thinking. That gives us some options. All right, children. Sleep well. Tomorrow's a new adventure. Goodnight, girls. Goodnight, Books."

Buttons cleared her throat pointedly.

"Oh," Zeek said, "I nearly forgot. Goodnight, ponies!"

The ponies waved goodnight as Zeek and the other boys left.

The girls and I settled down for the night. The only available camp cot was the one next to me, so Carra stowed her gear underneath, took off her boots, and unrolled a kind of bedroll I'd never seen before.

Unlike our rough woolen blankets, Carra's bedroll was a kind of a big bag. It was canvas on the outside, but soft on the inside, like a shirt, and it was padded, all fluffy. She wiggled into it, feet first, then pulled it up around her chin.

When she saw me watching her, she whispered, "It's called a sleeping bag. Haven't you ever seen one before?"

"No," I said. "We only have blankets."

"This is much better than a blanket. It doesn't come off in the night, and the cold air can't get in. It's warm and comfy."

"It looks like a good idea," I said. "I suppose we could make something like it out of our blankets, if we worked at it."

"Or you could buy some," Carra said.

"Sure," I was glad she couldn't see my sour face in the dark. "That's a great idea. We'll take our loads of money and buy ourselves some, next time we're in New City Market. Thanks so much for the tip. Good night, Carra. See you in the morning."

"Goodnight, Books."

Carra Trenta Wolcutt (of the Tumberland Wolcutts)

— 17 —

CARRA JOINS THE WORK CREW

THE NEXT MORNING, Zeek put his head into our tent well before dawn. "Wake up, children. We have a big day ahead of us."

Sable, Buttons, and I rolled out of our blankets. Carra Trenta Wolcutt (of the Tumberland Wolcutts) wriggled little by little out of her sleeping bag, still fully dressed in her tan pseudo-uniform, except for her boots. She smoothed her clothing, shivered, and remarked, "My! It's chilly out here this morning."

Zeek watched her, eyebrows raised. "That's a nifty bedroll, Miss Wolcutt, as long as you're not in a hurry."

"Why, thank you, Zeek. I was telling Books last night that he ought to get some for his group."

"Excellent idea, girl. I'm sure he'll pick up a half dozen the next time he's at New City Market."

"Why, that's exactly what Books said last night!" Carra smiled, obviously pleased with herself for having made such an excellent suggestion.

I kept my face straight, but Buttons rolled her eyes. The ponies exchanged a significant glance.

"By the way, Miss Wolcutt," Zeek said, "Do you happen to have a change of clothes? Something less… flamboyant, perhaps? I'm afraid your… um… outfit will be… um… out of place here in the salvage camp. We wouldn't want to attract unnecessary attention, would we?"

"Well, no, I don't have anything else. I do have a change of clothes in my pack, but it's much like this one. I wasn't expecting to join a salvage party."

"Of course, of course," Zeek said. "Perfectly understandable." He thought about the problem. "Wait here, Miss Wolcutt, if you please. I have an idea."

Zeek returned shortly with a bundle under his arm, which he handed to Carra. "Here you are, Miss Wolcutt. They might be a little big for you, but they're the best I could do on such short notice. If you roll up the sleeves and the pant legs, I'm sure they'll be fine. Come with me, Books, and let the ladies get dressed. We'll get started on breakfast, and they can join us when they're ready."

I grabbed the empty bowls from the night before and followed Zeek outside. The other guys were up and waiting for us. They were, all three of them, wearing funny little smiles, but they didn't explain and I didn't ask.

I turned the bowls in at the mess tent and got in line with the guys.

"Easy on the biscuits and such," Cheff said. "Remember how loopy Tocette was last night. We'll need to be extra sharp today."

We loaded up on eggs and meat, but only one biscuit each.

Zeek said, "Be sure to take some hard-boiled eggs and some dried meat for lunch. Don't worry about getting into trouble—it's expected and all the crews do it."

We were working on our second helping when the girls arrived. Buttons and Sable both had deadpan expressions. Carra was lagging behind a little bit.

When she caught up, I froze with my fork halfway to my mouth and did a double-take. Yes, that was Carra, but barely recognizable. She resembled a scarecrow dressed in a giant's clothes.

She saw me gawking at her. "Shut it, Books!" She scowled and followed the girls to the chow line.

After she was gone, Zeek started chuckling which set the rest of us off. I couldn't catch my breath. Lery laughed so hard that his felmoss tea shot out of his nose.

"What in Andaran happened to her?" Mid asked.

Lery said, "Zeek… borrowed my… my extra shirt and… overalls."

"Andaran's bones!" Zeek said. "I didn't think she'd look *that* bad."

We looked at Carra over our shoulders and started laughing again. From the chow line, she shot us a glance that promised death and destruction when she caught up with us.

The girls joined us at the table. All of us, including Zeek, kept perfectly straight faces and studied our trays intently. Zeek said, "Good morning, girls. Good morning, Miss Wolcutt."

"Good morning, Carra," I said.

"You look lovely today," Mid added.

"I… I like your… overalls," Lery said. "I… I have… a pair… exactly like them."

I almost choked on a bite of bacon.

"Yes," Cheff said. "They're nice. They go quite well with your—"

Carra flung her gravy-covered biscuit at Cheff, which hit him square in the center of his forehead, gravy running down his nose. He sat stunned, then stuck out his tongue and licked the gravy away. "Thank you, Miss Wolcutt. The gravy is delicious." He plucked the biscuit from his face and nibbled it. "Ahhh, nothing like the taste of jexan in the morning."

That did it—we cracked up. Even Sable smiled. Carra sat there, fuming, until she, too, gave in and laughed. Then she picked up her tray, went round the table, and sat down next to Lery.

He scooted over to make room, avoiding eye contact with her. But she leaned over and kissed him on the cheek. "Thank you, Lery, for loaning me some work clothes. I'm afraid I didn't come prepared. Buttons offered me hers, but the ponies said that they wouldn't fit. I don't know what I'd have done without you."

Lery blushed purple. "You're… welcome, Miss Wolcutt."

"Call me 'Carra,' Lery, if you please."

"Okay."

Cheff's eyebrows arched. He looked, well, jealous, but quickly recovered and composed himself.

Zeek clapped his hands. "Fine, fine, everybody gets along. That's wonderful." He leaned close and whispered to Carra, "In case you don't already know, any white food—flour, sugar, and the like—is likely laced with jexan. A little bit won't hurt you, but you'll need to be cautious."

Carra nodded. "Thank you, Zeek. I'll be careful."

Mid asked, "Carra, where did you get your ID badge?" He peered at it. "It looks authentic."

"It was in the bundle with Lery's clothes. I don't know where it came from."

"I have my ways," Zeek said. "Now you're official. See? It even has your new name on it: Carra Trent. If you're stopped at the gate, don't worry—your new name is on the official list, now, too. And your pass is already stamped once, a most sincere stamp showing that you entered the camp with us last night."

"Thank you, Zeek," Carra said again.

"You're quite welcome. But do me a huge favor and remember your new name, okay? Now, children, let's discuss our strategy for today. Obviously, our objectives have changed, and we have several options."

"If we can," Mid said, "we should make an appearance somewhere Brex can see us. Maybe that will put her off our trail for a while."

"We need to get Carra to Meltern's, too," Cheff added.

"Well, I have a load of scrap that needs to go back to the yard," Zeek said. "Willam's full to the top. And I suppose there's nothing to keep me from buying my helpers a mug of ice-cold cider at

Meltern's Guest House on the way back. He has the best cider in Fellstone City, you know."

Buttons said, "Maybe some of us should stay here for Brex to see, and the rest go with Zeek?"

"D.B.U.T.T." Sable said.

"What was that?" Zeek asked.

"D.B.U.T.T." Cheff said. "Don't Break Up the Team. It's one of the rules from Sable's Naval Officer's manual, written by Admiral Pitr Karlsin."

Zeek thought this over. "I agree with Sable," he said. "If we split up and Brex asks about the others, it could be awkward. We should stick together. Besides, we don't know what instructions we'll get from Meltern. He might have some other mission for you. So, let's make sure Brex sees us heading down to the stern section of the wreck. We'll go in Willam, all together."

I asked, "Won't Brex wonder why we're going to work in the stern again, if Willam is already full?"

Zeek rubbed his chin whiskers. "Good question, Books. Well, if she asks, I can tell her that I'll be dropping you kids off at the stern, while I drive to town alone. But let's make sure she notices us. Then, when we drive out of camp, you kids can duck down so it looks like I'm by myself in Willam. Brex will think you're still working in the stern." He shaded his eyes from the morning light and looked across the mess area. "Here come the fellows who helped me yesterday. Hello, men! Had your breakfast, yet?"

"Mornin', Zeek," one of them said. "Yes, we've eaten and we're ready to go. Got all our tools right here."

"Splendid!" Zeek said. "Hop in, you can ride with me." He pointed to a group of Bluebands at a table on the opposite side of the mess area. "Isn't that Tocette over there?"

"It certainly is," Cheff said. "How about Buttons and I go have a neighborly chat, and you can swing by and pick us up?"

"Will do," Zeek said. "Tell Miss Brex I said hello!"

"I'll go with Cheff," I said.

The three of us casually crossed the mess area, and 'just happened' to run into Tocette.

"Ah, good morning, lovely Tocette," Cheff said.

Tocette blushed. "Shh, Cheff, not so loud. People will get ideas." But she was smiling.

"Right," Cheff said in a stage whisper. "We wouldn't want that to happen, would we?"

Tocette giggled, then turned to me. "Hi, Booksie! How's my little Booksie Buddy today?" She put her arm around me and crushed me in a squeeze.

"Fine, Tocette, thank you for asking," I gasped and wriggled free.

"Hi, Buttons!"

"We're off to our assignment in the stern section," Buttons said. "Zeek's going to take us in Willam. I'm going to help shift again."

"Oh. I wish I was going with you, Shifter Sister," Tocette said.

"Why?" Cheff asked. "Miss Averith Brex in a cranky mood again today?"

"When is she not?" I asked.

Tocette giggled again. "Shh, little Booksie Buddy. If she hears you, she'll pick on me all day."

Cheff said in a low voice, "Speaking of Brex…"

Miss Averith Brex, in a crisp, fresh uniform, stalked up to Tocette, ignoring the rest of us. "Cadet Moron, there you are. I've been looking for you. It's time to leave for the ship."

"Don't call me that, please, Miss Brex," Tocette said. She glanced at Cheff. "Please."

"Then don't act like one!" Brex snapped. She turned on Cheff. "Don't you have somewhere to be, Karfendek?"

"Why, yes, Miss Brex. We're on our way to our assignment in the stern."

"Then get moving, and take your brat sister and your"—she looked at me—"despicable Lildur runt with you."

"I wish people wouldn't keep calling me that," I mumbled.

Zeek roared up in Willam, sunlight glinting off the scrap metal piled high in the bed. Carra wasn't in sight—she must have ducked down below the dashboard. Zeek slid his window open. "Ready, children? Hop in! Good morning, Miss Brex. You're looking crisp and professional this morning, if you don't mind me saying so."

"Hmmph!" Brex said, then spun around and marched off, Tocette in tow.

"Starry says, cranky Miss Brex needs another cup of felmoss tea."

The cab was full, so Cheff helped Buttons and me into the engine area in the back of the truck, then climbed up after us. He thumped the cab of the truck twice to let Zeek know we were in and we rumbled off toward the stern section.

When we got there, we all piled out, including Carra, who groaned and stretched, then complained, "My back is cramped from all that crouching."

Buttons said, "Andaran's bones! What a whiner! It was all of ten minutes." The ponies glared at Carra, who glared right back at them, until Sable stepped between them.

Zeek said to the three helpers, "Okay, men. It'll be up to you again today. You'll be on your own—my crew and I have an errand to run. We'll be back as soon as possible, then we'll fill good old Willam to the brim again this afternoon." He patted Willam fondly on the fender.

"No worries, Boss," their leader said. "We'll be ready for you. Off we go, men!"

"So far, so good," Zeek said. "Now, let's see if we can get out the gate without attracting undue attention."

After a quick look around for any sign of Brex or Tocette, we got back into the cab. "Is my trusty shifting assistant ready?" Zeek said.

"Ready!" Buttons said.

"Let's go!"

Buttons shoved the shifter into first gear and off we went. Zeek took a more circuitous route back, skirting the southern edge of the salvage operation. We topped off Willam's water tank at the camp water tower, then drove to the front gate.

Zeek slid his window open. "Eight leaving camp, officer," Zeek said.

The guard checked all of our name badges against his checklist and stamped our passes. I felt Carra holding her breath, but the guard checked off her name and stamped her pass without a word, the same as the rest of us. The front gate swung open, and out we went. Carra let out a huge sigh of relief.

"What's this? You were worried?" Zeek said. "I told you, you're all official now."

"I know," Carra said. "Still."

"It's not going to be that easy getting in and out of the Labor Compound," Cheff said. "Even if she is beautiful."

Buttons dug him in the ribs with her elbow.

"Cheff's right," Mid said. "We'll never get her past Manyard."

"Well," Zeek said, "maybe we should take her to Meltern's first. She can stay with him while we unload."

"That sounds good," Mid said.

"Anyway," Zeek said, "I'm sure Meltern's going to want a private word with you, Miss Wolcutt."

Carra looked serious, but confident. "I'm ready," she said, "for whatever comes next."

— 18 —

CARRA MEETS MELTERN

WILLAM ROLLED TO a stop in the alley behind Meltern's guest house, where we waited briefly while Zeek escorted Carra in through the back door. Meltern didn't even glance in our direction. Then we drove to the Fellstone Labor Compound. There was no trouble at the gate. Manyard wasn't on duty and a guard we didn't recognize admitted us with hardly a glance.

Zeek drove straight to his scrapyard, where we unloaded Willam as fast as we could, refilled Willam's water tank and coal bin, then hurried back to Old City. Altogether, we had spent slightly under an hour inside the Labor Compound.

This time, Zeek parked Willam on the Boulevard right in front of the main entrance of Meltern's Guest House. "Come inside, children," he said loudly, though no one on the street seemed to be paying the least bit of attention. "We've worked hard already today. Let's celebrate with a nice, cold glass of apple cider."

We followed him inside and were seated at a table in the main room. Meltern himself, a rotund, clean-shaven, apple-cheeked Fruen with reddish-brown hair parted neatly down the middle of his characteristic Fruen white stripe, came to the table carrying a huge tray with seven frosty mugs.

He slapped Zeek on the shoulder. "Hello, Zeek, my old friend. Good to see you again. It's been a while. Hello, children," Meltern said as though he'd never seen us before. "Been working hard today? Well, you have a nice day for it. Not too hot, not too cold. Is this your first time working for Zeek? I'm sure you'll enjoy it— he's a good boss."

He set a mug in front of each of us children, then with great ceremony placed the last mug before Zeek. "This one's yours, Zeek. It has a little something special in it." He winked at Zeek, who waggled his eyebrows. "Enjoy your cider, children. It's a specialty of the house, you know. I make it myself in my cellar. Do you know why my cider is the best in Fellstone City? It's because I use only the best apples, of course! I get them fresh from the orchard, from a farmer named Klesky. Would you like to see how the cider is made? When you're finished, I'll take you on a tour. You can come, too, Zeek, if you want, even though you've seen it before."

"Sure, sure," Zeek said. "I'd love to. I'm sure the children will be interested."

After Meltern went back to the kitchen, I looked around the main hall. We'd been to Meltern's once before, but we hadn't seen this dining room. It was quite large, and filled with long, wooden tables and benches. Hundreds of artifacts covered the walls: old pictures, kitchen implements, a mounted bear's head, a stuffed animal of some sort, some pieces of harness, an old washboard, a battered stringed instrument I didn't recognize—a zither, maybe?—a two-headed lamb, a huge snake in a glass box, and countless other items.

The collection included various maritime items, too: a diving suit, a compass in a binnacle, a few ships' wheels of various sizes, and quite a few model ships, both steam and sail. I guessed Meltern had been collecting them for years. Not surprising, since the Guest House was only a short distance from the Old City docks. I supposed many sailors had eaten and drunk and slept there over the decades. Faintly visible on the walls were the outlines of old swords, shields, and other weapons, no doubt confiscated by Pallador's agents years ago.

After we finished our cider, Meltern returned and loaded the empty mugs on his tray. "Are you ready for your tour, children? All right, follow me." He threaded his way through the tables. We followed him, Cheff first with Zeek bringing up the rear, through the main hall, then through a door on the far side of the room. We found ourselves in the same room we'd been in a few weeks ago on our first meeting with Meltern. Carra sat in a chair along the wall.

"Be seated, Zeek, and BSI members. We have urgent business to discuss. Before we start, I'd like you all to know that I have contacted Carra's father through official FRM channels and let him know she arrived safely. Now, here is what we know so far: Carra told us of the death of Fentor Rignish. Sad. He was a fine man. He will be missed. She also said that you have both his shipment of anti-jexan compounds and hers. Is that right?"

"It is," Zeek said.

"Good. You may give them to me now."

Zeek reached deep into the front pockets of his greasy overalls and retrieved two small packets, which he handed to Meltern.

"Excellent," Meltern said. "I'll get these to the boys in the basement right away. They're eager to begin testing. We don't have the equipment in our lab to make the compounds, but we can test them. So far, so good. Now comes the difficult part. Carra related the request from the Tumberland lab for a quantity of the herb rovaldia. I verified the request with FRM headquarters. As far as anyone knows, rovaldia can be found only in the marshes of The Fel.

"I contacted Madame Entigy herself and asked for instructions. It seems that the rovaldia is of critical importance in the ongoing research for an antidote to jexan. By the way, children, this request for rovaldia is a direct result of the information you provided a few weeks ago. You can be proud—this could be a major breakthrough."

Carra didn't look too pleased with that announcement.

Meltern continued, "The lab boys in Tumberland have an idea that a refined version of rovaldia might counteract the mind-numbing effects of jexan. If they can learn how to synthesize it in quantity, we have a real chance of reversing the false sense of contentment, the complacency, that jexan has caused here in Fellstone City, and other cities, too. There's a new report that jexan is now being added to foodstuffs in Tumberland, Stoopone, and Cozzbole. So, you see, getting the rovaldia to Tumberland is urgent business.

"Madame Entigy has ordered that the BSI, all six of you children, along with Miss Wolcutt, enter The Fel. There you are to gather as much rovaldia as you can get your hands on in one day or even two, if necessary. Afterward, you are to escort Miss Wolcutt back to her canoe, whence she will return alone to Tumberland with the rovaldia."

"We don't even know what rovaldia looks like," Buttons said.

"I do, Sis. I've seen it before, once. Sarth had some he was using for seasoning. It has a rather distinct taste and odor."

Sarth was the old hermit that lived among the ruins between the Labor Compound and Old City. Cheff ran into him occasionally when he was hunting.

Meltern held up a drawing of a rovaldia plant for us to see. "It looks like this," he said. "Note the distinctive orange flowers, the spear-tip-shaped leaves, and the netted root system with bulbs at the tips. Look hard and memorize it as best you can."

We studied the drawing for a few minutes until we had it down pat. Cheff said, "If anyone sees anything even remotely like this drawing, bring it to me. I'll smell it."

"What's it smell like, Cheff?" Buttons asked.

"Hard to explain, Sis, but I'll know it when I smell it, so bring it to me."

"Okay."

Meltern continued, "Unfortunately, there is no way for us to excuse your absence from the salvage camp, so you will have to leave surreptitiously. In your absence, Zeek will cover for you as best he can. However, if your absence is discovered, you will be subject to whatever sadistic punishment the guards are meting out these days. Maybe you can convince them that you got lost in the woods." He looked grim. "I'm sorry, but that's the best that can be done on such short notice.

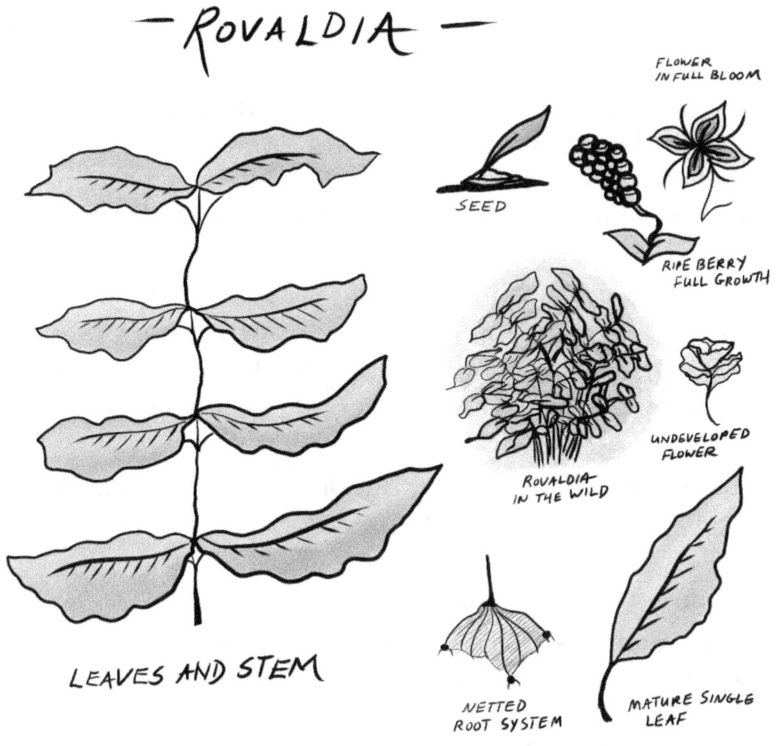

"It's worth noting, however, that Madame Entigy told me that, according to her calculations, your chances of avoiding being caught before you return to the salvage camp are reasonably good. She also said that you six—seven, that is, excuse me, Miss Wolcutt—are the only agents that have any chance at all. All adults suspected of being FRM agents are being watched carefully during the lockdown, and there's not one who could leave the city undetected." He paused and looked each one of us in the eye. "So, children, do you think the BSI is up to it?"

"I don't know," Mid said. "That seems like a lot of sneaking to me."

"What do you mean?" Meltern asked.

Mid enumerated on his fingers. "First, we have to sneak out of the salvage camp, again. Then we sneak out to The Fel, for a little camping vacation, collect a bagful of rovaldia—"

"—assuming we can even find any this time of year—" Cheff added.

—"without attracting any attention. Next we sneak Carra and the rovaldia back to where we found her, and finally sneak back into the salvage camp, where we pretend to have been there the entire time, all in the middle of a lockdown. Is that it? Did I miss anything?"

"No," Meltern said, "I think you covered everything."

"No disrespect, sir," Mid said, "but don't you think that's a lot of sneaking? How are we ever going to do that much sneaking in that many places, in the middle of the lockdown, and not get caught?"

In the silence that followed, Buttons held Starry Stargazer up to her ear and listened intently. "Starry says, by being very, very sneaky."

Mid buried his face in his hands.

We all laughed, especially Meltern. He said, "I think the ponies have hit on the solution. Good work, ponies!"

Buttons smiled proudly.

"I'm afraid that's the one and only answer," Meltern said. "Be very, very sneaky. Do the best you can. Besides, we know from your last adventure that you're all pretty good at sneaking."

Carra raised her eyebrows but didn't ask.

"Don't worry, sir," Cheff said, "of course we're up to it. We'll do our best. After all, the Fel is mostly empty, isn't it? I can't imagine we'll run into anyone more formidable than a marsh pig or two."

Meltern frowned. "*Mostly* empty isn't all the way empty."

"What do you mean, sir?" Cheff asked.

"Never mind. The chances of you running into anyone in the Fel are slim. The Fel is big, extremely big, and you don't have to go far. Get in, get the rovaldia, and get out. Get it?"

We got it.

"Good." Meltern said grimly, "This mission is critical, and all our hopes go with you. Here, you'll need these." He handed each of us a funny little bag made of some thick material coated with rubber on the inside. "They're for keeping the rovaldia in, when you find some. The coating is waterproof. It'll keep the rovaldia moist, and keep you dry. And they fold up quite small, see?" He demonstrated by folding a bag and putting it into his pocket.

"Okay, everybody have a bag? Everybody understand the mission? Good. Zeek will take you back to the salvage camp, where you can put in an appearance, gather your gear, then *sneak* out." He winked at Mid, who scowled. "Best get moving—you'll want to be out of sight of the road as quickly as possible."

Zeek rose. "No worries, Mel. Willam and I will have them on their way in an hour, two at the most."

"Perfect," Meltern said. He, too, rose, and we followed suit. He shook each of our hands and led us out of the room. When we returned to the main hall, he said loudly, "Well, I hope you enjoyed your tour, young ones. Now you can tell all your friends exactly why Meltern's Apple Cider is the best in all Fellstone. Come back and visit me again, soon."

No one so much as looked in our direction. If anyone noticed that seven children came out whereas only six went in, they kept it to themselves. We filed out quickly, before anyone had much of a chance to look us over, and got into Willam the Wheezer. Meltern stood on the porch smiling and waving goodbye. We waved back, then Zeek turned Willam in the direction of the salvage camp.

We rode in silence for a while, then Zeek said, "Well, children, I have to admit I didn't see this coming. Your first assignment has turned into a lot more than you bargained for."

"True," Cheff said, "but I'm not too worried. Actually, I'm more worried about explaining our absence if Brex gets wind of it."

"Don't worry about that, anyway," Zeek said. "I'll think of something before it becomes a problem."

"In any case," Mid said, "it's quite an honor that Madame Entigy considers us capable. I wonder who she is, anyway."

"Stop wondering," Zeek said. "Her true identity is probably the best-kept secret in all of Andaran. I don't know anyone who knows who she is or where she is. I've never even heard of anyone who knows. But you're right—it does seem she has taken a special interest in you. Now let's hope that her special interest doesn't get you killed."

I said, "I'd rather die trying to do something to help people than die for nothing in that stupid Labor Compound."

"Well said, Books!" Cheff clapped me on the back. "We all feel the same. Plenty of kids our age have been killed by Emperor Pallador for no reason, no reason at all. If we must die, better we should die for a good cause."

"If it's all the same to you, Cheff," Buttons said, "I'd rather keep living for a good cause. And the ponies agree."

We laughed.

"Too right, Sis," Cheff said, "too right."

— 19 —

INTO THE FEL

THERE WERE NO complications getting back into the salvage camp. First, we swung by our tents where we gathered all of our mission gear and stowed it out of sight in some of Willam's many side compartments. Then we drove down to the shipwreck once more.

Zeek's three helpers had a huge pile of assorted scrap waiting for us. We all pitched in and in minutes we had Willam loaded to the brim.

"This time," Zeek said, "I'll take the load out by myself. If you were to go with me, your absence would be noted when I returned alone. I'll tell the guards that I hired a couple of helpers back at the salvage yard this morning who will help me unload. Meanwhile, you children work in the stern section for a few minutes, then make your way outside of the camp to the south. I'll meet you at the first bend in the road. Uh-oh, watch out. Here comes your Blueband buddy. Get Carra out of sight, fast!"

Lery took Carra by the hand and disappeared into the wreck, shielding her from Brex's view with his bulk.

Miss Averith Brex strode up to us. "Hmpf! Hard at work, I see."

"That we are, Miss Brex," Cheff said. "Thank you for noticing. We've loaded the truck again and Zeek is going to take it to his salvage yard."

"And you're going with him, I suppose?"

"No, Miss Brex. Zeek hired a couple of kids at the salvage yard this morning, so our time wouldn't be wasted driving back and forth when we could be working here. Much more efficient this way."

"After all, Miss Brex," Mid said, "our beloved Emperor Pallador wouldn't be pleased with inefficiency. Excuse me, Miss Brex. Nature calls." He went around Willam, out of sight.

"Hmmph! That's true, I suppose. Well, I'm keeping an eye on you. At the Blueband leaders' meeting last night, we received special instructions to watch all suspicious persons carefully. Your name was mentioned, Karfendek. I'm going to be watching you *exceedingly* carefully from now on."

"Why, thank you, Miss Brex," Cheff said. "It's a comfort to know that I'm being looked after. I'm sure you'll be pleased with my work. All of our work, in fact." He smiled innocently at her.

A voice came over the camp loudspeaker. "Miss Averith Brex to the Administration tent, immediately. Miss Averith Brex to the Administration tent."

"Better hurry, Miss Brex," Buttons said. "It sounds like you're needed for something important."

Brex narrowed her eyes at Buttons, then at the rest of us. "Hmmph!" She turned and strode off toward the camp offices.

When she was out of sight, Mid came back from behind Willam, looking pleased with himself. "What did I miss? Was Brex called away? I wonder what for?"

"Careful," Sable murmured. "Too much."

"Sable's right," Cheff said. "One too many false alarms and Brex is bound to figure out that something's not right. You'd better save that voice-changer of yours for a real emergency."

"Aw, all right," Mid said. "Still, it was funny."

"I don't know what you're talking about," Zeek said, "and I don't want to know. Not right now, anyway. Right now, you're all going to make your way out of the camp, and I'm going to make an appearance at the mess area then go on up the road. I'll wait for you at the bend, but don't take too long, okay? Someone might see me and get suspicious."

"Okay," Cheff said. "Give us enough time to circle around. Ten minutes should do the trick. Ready, everyone? Let's go!"

Zeek got into Willam and rumbled off to the mess area.

The rest of us went inside the wreck and worked our way around to the southernmost part of the hull. We worked long enough for several people to notice our presence, then we exited the stern section through a side-hatch, slipped under the fence, and disappeared into the woods. Ten minutes later, we were waiting for Zeek inside the edge of the forest at the bend in the road south of the camp entrance. Presently, Willam the Wheezer came chugging cheerfully along and rolled to a stop in front of us. We checked the road in both directions, dashed into Willam's cab, and put our heads down. Once more, Buttons shoved the shifter into gear, and we were off to The Fel.

Zeek avoided Old City on our way to The Fel. Instead, we took a scarcely populated back road that eventually connected with East Road, the easternmost boundary to Old City. It was all in ruins, with only the occasional squatters visible. There wasn't much traffic. Every time Zeek saw a car coming or spotted some squatters by the roadside, he said, "Get down, children," and we hid below the dashboard. As far as any casual observer could tell, Zeek was driving alone. We had no trouble passing the check-point south of town—one bored guard barely looked up and waved Zeek on.

A few miles south of Old City, the road rose about twenty feet or so (6m)', and became a 'levee road,' running along the top of the levee.

"This levee was built by Sevros, many decades ago," Zeek told us. "The idea was to keep The Fel on one side, during the rainy season. The other side, as you can see, is farmland. Wouldn't do to have The Fel flooding into the crops, now, would it?"

"Why was the levee built by Sevros?" I asked.

"Nobody knows anymore," Zeek said. "Traditionally, many of our so-called 'public works' were built by the Sevro People."

"What's 'public works?'" Buttons asked.

"Good question, Sis," Cheff said. "Public works usually refers to things too big for one man or even one family to build by themselves, such as roads, bridges, levees, things like that."

Mid added, "I've heard that most of the docks in Old City were originally constructed by Sevros."

"The Sevros do a lot of things that the other Peoples prefer to avoid," Zeek said. "Building this levee was a lot of hard work! It was built shortly after The Fall, in the years following Pallador's takeover of Fellstone City. Pallador rounded up as many Sevros as he could and put them to work." He scoffed. "'Work', indeed! Slave labor, more like. They worked long days in the hot sun, were given little to eat, and were barely paid at all. Many of them died from sheer exhaustion and malnutrition during the construction, I'm told."

"Where… where did… they all… go?" Lery asked.

"The Sevros?" Zeek asked. "Why, I don't know. There used to be a number of small Sevro villages and construction camps all along this levee road. When I was a boy, you could still see the ruins, but they're all gone now, I'm afraid."

"But where did all the Sevros *go*?" Buttons asked. "We've only ever met a few around here. They seemed nice enough."

"No one knows," Zeek said. "Most Sevros don't like to get too far from home." He reflected. "Which seems odd, when you consider what their homes are like, for the most part."

"What are their homes like?" Buttons asked.

"Well, how should I put it?" Zeek asked. "They tend to be not, um, as… tidy… as they might be."

"Tidy?" Buttons asked. "What do you mean?"

Zeek shrugged. "There's no nice way to put it. They don't seem to care about cleanliness as much as they might—dirty houses in need of painting, unkempt yards full of rusty junk and other trash. Those who keep dogs don't seem to pick up after them. As for personal hygiene…"

"Don't they take baths?" Buttons asked. "They teach us personal hygiene in school."

Zeek wrinkled his nose. "Let's just say that when someone spots a Sevro on the street, he'll check to see which way the wind is blowing."

We laughed.

Zeek added, "They're not all like that, though. There are plenty of Sevros who don't fit the stereotype. One often finds them in towns and cities. They're noted for being excellent merchants and traders. There are a few successful Sevros in the market in New City. Next time you're there, look for them. But they are the exceptions, not the rule. Anyway, for whatever reason or reasons, Sevros tend to be poor, tend to live together in squalid little communities, and tend to stick to themselves."

"Why are they poor?" Carra asked. "Don't they care about money?"

Zeek thought this over. "As far as I can tell, Sevros care about money as much as anyone. But they have a reputation for taking a less-than-straightforward approach. Instead of working hard at some useful occupation, they always seem to be working some angle, some way to get rich quick, some kind of deal. It backfires on them more often than not. There's no substitute for good old-fashioned hard work. Of course, I'm only talking about *some* of the Sevros I've known personally, in and around Fellstone City. I have no idea what Sevros are like in the rest of Andaran. Probably pretty much like everyone else."

Buttons asked, "Are they that way *because* they're Sevros?"

"Of course not!" Zeek answered. "There are plenty of individuals from all the other Peoples who behave exactly the same way or even worse. People are what they are for lots of reasons—culture, upbringing, opportunity, education—too many to count. Species itself doesn't figure into it."

"Except for the species with Abilities, right?" Buttons asked. "Torphs and Sephs?"

"That's true, Miss Buttons. The Torph Ability and the Seph Ability are species' attributes. As is the Fessals' susceptibility to the Seph Ability. But the qualities we're born with, no matter what species we are, aren't what counts. What's important is what we make of ourselves on the inside, in our minds and hearts."

We drove for quite a while, mulling this over. The farther south we went, the wetter and flatter the terrain got. The Fel was a large, marshy, windswept plain, covered in tall marsh grass, cattails, and reeds. Whenever a gust of wind whooshed by, it set the entire Fel to waving like waves in the ocean. In places, apparently following hidden waterways, were dense stands of tall trees.

"It's windy out there," I said.

"It's the openness of the country," Cheff said. "There's nothing at all to slow the wind down. It blows like this from Fellstone Bay until it hits the Minara Mountains to the South."

"The ground out there looks pretty squishy," Carra said. "Is it safe to walk on?"

"It *should* be squishy," Buttons said. "It's a marsh. Aunt Dee says that's what Fel means in the old Lora tongue: marsh."

"That's right," I said. "I read once that The Fel is basically a shallow, hugely wide river, flowing slowly toward the Fel River. All the water from the surrounding mountains drains into it. It's full of all kinds of wildlife, too—mostly birds." As if they had heard me, a flock of hundreds of large, long-legged white birds rose from The Fel and glided to a new spot farther from the road.

"Is it safe?" Carra asked.

"It's safe enough," Cheff said, "if you know how to find the higher ground. There are old trails crisscrossing the entire Fel. Don't worry, lovely Carra—I'll keep you safe."

"Uh-oh," Buttons muttered, "here he goes again." She gave Cheff another poke in the ribs.

"I'm sure," Carra said. "And I suppose *you*, in your wondrous teenage wisdom, are completely familiar with The Fel."

"I am indeed," Cheff said. "I've hunted out here lots of times. That's why I know how to find rovaldia."

"First I've heard of it," Buttons grumbled.

Carra rolled her eyes. "Oh, wonderful."

It was mid-afternoon by the time Zeek said, "We're well south of the Market District, now, I think. Let's find a landmark that will be our drop-off point. Perhaps that tree on the left?"

A huge, gnarled tree, with dark brown bark and a big canopy of small, curly, green leaves stood alone by the edge of the road, its mighty branches waving in the strong wind.

"I won't have any trouble finding this tree again," Zeek said. "It's the first big tree we've seen south of Old City."

"It's a Fel oak," I said. "Keeps its leaves the entire year, unlike all the other kinds of oaks. Nobody knows why. They only grow in The Fel."

Carra gave me a peculiar look.

"What? I read a lot," I said.

Zeek brought Willam to a stop. "Okay, children, this is it."

We got out and waited between Willam and the edge of the road, trying to keep out of the wind.

Carra was wearing her ridiculous camping hat again, which blew off as soon as she stepped out of Willam and skittered away down the road. She ran after it, then returned. "I'm going to have to tie this on. Fortunately, it has a chin strap built in. You children should get some for yourselves. You'd look great in them!"

"That's a great idea, Carra," Cheff said.

"Oh, yeah," Mid said, "great. We can get them in New City when we buy our new sleeping bags." He took his dark glasses from his tech bag. "Bright out here."

Zeek opened Willam's side compartments, and we took out our packs and bags. Buttons made sure both ponies were secure in their special backpack. "Ponies belted in and ready, Cheff!"

Zeek shouted over the roaring wind, "I'll wait for you right here tonight at sunset. If you're not here, I'll wait for a half hour, then come back tomorrow night, and every night until you show up. Got it?"

We got it.

Zeek shook hands solemnly with each of us. "Be careful, children. Be safe."

As he took Buttons' hand, she threw her arms around Zeek's enormous waist. "The ponies say they're going to miss you!"

Zeek hugged her and smoothed her hair. "And I'm going to miss them and you, too. Okay? Run along, now." He stopped abruptly. "What was that?"

"What was what?" Cheff asked.

"I thought I heard something like a door slamming. Did someone leave one of Willam's compartments open?"

No one had.

Zeek walked completely around Willam. "Everything looks okay," he said, frowning, "but I was sure I heard something." He shrugged. "It must have been the wind."

We entered The Fel by walking straight down the levee to the Fel oak, our boots and shoes making seeping footprints in the mud.

"Good thing I… I wore my… army boots," Lery said.

"My boots are completely watertight," Carra said. "You should get some. Maybe at that market you mentioned."

We ignored her, except for Buttons, who made a sour face.

Cheff merely said, "It's your show, Sable. Do your thing."

Sable took a professional-looking military compass from her mission bag and a small clipboard with a blank sheet of paper. At one corner, she drew a tiny tree and labeled it 'Fel oak.' Then she scouted around. "Trail. Southeast."

It didn't look like much to me, but Sable seemed pretty sure of herself. She made a note on the little clipboard, then took the lead, and we marched off into the tall grass. Mid was right behind Sable, then Carra, Buttons, and Lery. I came next, and Cheff brought up the rear.

Sable's map was great idea. From up on the levee, The Fel looked completely flat. But now that we were down in it, it was full of clumps of alder and willow, little islands, and winding waterways, all of which were hidden by reeds well up over our heads.

Cheff said, "Everyone keep an eye out for rovaldia. It'll grow at the waterline. Its roots like to be wet. If you think you found some, call out, and I'll check its smell. When we find one, we'll all know how to recognize it. Hopefully, it won't take us too long to gather a couple of bags full. We'll probably be back at the Fel oak by tonight or tomorrow afternoon, at the latest."

"I hope so," Carra said. She brushed a buzzing insect from her face. "I don't think much of this swamp of yours."

"At least we have it to ourselves," Mid said. "It's nice not to be under Miss Averith Brex's watchful eye for once."

"That's for sure," Cheff said.

"We entered The Fel… making seeping footprints in the mud."

— **20** —

REFLECTIONS

WE TRUDGED ALONG behind Sable, carefully scanning the plants growing along the waterline. There were dozens of varieties, but nothing that looked like Meltern's drawing of rovaldia. Every fifteen minutes or so, Sable stopped, took a bearing on the Fel oak with her compass, and made a notation on her clipboard.

"What's that you're making, Sable?" I asked.

"Map," Sable said, holding it up for me to see. "Bearing. Distance—estimated. Landmarks."

"What landmarks?" I asked.

"Fel oak," she said. "So far. Eyes out."

"Good point," Cheff said. "Along with the rovaldia, we need to watch for landmarks Sable can add to her map."

"Like what, Cheff?" Buttons asked.

"Anything tall enough to see above this grass for a distance." He stood on his tiptoes, shaded his eyes, and looked all around. "I don't see anything yet, but if we do, we should let Sable know."

Carra looked impressed, in spite of herself. "How did she learn to do that?"

"It's part of her military training in the Advanced School," Cheff said. "She's on the Military Officers Track. She showed me the book, once. There's a chapter on Land Navigation. It was all about how to find your way around wild country, using only a compass and a map, if you have them, or how to make a map if you don't have one. What Track were you on in school?"

"We didn't get Pallador's new 'Paths of Destiny' academic program in Tumberland until after I finished school." She watched Sable's note-making wistfully. "I used to be glad I missed it. Now I'm not so sure."

Sable took up the trail again, following the waterline.

"It has its uses," Cheff said. "I'm in Civilian Leadership and Management. Books is studying Archiving and Library Management. Mid's going to be an engineer. Buttons won't be in Advanced School until next year, but she wants to study Political Leadership. She's good with people."

Carra raised her eyebrows. "You're joking."

"She is," Cheff said. "You'll see. She has her ways."

"How about Lery?" Carra asked.

"Lery is a special case. He's in Regular School. Right now, he helps Mid after school, until he gets his own work assignment."

"I see," Carra said. "That's a pretty strange combination of skills, if you ask me. How did you all get together?"

"Mostly coincidence," Cheff said. "I've known Sable since my first day in the Labor Compound. Mid lives a block away from my house. And Books moved in two doors down from me a few weeks ago. We hit it off."

"What about Lery?"

"As I said, Lery's a special case. We met him during our first, um, mission. Unofficial mission. I can't talk about it. Anyway, on that mission, he got noticed by Madame Entigy. We all did. Shortly after, we were invited to join the FRM."

"Even Lery? He's a… well, you know, he's a"—she looked to make sure that Lery wasn't within earshot—"*Fessal*. There aren't many Fessals in the FRM. I certainly don't know any."

"Special case, I told you. He's not your ordinary Fessal. Among other things, he specializes in tools. You'll see. Besides, Fentor Rignish was a Fessal."

"True, but that's… different. Isn't Lery, you know, slow?" She tapped her temple.

"Nah, he just talks like that," Cheff said. "He's smart, but a very different kind of smart. I've never met anyone like him. Plus, he has other redeeming skills. Wait until you get to know him."

We walked in silence for hours, without spotting either rovaldia or any new landmarks. From time to time, Cheff picked up a smooth, round stone a little larger than a walnut.

"What are the stones for," I asked him.

"For my hunting sling," Cheff said. "I like to keep about five large stones in my pocket at all times. You never know when you might need one."

The sun was setting behind us, and our shadows, marching along in front of us, were getting longer.

"Camp soon," Sable said.

"Good idea," Cheff agreed. "We'd best make camp early if we can. It's going to be dark out here in The Fel before long."

Mid checked the eastern horizon. "No moon until late tonight."

"We'll make a campfire," Cheff said. "We can keep it small, but it'll give us some light."

"Won't someone see us, Cheff?" Buttons asked.

"They'd have to be extremely close," Cheff explained. "The tall grass will shield the campfire. Besides, Sis, I don't think there's anyone out here *to* see us."

"I hope not," Buttons said. "I'm glad we'll have a fire. The ponies get nervous in the dark."

A large *something* bolted out of the reeds, crossed our path, and disappeared. We nearly jumped out of our skins.

"What in Andaran was that?" Mid asked.

"Marsh pig," Sable said. "Harmless."

"*Harmless*?" Mid said. "It nearly gave me a heart attack. You call that harmless?"

"Vegetarian," Sable said.

I tried to remember what I'd read, if anything, about marsh pigs. I concentrated, then called up an old book from long ago. In my mind, I saw a picture with an explanation. "Marsh pigs aren't true pigs. They're a kind of big rodent. They're only found in The Fel and surrounding areas. They're good to eat. If we can catch one, we can cook it over a fire. The article says not to eat them raw, because they can make you sick. You have to make sure the meat gets cooked all the way to the bone."

"Article?" Carra asked. "What article?"

"It's from a schoolbook I had years ago, back in Tumberland."

"And you can still remember it? Remarkable."

"Books has a special talent for remembering things he's read. That's why we call him 'Books,' see?"

"I do not," Carra said.

Cheff laughed. "Books doesn't merely remember things, he sees pictures of them in his mind exactly as they were when he read them. It comes in handy from time to time."

"I don't mean to," I said. "It just happens."

"Okay," Carra said. She looked around at each one of us, then shook her head. "You truly are a strange bunch, aren't you?"

Cheff smiled, but didn't reply.

We slogged through the marsh for another hour or so, until the sun was nearly touching the western mountains.

"Tree," Sable said, and pointed.

Off in the distance, maybe a few hundred yards ahead, was another Fel oak, much smaller than the one by the levee road. When we reached it, we were pleased to see that it was growing on a little mound of dry ground in a small clearing. The ground was littered with oak leaves that gave off a pleasant aroma as they crackled under our feet.

"Perfect," Cheff said. "We can camp here, I think. Sable? Mid?"

Sable said, "Good spot."

Mid said, "Fine by me."

"Looks good to me, too," Carra said too loudly.

"Okay," Cheff said, "let's gather some, uh, whatever we can find that's dry enough to burn."

"Twigs," Sable said. "No grass. Smoky."

We got busy looking around. Plenty of twigs and small branches had fallen from the oak tree. Buttons found some dry, dead leaves still attached to the lower branches of the tree.

I recalled something I'd read long ago and went down to the waterline. I cut a cattail with my camping knife and took it to Sable.

Sable smiled. "Good!" She broke open the brown sausage-shaped section at the top. It came apart into mounds of white, fluffy fibers. She formed them into a little pile, then carefully stacked the thinnest of the twigs in a cone on top of them. Next, she sorted the larger branches by size and placed them within easy reach. "Ready," she said. "Wind shield."

I wasn't sure what that meant, but followed Cheff's example. We formed a tight circle around the little fire-to-be to block the wind with our bodies.

"I'll light it," Carra said. She unfolded a shiny metal object into a bulky, odd-looking contraption. She pointed one end of it at the pile of fluff and cranked the handle at the other end. Nothing happened. She tried again. "I don't know what's wrong with it—it worked the night before last."

"Here, let me," Mid said. "I have a new invention I've been wanting to test."

"It's getting late for experiments, Old Son," Cheff said. "Maybe let Lery do it, like always."

"This will only take a sec." Mid took a small metal tube from his tech bag. It came apart into two pieces: 1) a piston that slid inside 2) a cylinder. He took a round piece of black cloth from a little metal box and inserted the cloth into the cylinder. He inserted the piston into the cylinder, then smacked the piston on its end. It went in, then bounced back again. Mid removed the piston and shook a tiny burning coal off the end of it into the pile of fluff.

Sable blew gently on the fluff and it burst into flame. She added more twigs, then larger branches, until we had a cheerful campfire.

"That was amazing!" I said. "What was that thing?"

"I call it my Fire Cylinder," Mid said. "The sudden compression ignites the K-cloth."

"K-cloth?"

"Well, that's what I call it. K for Karfendek, because Cheff gave me the idea."

"I did?" Cheff asked. "How so?"

"You know how you make your charcoal sticks? The ones you use for drawing? You take some willow sticks, put them in an airtight can, and cook them on the coal stove. They turn into charcoal, right?"

"Right."

"Well, I did the same thing with little bits of cloth, some bits of old cotton rags. And they turned into charcoal cloth. But I call it K-cloth, because you gave me the idea."

"Wonderful!" Cheff said. "I'm honored, Old Son!"

"My pleasure, Old Man," Mid said.

"Hurray for the techie!" Cheff shouted.

Mid took a bow. "Thank you, thank you."

We gave Mid a brief round of applause.

Carra, frowning, watched this exchange in silence, then asked, "So, Mid, you *invented* this? All by yourself?"

"Yes and no," Mid said. "All great inventors build on the work of their predecessors. I noticed how hot the air compressors at the factory got and figured it might work on a small scale. I got permission to use the metal lathe after hours and made this little gadget. Then I tried charcoal, but it didn't work too well, because the piston kept crushing it. So then I thought of cloth. And the rest, as they say, is history."

"So you invented a tool," she said airily. "Am I supposed to be impressed? Why don't you just use matches?"

"Matches are… are expensive," Lery said.

"And they don't work when they get wet," Buttons added.

"Besides," Mid said, "tools are important."

"The right… tool… for the right… job," Lery said, caressing the pipe wrench in his belt.

"Right," Carra said. She moved a few feet away and started setting up her bright red tent.

"Seriously?" Mid said. "You're going to set that gaudy thing up here?"

"Sure, why not?" Carra asked.

"Haven't you folks up there in Tumberland heard about camouflage?"

"Of course," Carra said. "But it's so… tacky."

"'Tacky.' Right." Mid shook his head.

"Besides," Carra said, "Cheff said it himself: there isn't anyone out here to see. So why not get out of this miserable wind for a while?"

We watched her putter around, fussing with tent pegs and poles and guy lines. When she was satisfied that all was in order, she disappeared into the tent and sealed the flap behind her without so much as a word to us or even a glance in our direction.

Cheff shook his head. "There's something wrong with that girl. I can't put my finger on it." He frowned, then added quietly, "Although, whenever I get close to her, I don't seem to notice as much."

"No kidding," Buttons said. "Brother!"

"Could it be," Mid asked thoughtfully, "that when she was a baby, somebody dropped her on her head?"

Lery snorted. "That's... not nice, Mid. But it's... funny."

Buttons sat by the fire, holding Starry and Moka in her lap, out of the wind. The ponies consulted together, then whispered in Buttons' ear. "The ponies agree with Lery," Buttons said, "it isn't nice. But they also agree that she may, indeed, have been dropped on her head. Perhaps more than once."

Cheff and Mid laughed. Sable permitted herself an agreeable smile.

"Well, Lery," Cheff asked. "What incredible culinary concoction do you have in mind for us tonight?"

Lery took a stew pot and several small packages from his pack. "Not much," he said. "Everybody... give me... your leftovers from... breakfast."

We gathered our leftover bits from the salvage camp's breakfast chow line and handed them to Lery. He chopped, mixed, and added mysterious powders and crushed leaves to the pot. A tantalizing smell pervaded our little camp.

Miss Carra Trenta Wolcutt emerged from her red domicile and approached the fire. "What, um, is that smell?"

"Lery's making stew," Mid said.

"Lery cooks, too?"

"Sure," Cheff said. "After he joined the FRM, he did a temporary stint as a short-order cook."

"He's not all *that* short," Buttons murmured.

"At Meltern's, in fact," Cheff continued. "Meltern taught him to cook."

"I see," Carra said.

"But... I used to cook... at the Fortress... remember?"

"The fortress?" Carra asked. She mulled it over. "The *Iron* Fortress?"

"And a... little bit... in the army."

"You were in the army?" Carra narrowed her eyes. "How old are you, exactly?"

"Forget it… Miss Carra…" Lery said. "I… I shouldn't have said anything."

Carra frowned, but didn't press the issue.

"Anyway," Cheff said, "that was before he moved in with Mid."

Lery stirred the pot with a big wooden spoon, then offered a spoonful of broth to Carra. "Blow… hot…"

Carra blew, then tasted. "Why, that's incredible! I've never tasted anything so good in my life. How did you do that with leftover breakfast?"

Lery smiled. "The right… spices… for the right… stew." He patted his bag fondly. "Cups… please."

We passed Lery our tin camp cups, and he filled them with his wooden spoon and handed them back.

I tasted mine. Carra was right—it was the best thing I'd tasted since I had supper with Cheff's Aunt Dee. Far better than anything we'd had at the salvage camp or even at Pallador's Bounty on our last field trip. No doubt about it—Lery had a talent for cooking.

When we finished eating, we sat companionably by the fire. The wind had diminished after the sunset. Lery cleaned and re-packed his cooking utensils, but left the stew pot covered and warming over the coals. Cheff and Mid discussed the particulars of rovaldia. Sable cleaned and checked her mission gear. Carra ostentatiously shined her huge silver belt buckle so vigorously that soon everyone's attention was riveted on her.

"Reflections," Sable said.

"I beg your pardon," Carra said. "Did you say something?"

Cheff said, "Tomorrow, while we're hiking, you'll need to cover that shiny belt buckle. Hide it under your shirt or something."

Carra arched her eyebrows. "Why, whatever for? Don't you like it? I think it's rather pretty, myself. It was a gift, you know, from the Mayor of Tumber—"

"Yes, I'm sure it's quite nice," Mid said. "But it's also shiny. We don't want any reflections of sunlight to give away our presence."

"Refer to previous conversation about camouflage," Cheff said.

"Hmmph!" Carra's face flushed, but she didn't reply—she just kept polishing.

While all this was going on, I observed that Buttons had quietly opened a seam on Starry's left hind leg. She took from her pocket the pieces of scrap she'd picked up at Zeek's scrapyard and inserted them into Starry. When she finished, she stitched Starry's leg closed. Then she hefted Starry a few times and appeared satisfied. She saw me watching her and smiled sweetly. "You never know," she mouthed silently, then held a finger to her lips.

After what I'd seen Starry do at the Iron Fortress, it seemed like a pretty good idea to me. "Right. You never know when you'll have need of a scrappy little pony."

Buttons giggled. "She is that, isn't she?" She kissed Starry's leg where it had been repaired.

Sable shook the last cold drops from her mug and stowed it. She went to the west end of the clearing, cupped her hands around her ears, and swiveled her head back and forth.

"What is it?" Cheff asked.

"Heard something."

Cheff went and listened with her. "I don't hear anything."

"Marsh pig?" Mid asked.

"Maybe," Sable said. "Not sure. Watch tonight."

"Good idea," Cheff said. "Okay, gang, listen up. We're going to post a watch tonight. We'll take turns. Every two hours we'll change. There are seven of us, so that'll cover fourteen hours. Seems unlikely that we'll sleep that long—it'll be dawn before then. I'll go first, then Mid, Sable, Books, Lery, Carra, and Buttons. The ponies will watch with Buttons."

Starry and Moka consulted each other silently. They seemed satisfied with the arrangements.

"Lend me your watch," Cheff said. "I'll wake you in two hours."

"Good enough," Mid said, handing over his timepiece. "Let's hit the hay."

Carra disappeared into her tent, again without a word. Even though it was a pretty big tent, she didn't invite Sable or even Buttons to share it. I'm not sure they would have if she had invited them. The rest of us wrapped ourselves in our blankets and settled around the campfire. All in all, it was a good first day in The Fel.

Operation Lockdown

— **21** —

NIGHT VISITOR

SOMETIME IN THE middle of the night, Sable gently shook me awake and handed me Mid's timepiece. It was my turn on watch. I wrapped my blanket around me and went to stand by the Fel oak. It was still dark, as the moon hadn't risen yet, but I could see the glow of it over the Lassa mountain range to the east. In another hour, there would be plenty of light.

I strained to hear anything unusual, but the night was silent, except for the occasional drone of a nocturnal insect or the hoot of an owl. From time to time, I heard the soft swish of bat wings. The wind had died down somewhat, so I wasn't too cold.

I was having difficulty staying awake, so I walked around the Fel oak tree a few times, then I went to the edge of the camp and circled it, being careful not to step on a twig or make any other sudden noise. I was pretty sure that Sable's training enabled her to sleep with an eye and an ear open, and I didn't want to rouse her.

Once, more than halfway through my watch, I thought I heard sounds of something moving from the direction we'd come. I walked a short way down our back trail and listened for ten min-

179

utes or so, but the sounds never came again. I thought perhaps that it was another marsh pig or some other nocturnal wanderer.

In due course, my two hours went by. I woke Lery and gave him the watch. I returned to my place by the fire, rolled up in my blanket, and was instantly asleep.

The next thing I knew, it was daylight, and there were voices. I sat up and looked around. Lery stood by the fire with his stew pot in his hand. Sable and Cheff squatted, examining the ground around the campfire. "What's going on?" I asked.

"Footprints," Cheff said. "Someone was in the camp last night."

"We all were, Cheff." I wiped the sleep from my eyes.

"I mean someone *not* us. Someone else. They came down the trail we came in on, messed around by the campfire for a while, then left the same way."

"I think they took some food," Mid said from the edge of the clearing. "Look here—are these some bits of the stew Lery made last night?" He picked up something from the ground, sniffed it, and put it in his mouth. "Yep, that's Lery's stew, all right." He smacked his lips a few times. "It was better warm."

Lery lifted the lid of the stewpot. "Empty."

"I thought I heard something from that direction during my watch," I said. "I walked back along the trail a short distance and listened, but I didn't hear anything, so I figured it was a passing marsh pig or some other animal."

"Torph," Sable said, pointing at a footprint. "Webbed."

"Huh," Mid grunted. "What would a Torph be doing way out here, and barefoot at that?"

"Yeah, Cheff," Buttons said. "I thought you said there wasn't anyone out here in The Fel."

Instead of replying, Cheff merely scuffed his feet and turned away.

"Out with it, Cheff." Mid demanded. "What do you know? You *did* say The Fel wasn't inhabited."

"Well," Cheff said, "that's not *entirely* true."

"Uh-oh," Lery said.

"Yeah, Cheff, 'uh-oh' is right!" Mid said. "What didn't you tell us?"

"The Fel *is* uninhabited. Mostly."

"*Mostly?*" Mid asked.

"Yes, *mostly*," Cheff said. "I didn't mention the Fel People."

"Fel People," Mid said in a flat tone. "Naturally, you didn't mention the Fel People. Of course not, why would you?"

Carra barged out of her tent and marched up to Cheff. "Who are the Fel People, Cheff? And why didn't you mention them earlier?"

Cheff sighed. "I ran into them once when I was hunting out here. It was a few summers ago, when game was practically non-existent around the Labor Compound. I came on the night before Day Six, so I could hunt the whole day and not worry about being missed at school. You might remember a week back then that we had plenty of meat? I killed a marsh pig, a pretty big one. Had to lug it all the way back home in the dark, too. It was a long hike, longer than I had thought, and I never hunted here again."

"Not 'lots of times'?" Carra asked, her eyebrows arched. "I distinctly remember you saying that you hunted out here 'lots of times.'"

Cheff scowled, but didn't answer.

"Excuse me… Cheff…" Lery said. "Is it… okay… for me to… cook breakfast now?"

"Are you done examining the footprints, Sable?" Cheff asked.

Sable nodded. "All clear."

"Sure, Lery, go ahead. What's for breakfast, by the way?"

"Eggs."

"Eggs!" Cheff said. "Where in the world did you find eggs out here?"

Mid said, "You can talk about eggs later, Cheff. Right now you're telling us about the Fel People."

"Right," Cheff said. "As I was saying, I was hunting, following paths at random through the marsh. On one path, I turned a corner and ran smack into a family of Torphs—a man, a woman, and two small children. I think I frightened them pretty badly, but not nearly as badly as they frightened me. They were fishing in a little pool. I distinctly remember that the little boy and girl had kid-sized fishing poles.

"When I caught my breath, I said to them, 'Excuse me, I didn't know there was anyone out here in The Fel.' 'That's the idea,' the Torph man said sourly. His name was Bors, or Boran, or something like that." Cheff searched his memory. "Yeah, Boran, that was it. I'm pretty sure. Anyway, this Boran said, 'We'd like to keep it that way, if you don't mind.' 'Of course,' I said. 'I'm pretty good at keeping secrets.' 'I'll bet you are, at that,' Boran said. And then he surprised me. 'Come sit down with us. We're about to have our lunch. You're welcome to join us.'

"So I sat with them a while, and they shared their lunch with me: some dried meat and a kind of odd cheese. Marsh-pig cheese, he said it was."

Buttons made a face. "Eww!"

"It wasn't bad, Sis. Tasted kind of sharpish, but not unpleasantly so. Anyway, he told me that there was a small community of refugees living in a sort of camp out here. He said they were mostly Torphs, but that anyone who would rather not live under the law of Emperor Pallador was welcome."

"Why mostly Torphs?" Carra asked.

"He said it had to do with the Torphs being rounded up and put into Torph Camps, where they are tested for the Ability. So, when Pallador instituted Torph testing, a lot of Torphs left Fellstone City. Anyway, Boran invited me to go back to his village with him, but I hadn't gotten my kill yet, so I didn't go."

"Why didn't you tell us about it, Cheff?" Buttons asked.

"Because I promised Boran I wouldn't. I never told anyone. The 'best way to keep a secret' and all that. You were a lot younger, then, Sis. I would have felt terrible if you had accidentally blurted it out. Besides, that was a long time ago—I haven't thought much about it since."

"I mean," Buttons said, "why didn't you tell us about it *yesterday*?"

"Oh. Well, I didn't expect to run into them. Back then, the camp was far northeast of here." He thought about it. "Boran did say they moved the camp, sometimes. Maybe it's closer to here, now."

"So," Mid said, "why would a Torph from a village sneak into our camp and steal stew? Especially if his village was nearby. Wouldn't he go home and eat, rather than risk an encounter with strangers?"

"I suppose so—I don't understand it, myself."

"And another thing," Mid said. "If we had an undetected visitor, that means that someone was asleep on their watch. I know it wasn't me. How about you, Cheff?"

"Not me—I was on my feet the whole time."

"Me, too," I said. "I never sat down once."

"Sable?" Cheff asked.

Sable snorted.

"Right," Cheff said, "of course. Lery?"

"No… Friend Cheff…" Lery said. "I walked… around and… around…"

"I never got my turn," Buttons said. "It got light first."

"Okay," Cheff said, "then…"

Everyone turned and stared at Carra. "I didn't mean to," she whined. "I only closed my eyes for a tiny bit. I was sooo sleepy."

Sable snorted again.

Mid shook his head. "It must have been longer than a minute. Somebody, apparently a Torph, had time to decide you were sleeping, slip into camp, help themselves to a mug of stew, and sneak out again."

"Aw, Mid," Cheff said, "she didn't mean to." He was gazing at Carra. "I'm sure she won't do it again."

"Stow it, Cheff," Mid said. "Get hold of yourself. This is a serious breach of discipline. We all put our lives in her hands last night, and she let us down. I'm sorry, Carra, but that's the way it is."

Carra hung her head. "I'm so sorry. And I promise I won't let it happen again."

"No," Mid said, "you won't. I'm not sure what to do about this. We'll have to talk it over and decide before night, though. For now, let's eat our breakfast, break camp, and find some rovaldia."

"Thank you, Mid," Cheff said. "You're absolutely right. We did, all of us, put our lives in Carra's hands. If our visitor had been hostile, we might well have woken up this morning with our throats cut."

Buttons giggled at that, then caught the ponies' serious look and straightened up.

Cheff whirled on Carra and waved his index finger in her face. "Frankly, Miss Carra Trenta Wolcutt of the Tumberland Wolcutts, I've had a bellyfull of your antics. I expected better from a *real* FRM agent." He turned his back on her, and plopped down by the fire, scowling.

We passed Lery our cups, and he filled them with scrambled eggs and some reconstituted dried meat which he had spiced like sausage. Carra waited until everyone else was served, then took her cup into her tent and ate by herself. Yesterday's happy mood had turned into a grim seriousness. I hoped Cheff thought of something to raise our morale before too long.

We finished eating quickly, then broke camp.

"All right, everyone," Cheff said. "let's look sharp and find that rovaldia. We have bags to fill. Sable, let's go south for a while. Maybe we'll hit a patch that way. Ready? Let's move out!"

We went southward in the same formation as yesterday, with Sable in the lead and Cheff bringing up the rear. I had a feeling that Carra Trenta Wolcutt was going to look exceptionally hard for rovaldia today.

— 22 —

ROVALDIA

I WAS RIGHT.

We'd only been hiking an hour or so when Carra called out, "Rovaldia! I think it is, anyway."

She was squatting by the waterline. Cheff compared the little plant with his rovaldia diagram.

"Sure looks like the picture," Buttons said.

"I think it's the real thing," Cheff said. He broke off a leaf, sniffed it, and put it in his mouth. He smacked his lips a few times. "Yes, that's rovaldia. It has the characteristic smell and taste."

We all sampled some. It did, indeed, have a distinct flavor, a little like licorice candy.

Cheff pulled it up and shook the wet mud off its roots. "Good work, Carra. Everyone, remember how it looks, smells, and tastes. Here—everybody put a twig of it in your pocket." He stashed the plant in one of the special rovaldia bags. "It's a big plant—won't take too many of these to fill our bags."

"And then we can go home!" Buttons said.

"Well, back to the salvage camp, anyway," Mid said.

We hiked for another few hours and found four more rovaldia plants. At that rate, there was a real possibility that we might finish by evening. I asked Cheff, "Do you think we should start back toward the road?"

"Maybe," he said. "Or maybe we should keep going until we fill all the bags. We're doing pretty well, so far."

"I have to go," Carra said.

"So go," Mid said.

Carra glared at him.

"Ten minute break," Cheff called out. "Girls that way, boys over here. Lery, are there any more of those biscuits in your grub sack?"

We trotted off in our respective directions. We hadn't been gone two minutes when we heard Carra scream.

"What is it?" Cheff yelled.

"Bear!" Carra cried.

We ran in her direction. Lery held his pipe wrench in his hand, ready for action. We ran smack into Buttons. She was fastening her pants. "Hey, this is the girls' side! What's the big idea?"

"Sorry, Sis," Cheff said. "Didn't you hear Carra scream?"

"I heard something," Buttons said. "Carra went that way." She pointed southeastward.

We ran that way, Buttons close behind. We burst into a little clearing and found ourselves face-to-face with a bear. The bear put his head down and growled at us. We stopped dead in our tracks.

"That's a Fel bear," I whispered. "I recognize it from a textbook I read."

"Oh, wonderful," Cheff whispered back. "Vegetarian, I hope?"

"Not so much," I said.

"Wonderful," Cheff said again. "First, we stop for a snack, then we *are* a snack."

"Don't be silly," Buttons said. "He looks friendly to me." She slowly approached the bear, her right hand extended.

"Buttons, don't!" Cheff hissed. "It's a wild animal." He tried to grab her arm, but missed.

"Hello, Mr. Grumbles," she said. "I'm Buttons, and these are my friends, Starry and Moka." Buttons held out her ponies for Mr. Grumbles to examine. He sniffed them both and seemed satisfied. Then he sat down and scratched his left ear with his hind paw.

"Do you have an itch?" Buttons asked. "Here, let me see."

"Buttons, leave him alone." Cheff said. "Let's get out of here before he eats us!"

"Oh, Cheff!" Buttons said. "He's harmless. Can't you see that?" She scratched behind Mr. Grumbles' left ear. Mr. Grumbles lay down, rumbled, and rolled his eyes blissfully. Buttons switched to his right ear. "See?" she said. "He likes it."

"Okay," Cheff said dubiously. "But seriously, Sis, you need to be more careful. One of these days, you're going to meet some creature that isn't so agreeable."

"Andaran's sake, Cheff," Buttons said, "don't be so silly."

"Yeah," Cheff said, "that's me, all right—just plain silly." He shook his head.

"Where's Carra?" Mid asked, looking around.

We'd no sooner started searching again than there came a shrill, piercing scream from the grassy area to the south. We ran toward the scream. Carra sat, heedless of the wet ground, holding her leg.

"What is it?" Cheff asked.

"Snake bite!" Carra wailed. "I was running from that horrid creature, that awful *bear*, and I ran into the water, and a snake bit me."

Sable and Buttons knelt next to her. There was a ragged hole in Carra's right trouser leg. Sable slit the trouser leg from the bottom cuff up to her knee, revealing two puncture wounds close together on the back of her calf.

"Is that a snake bite?" Buttons asked.

"Could be," Sable said.

"Of course it is!" Carra howled. "I told you it was! It was a water snake! I ran into the water, and it bit me!"

"Books," Mid said, "do you have any information on snakes in The Fel?"

I squeezed my eyes shut and called up a mental image of a book my father had back in Tumberland, a banned book called *Fauna of Andaran*." It had pictures of hundreds of animals from all over Andaran. There was an entire chapter on The Fel. "There are two snakes native to The Fel," I told Cheff. "Both are poisonous."

"How poisonous?" Cheff asked.

"Extremely. Death occurs within minutes."

Sable removed one of Carra's bootlaces. Lery found a short stick. They made a tourniquet right below Carra's knee.

"We'll have to… to open… it a little… every ten minutes… or so to… to keep… the leg… alive," Lery said. "Meanwhile… we have to… to get the… the poison out. I learned that in… in the… army… Basic Training… first-aid."

Sable gave Lery an approving nod then cut two X's in Carra's leg, one over each puncture wound, and squeezed. Carra screamed. Sable sucked each wound and spat it onto the ground. She repeated this procedure many times, then leaned back.

"My leg's going numb," Carra sobbed. "I'm *dyyying!*"

"We'll probably have to amputate," Buttons said cheerfully.

Lery loosened the tourniquet a little.

Carra screamed. "Ow! It hurts! I'm going to die."

"Not so numb, then?" Buttons asked, smiling sweetly.

Sable ran her tongue over her lips and around the inside of her mouth. "No poison."

"What?" Cheff asked. "Are you sure? Books said that—"

"Sure," Sable said.

Mid was knee-deep in the marsh, poking around.

"Hey!" Cheff said. "Get out of there, Mid! You'll get bit, too. That's the last thing we need."

Mid picked up a broken tree branch that had been in the water for some time. He held it up for us to see. Hanging from two small prongs was a tiny scrap of Carra's trouser leg. Mid waded out of the water and threw the stick at Carra's feet. "There's your poisonous snake," he said. "I think you're going to recover."

Sable stood up and spat once more on the ground. She walked a few steps away and stared off into The Fel, spitting occasionally.

Buttons took off the tourniquet and handed Carra her shoelace. "Better lace up, Wolcutt. We have rovaldia to find."

"But," Carra cried, "I'm dying! I'm sure of it! I'm dizzy and I feel faint!"

Buttons picked up the branch, waved it in Carra's face, and dropped it in Carra's lap. "Oh, I don't know," Buttons said. "I think you'll be fine."

We started laughing, except for Sable, who was still spitting.

Carra blushed violently and hid her face in her hands.

While we were laughing, Mr. Grumbles nosed his way through the tall grass. He ambled over to Carra, still sitting with her face in her hands. He sniffed her head thoroughly and moved on to her neck. "Stop it, Cheff!" Carra said. "You're just a little kid!"

Cheff's eyebrows shot up, Sable snorted, Buttons rolled her eyes, and we laughed.

Carra uncovered her face and looked up to see what was so funny. She found herself staring right into Mr. Grumbles' eyes. He began systematically licking Carra's face. She let out a piercing scream and wrapped her arms around her body. "Bear! I'm getting eaten by a bear! Help!"

Mr. Grumbles plopped down heavily almost on top of Carra and scratched his ear again.

Lery offered Mr. Grumbles a biscuit from his bag. Mr. Grumbles accepted the biscuit happily and trundled off to munch on it.

"Think the jexan will hurt him?" Mid asked.

"I don't have a problem with a Fel bear in a good mood," Cheff said.

"The right… tools…" Lery said.

"What's the matter with you *now*?" Cheff asked Carra, who was still sitting on the ground, crying a little, her face in her hands again.

"I'm going to die," she howled. "First a snake poisoned me, then a bear tried to eat me."

Buttons said quietly to Sable, "I've had worse bug bites — in my own bed!"

Carra ignored Buttons and laced up her boot. Then she glared up at Sable. "You've ruined my trousers. I expect you to reimburse me the cost of replacement."

"Drop it, Carra," Cheff said. "She was saving your life, remember?"

"But—"

"I said drop it. Now get yourself ready to march. *Move!*"

Carra moved.

"Anyway…" Lery said, "they're my… my trousers."

We laughed again. Except Carra, of course.

Cheff turned to the rest of us. "Everyone about ready? As Buttons said, we have rovaldia to find." He strode toward the vague trail we'd been following all morning.

"I'll be right with you," Carra said. "I still haven't… you know."

"Oh, for—" Cheff took a long, deep breath. "Hurry it up, okay?"

"I will."

The rest of us, including Mr. Grumbles, followed Cheff to the trail and waited for her. Mr. Grumbles followed Lery, hoping for another biscuit.

"She's a real pain," Mid said. "I'll be happy to see her back in her little yellow canoe paddling off across the bay, disappearing into the fog."

"Her sacks of rovaldia bulging," Buttons added. "The ponies say, the sooner the better."

Lery dug into his bag and handed Buttons a biscuit. Buttons fed it to Mr. Grumbles, then scratched his ears some more.

"Carra does seem to cause a great deal of trouble." Cheff said. "But she *is* kinda cute. And she's trying her best."

"You still think so?" Mid asked.

Cheff shrugged. "It comes and goes."

"I think you're kind of cracked, Old Man," Mid said.

Sable said, "Time."

"She is taking her time, isn't she?" Cheff asked. "I hope she's okay. Maybe we should check on her."

"The last thing I want to do is walk in on her when she's… you know," Mid said.

"You go, Buttons," Cheff said. "You can take Mr. Grumbles with you."

"Okay." She disappeared into the reeds with the huge bear right behind.

Sable shot Cheff a look, then followed Buttons. A minute later, Sable's voice came over the wind. "Gone!"

We rushed back to the water's edge. Sure enough, there was no sign of Carra.

"Where could she have gone?" Cheff asked.

"Do you suppose she was captured by The Fel People?" I asked. "Maybe the one that was in the camp last night?"

"Could be, Cheff," Mid said.

Sable was walking the waterline, studying the ground. "Footprints," she said. "Boots."

"Army boots," Lery said.

Cheff said, "The Fel People don't wear boots, as far as I know. There are at least two sets here, two different sizes."

"Three," Sable said.

Lery came over and showed Sable his army boots.

"Same," she said.

"What do you suppose the army is doing out here?" Mid asked. "And why would they kidnap Carra?"

Cheff turned away.

"What is it, Cheff?" Buttons asked. "What are you not telling us?"

"Remember I was telling you that Boran said that the Fel People move their camp from time to time?"

"What about it?" Mid asked.

"He said it was because the Sephs hunt out here sometimes."

We stared at him. Mid asked, "And exactly when were you planning to tell us about that, Cheff? Or were you even *going* to tell us about it?"

"I wasn't," Cheff said. "I didn't see any reason to worry everyone."

"Didn't see a reason—are you out of your mind? If you'd told us, we could have been a lot more careful. Posted a double watch. Insisted on the buddy system at all times. Things like that." Mid walked away a few yards, shaking his head.

"He's right, Cheff," Buttons said. "We're all in this together. You should have told us."

"Yes," Sable said.

"I… think so… too." Lery said.

"I agree," I said. "Ignorance is never helpful. Knowledge is powerful."

"I'm sorry, everyone," Cheff said. "I meant well, but I see now that you're right—I should have told you. I promise, from now on, everything I know, you'll know."

"Fair enough." Mid pointed to a triangular indentation in the mud, right at the waterline. "What do you suppose this mark is?"

Sable examined it. "Boat. Canoe, maybe."

"What?" Cheff frowned. "Are we saying that Carra was taken by someone in a canoe?"

"Three someones, Cheff," Buttons said. "Maybe more for all we know. Try to follow along."

Cheff covered his face with his hands. "Oh, my sweet Carra! Where have you gone?"

"Can it, Cheff!" Mid snapped. "Your 'sweet Carra' is a sweet pain in the—" He paused and took a deep breath.

Sable murmured, "Mission."

"Sable's right," I said. "This is about far more than Carra. This is about the entire mission. It's up to Carra to take the rovaldia to Tumberland. No Carra, no mission."

Cheff looked at me funny, then said, "Thank you Books, Sable. Of course you are both right."

"Yes, they are," Mid agreed. "Anyway, the question now is, how are we going to find her and get her back?"

"I don't know," Cheff said. "We can't catch up with a canoe, that's for sure."

"But if they're taking her somewhere, and we can find out where, maybe we can rescue her," Mid said.

"Not if… they took her… to the… Fortress," Lery said.

"No, but we can't assume they did," Cheff said. "For all we know, she's still in The Fel somewhere."

"Fel People," Sable said.

"What?" Mid asked.

Cheff said, "Sable means that we're going to need some help. It's time for us to find The Fel People."

OPERATION LOCKDOWN

— 23 —

THE FEL PEOPLE

"FIND THE FEL People!" Mid said. "How in Andaran are we going to do that?"

"How hard could it be?" Buttons said. "They seem to have found us already."

"Maybe," Mid said, "but we don't know that for sure yet."

"We don't know much of anything for sure, yet," Cheff said. "I wish I had gone back to Boran's village with him."

"I thought you said it had moved," Buttons said.

"No, I said that Boran said they move it sometimes on account of the Sephs, and that *maybe* they've moved it."

"If the Fel village were around here somewhere," Mid said, "and I'm only saying *if*, how would we go about finding it?"

"Good question," Cheff said. "I wonder how *they* find it? You know, when they go out hunting, or gathering, or fishing, or whatever they leave their village to do. They must have some way of getting home again, right?"

"Right," Mid agreed. "But what?"

"Everybody gather around," Cheff said. "Let's sit down, have a bite to eat, and think this through."

"Shouldn't we go after Carra?" Buttons asked. "The ponies think that the longer we wait, the farther away she'll be."

"That might be true, Sis. But since we don't know where they're taking her, or why, there's not much point in running off in some random direction."

"T.B.A." Sable said.

"What's that?" I asked.

"Think Before Acting," Cheff said. "It's another principle from Sable's military training manual. You know—the one by Pitr Karlsin."

"I'd like to memorize that book someday," I said.

"Read mine," Sable said.

"Thanks, Sable! I'll do that when we get back."

"For now, though," Cheff said, "come and help me make a place for our break."

We stomped down a little circle in the tall grass, only big enough for the six of us to sit around a tiny cooking fire. The tall grass blocked most of the wind.

Buttons and I gathered all the dry twigs we could find and took them to Lery and Sable, who were preparing a safe spot for a fire in the center of our little clearing.

In a few minutes, we were warming our hands over a cheerful little blaze, sipping piping-hot felmoss tea and nibbling on biscuits and jerky.

"I know these have jexan in them," Mid said, "but in small quantities, they sure can give a guy a boost."

"It's true," Cheff said. "Between the felmoss tea and the jexan biscuits, I'm feeling considerably better." We nibbled and sipped a little more, then Cheff said, "Okay, everyone. Let's pool our knowledge and see what we know."

"Village," Sable said.

"Good start," Cheff said. "There used to be a village out here somewhere, and maybe there still is. When I met Boran, he said the Fel People were mostly Torphs, but also a few from the other Peoples."

"They go barefoot, as far as we know," Mid said.

"They fish," Buttons said. "Boran and his family did, anyway."

"Good!" Cheff said. "What else?"

"They move the village sometimes, because of the Sephs," Mid said.

"How about what we don't know," Cheff asked, "but can guess?"

We thought about it, then Mid said, "They must be pretty familiar with the waterways. This place is all high spots and low spots."

"Rain," Sable said.

"That's right," Cheff said. "There's probably a lot less dry ground after a storm. They must have some way of getting out of the mud."

"Houses on legs?" Mid asked.

"Maybe. But if their houses are on legs, wouldn't they stick up above the grass? That would make them too easy to find."

"Camouflage," Sable said.

"Of course!" Mid said. "Grass roofs, or reeds, or something."

"Even so," I said, "they'd stick up above the grass line, right?"

"They'd have to, wouldn't they?" Cheff mulled it over. "Let's see, Torphs are shorter than most Peoples, except Troh. No offense, Mid. Stand up for a moment."

"None taken." He stood up. "I'm short, but my head is only half a foot below the top of the grass. And I'm not full-grown yet."

Cheff raised his eyebrows.

Mid said, "I *hope* I'm not done growing yet." He stood as tall as he could on his tiptoes.

"So, what does that tell us?" Cheff asked. "Even if they used short little houses, barely big enough to stand up in, the roof line would be above the grass line."

"Which means," Mid said, "that if we could get even a little elevation, we could possibly spot the roof line. You'd be amazed at how little elevation it takes to extend the horizon, especially on flat ground. Even a stepladder can add several miles."

"Unless they hide their village in a grove of trees. Anything else?" Cheff asked.

"They have to cook," Buttons said. "No matter how careful they are, there will be a little smoke, at least sometimes."

"Excellent!" Cheff said. "So, now, all we need is a stepladder."

"Tree," Sable said.

"There must be a Fel oak around here somewhere," Cheff said. "I mean, there has to be. Right?"

Mid shrugged.

"Lery," Sable said, "help."

Sable stood up. From her mission bag, she took a pair of folding binoculars, then spread her feet. "Lift."

Lery squatted down behind Sable, got into position, then stood up with her sitting on his shoulders. Sable raised the binoculars to her eyes. "Turn. Slowly."

Lery rotated slowly. He'd turned more than halfway around when Sable said. "Stop. Tree. Mark."

Cheff scuffed an arrow in the ground pointing the way Sable was looking. "Got it. You can let her down, Lery."

Lery gently lowered Sable to her feet.

Sable said, "Thank you, Lery."

"How far?" Cheff asked her.

"Ten, fifteen minutes."

"How tall?"

"Tall enough." Sable aligned her compass with Cheff's arrow and made a note on her little clipboard.

"Excellent!" Cheff said. "Okay, gang, pack it up. We're moving out."

Five minutes later, we followed Sable through the marsh. Traveling in a straight line was a lot harder than following a trail on dry ground. We had to keep crossing wet spots. The shallow ones we could step through, but the deep ones required us to wade with our packs held above our heads.

Three times we stopped and waited while Lery lifted Sable on his shoulders again to take a fresh bearing. By the time we reached the tree, we were tired, cold, wet, and muddy from head to toe.

"Should we make another fire?" Buttons asked. "The ponies are freezing."

"I don't think we're going to be here that long, Sis," Cheff said.

Sable fastened a grappling hook to a coil of rope and tossed it over a stout branch near the top of the oak. She climbed the rope, scanned The Fel, and noted a compass bearing on her clipboard. She rappelled down the long trunk, then gave the rope a peculiar flick. The grappling hook detached itself and fell at her feet. Sable folded the hook and returned it to her tool belt along with the coil of rope.

"How far?" Cheff asked.

"That was amazing, Sable!" I said.

She allowed herself a tiny smile. "Naval Cadet training."

"How far?" Cheff asked again.

"Far."

"Are you sure it's the village?"

Sable shrugged. "Possibly."

"Roofs?"

"Trees."

"Was there smoke?"

"Maybe. Hard to tell. Sorry."

"That's okay," Cheff said. "It's better than nothing, which is what we had five minutes ago. Brace yourselves, crew. It's going to be like what we just did, but a lot more of it. Everyone ready? Let's go!"

But before we could start, Mr. Grumbles wandered out of the weeds and walked straight up to Lery. He sat back on his haunches and waved his paws in the air.

We laughed, forgetting briefly how tired we were.

"Hello, Mr. Grumbles!" Buttons said. "Have you been following us the whole time? The ponies are glad to see you." She scratched his ears.

Lery dug into his pouch and found another biscuit for Mr. Grumbles, who accepted it eagerly, crunched it down, then snuffled the ground for crumbs. He gently sniffed Starry and Moka and gave Buttons a lick on her cheek.

"He kissed me!" she said, then threw her arms around him and kissed him back.

"Okay, Sis, unhand that bear and let's get going. We have a long way to go."

"That is," Mid said, "if you can *bear* to leave him."

Buttons giggled. "Goodbye, Mr. Grumbles. Be safe!"

Sable checked her compass, then headed southward through the deep grass. Cheff was right—it was some tough going. We trudged through that swampy marsh for several hours. Cheff allowed a five-minute break every half hour.

Somewhere in the middle of the third hour, a horrific growl that raised the hair on the back of my neck froze us solid. An enormous marsh pig, eyes red, spittle dripping from its huge, yellow fangs, rushed across the clearing and stopped at Sable's feet, menacing.

"Nest," Sable said.

Sure enough, in the center of the clearing was a mound of dry grass and reeds. Barely visible over the rim were a half-dozen tiny snouts, moving around, sniffing the wind. A second marsh pig lurched to its feet and charged in our direction, halting a few inches from Sable's boots. Both pigs pawed the mud and backed up a few feet, preparing for another charge.

"Back up," Cheff said. "Slowly."

"Not too slowly," Mid said.

"If we run, they'll chase us," I said. "I read it in that old fauna book."

We retraced our steps, but it wasn't easy backing up in the sludge. Buttons stumbled, which precipitated a second charge by the angry pigs. They stood defensively, pawing the mud and growling, preparing for a third run at us. I had a feeling that this time they wouldn't stop. I was right. They let loose an ear-splitting howl and made their run.

Right before they reached Sable, Mr. Grumbles lurched out of the grass. The marsh pigs skidded to a halt and whirled on this new threat. Mr. Grumbles stood on his hind legs, lifted his huge paws above his head, and roared. The marsh pigs scurried back to their nest, where they adopted a defensive stance.

We kept backing away. Mr. Grumbles kept roaring. Finally, we were far enough back that the marsh pigs decided we were harmless.

"That was close," Cheff said, wiping the sweat from his forehead with his shirttail.

"Too close," Mid said. "Mr. Grumbles arrived just in time." He gave the bear a tentative pat. "Good bear."

"We'll have to go around," Cheff said. "Can you adjust our course, Sable?"

"Yes," Sable said. "Tree. Lery?"

Lery lifted her on his shoulders and she located another tree. It was only a few minutes away, and, in short order, Sable was up the tree and taking a new bearing.

"How's it look?" Cheff asked.

"Close," Sable said.

We took advantage of the break to drink some water and relieve ourselves. It was the middle of the afternoon, so Lery gave each of us another biscuit, including Mr. Grumbles, who accepted his biscuit proudly this time, as a well-earned reward. Then we were back on the march.

Not for long, though. Less than a quarter of an hour later, we ran into marsh pigs again. Not only two this time, but an entire pack of them. The instant they spotted us, they ran over and encircled us, yipping, grunting, howling, and generally raising an enormous fuss.

We braced ourselves, but instead of charging, they held us in their circle. As long as we stood still, so did they. But every time we tried to move, they nipped at our feet. So we waited, trying to figure out our next move.

After what seemed a long time, a tall Torph man came out of the reeds. He wore sandals and a kind of leather tunic. Two long knives in leather sheaths hung from his belt. He assessed the situation: six kids, two ponies, and a Fel bear, surrounded by marsh pigs. He put two fingers in his mouth and whistled, then barked a command in a language I didn't recognize. The marsh pigs instantly stopped their racket and resumed rooting in the mud.

"WHAT ARE YOU KIDS DOING IN MY SWAMP?"

Rayce

— 24 —

RAYCE

CHEFF STEPPED FORWARD. "I'm Cheff Karfendek, sir, and these are my friends. We're from Fellstone City. I'm looking for a man I met here, once, Boran. Do you know him?"

"Maybe, maybe not. What do you want with him?"

"One of our party is missing," Cheff said. "We think she might have been taken by soldiers. We came to ask if Boran would help us find her."

"Soldiers?" he said. "It's not impossible—they come out here sometimes. Hunting parties. What makes you think they were soldiers?"

"We found boot prints where she was last seen. And there was a mark on the ground that we thought might have been made by a canoe."

"I see. Where was this, exactly?"

Sable showed him her notations on her clipboard.

"We've been tracking a hunting party out here for days," the Torph said. "That's right about where we spotted them."

"What kind of hunting party, sir?" Mid asked.

"Sephs. Well, Fessals. Facilitators, the Sephs' attendants, you know. They serve as the Sephs' hands and feet. They're Controlled. Sometimes the Sephs themselves go hunting, but only on the warmest days of summer. They don't like getting cold—but you probably know that. The Sephs have a hunting lodge south of here. They like to hunt for marsh pigs and sometimes bears. And sometimes other game."

"Nooo!" Buttons said. "Not *bears*! The ponies would be upset if Mr. Grumbles got eaten."

"Mr. Grumbles?" the Torph asked.

Upon hearing his name, Mr. Grumbles ambled into the clearing. At the sight of the Torph stranger, he stood up on his hind legs and roared.

The stranger said gently, "Easy, good bear. I won't hurt you or your friends."

Mr. Grumbles sniffed the air a few times, then wandered off to investigate the marsh pigs.

"His name is Mr. Grumbles," Buttons said. "He's our friend. Lery feeds him biscuits."

Mid said, "He scared away some gigantic marsh pigs, wild ones, when we stumbled onto their nest."

"They were going to eat the ponies," Buttons said, "but Mr. Grumbles wouldn't let them. Mr. Grumbles likes the ponies."

"I see." A ghost of a smile played about the Torph's mouth.

The Torph approached Cheff and spoke quietly in his ear. "Who's your other friend?"

"What other friend?"

"The one behind you, in the grass."

Cheff started to look, but the Torph stopped him. "Don't turn your head. Could it be the one you're missing?"

"I don't think so," Cheff said. "We haven't seen her for hours. If it were Carra, she would have said something by now."

"All right," the Torph said. "Walk with me, slowly."

He and Cheff moved across the clearing in the direction he'd come from. The Torph put his fingers in his mouth again and whistled, but this time it was a kind of warbling sound. Six Torphs armed with long spears burst into the little clearing. The Torph nodded in the direction of the mystery 'friend.'

The six Torph spear-carriers rushed into the tall grass behind us. They emerged with a sodden, bedraggled figure in tow. They hauled it to the center of the clearing and deposited it at Cheff's feet.

"Looks like a female," the Torph said. "A *Torph* female."

"That's a Blueband uniform," Cheff said, then looked at the Torph. "Bluebands are a kind of—"

"We know what Bluebands are, though I have to admit we don't see them out here often." With his foot, he gently rolled the muddy form over so we could see her face. "Recognize her?"

Cheff's jaw dropped. *"Brex?"*

We crowded in to take a better look. The sodden figure raised herself to a sitting position and wiped some of the mud from her face. "So what if I am, Karfendek? Huh? What are you going to do about it?"

Cheff grinned. "There's the Blueband squad leader we know and love. Why, Miss Averith Brex, whatever brings you out to The Fel?"

"Oh, shut up, Karfendek. Leave me alone."

"She's a friend of yours?" the Torph asked.

"Not exactly. We know her—she goes to the same school as we do. We had no idea she was following us, though I can't say I'm surprised." He turned and faced the Torph. "I'm sorry we led her here, sir. I'm afraid she could be a serious problem for you and your village."

"We've had intruders here before," the Torph said. "So far, no great harm has come from them. We have certain… procedures… we follow, to keep our people safe."

The way he said 'procedures' made me shiver.

The spear-carriers bound Brex's hands behind her back and, at a signal from the Torph man, they half-walked, half-dragged her away toward the village.

Cheff started to protest, but the Torph cut him off. "Never mind her, she'll be fine. For now, anyway. Tell me more about the missing one."

"Could they have taken her to the hunting lodge you mentioned?" Cheff asked.

The Torph's face darkened. "It's a possibility, yes. The Sephs don't limit their hunting to animals."

Cheff said grimly, "We understand, sir. We found out about their so-called 'dark food' a few weeks ago."

"Will you help us, sir?" Mid asked. "I'm afraid that the longer we wait, the less likely it is we'll ever see Carra again."

"Perhaps," the Torph said, "but first things first." He offered his hand to Cheff. "You may call me Rayce."

"Yes, sir. Thank you." Cheff shook his hand. "I'm Cheff, as I said, and this is my sister Buttons, and my friends, Sable, Mid, Lery, and Books."

We shook hands all around, then Rayce said, "I can't wait to hear what brings you youngsters to The Fel on a windy autumn day. Or why that muddy Blueband was following you."

"Well, you see, sir, it's like this—"

"Hold on, Cheff. It sounds like it could be a long story. Let's go somewhere we can refresh ourselves and warm up. Besides, if we're going to help your friend—Carra, was it?—we're going to need a plan and a lot of help. Follow me." He turned and led the way down a trail through the marsh.

It was a short walk to the Fel People's village—Sable's compass work had been brilliant. In ten minutes or so, the tall grass parted to reveal a surprisingly large group of structures hidden in a small grove of Fel oaks. Several dozen small houses encircled a central clearing, their rooftops only barely visible above the grass line. Small groups of poorly dressed children were playing games or interacting with tame marsh pigs. A dozen or so men and women dressed much like Rayce were scattered around the central common area, engaged in various tasks. Several men and women holding long spears stood guard. A few villagers tended small children. Several wove grass mats or square panels on large wooden looms. In the center of the common area, a couple of women and a man cooked over the edge of a rather large bonfire. As we entered, everyone stopped what they were doing and stared at us. Some of the children ran up to us, smiling, and tugged at our gear and clothing.

"I don't think they get too many visitors," I said. "We're a sensation!"

"Look!" Mid said. "The houses are on stilts like we figured. They seem to be made all out of poles and woven grass panels. I'll bet that's so the Fel People can fold the houses up and carry them away."

"Looks like there could be a couple hundred people living here," Cheff said, "maybe more. It's amazing they can live out here without getting caught. I wonder how they live?"

Rayce overheard and said, "We hunt, mostly, and fish. We also gather felmoss, which we sell in Old City to… well, you don't need to know that. The man we sell it to never asks who we are or where we live—he just pays us. He says that our tea is the best he's ever tasted."

Cheff laughed. "If Mr. Rishten knew where his felmoss tea came from, he'd be astounded, to say the least."

"Mr. Rishten is our teacher, Cheff's and mine," I said. "He drinks felmoss tea all day long. It makes him a little intense, sometimes."

"I have a question if you don't mind," Cheff said.

"Not at all," said Rayce. "Go ahead."

"I noticed as we walked through the village that the guards carry spears, and I see that you carry a pair of long knives, but I didn't see a single bow anywhere."

"Observant," Rayce said. "We learned long ago that ranged weapons aren't effective in The Fel. Can you guess why?"

Cheff considered. "The tall reeds don't afford much visibility."

"True," Rayce said. "But there's a more compelling reason."

Cheff thought some more. "You can't find your arrows."

Rayce laughed. "Correct! The Fel is mostly covered in water. Shoot an arrow, miss your target, and it's gone forever. Spears, on the other hand, are pretty easy to recover. Do you use a bow to hunt?"

Cheff took his hunting sling from his pocket and handed it to Rayce. "This tucks out of sight pretty easily. Also, most of the Bluebands have no clue what it is. It's at least as effective as a bow." He grinned. "With sufficient practice, that is. Also, it uses stones, not arrows. Arrows are time-consuming to make. Stones you simply pick up off the ground. I usually keep five well-shaped stones in my pocket."

"How interesting! Perhaps you would give us a demonstration while you are here?"

"Sure," Cheff said. "I'd be happy to."

"For now, though," Rayce said, "I'm going to take you to our longhouse."

"What's a longhouse?" Buttons asked.

"It's the largest building in the village. It serves as a meeting place, mess hall, dormitory, whatever we need it to be at any given time. Today it's our guest house. It's built like the other buildings and can be folded up and transported easily, but it's bigger." He gestured for us to enter.

Lery had to duck low to get in. The inside was dimly lit by a small charcoal brazier in the center of the floor. It was good to get warm again out of the wind. What a relief!

Rayce stuck his head into the room. "You six wait here. I'll have someone bring you some hot soup. I'm going to take your Blueband to the women and get her cleaned up. After a while, I'll bring some folks to talk with you and we can decide what we're going to do about Carra."

"Thank you, sir," Cheff said. "I'm rather worried about her—we all are."

"If she's still alive, she'll likely stay that way for several hours. The Sephs prefer to feed at night."

Cheff blanched. "We know. We watched them try to eat my uncle."

Rayce raised his eyebrows. "Try?"

"Yes, sir," Cheff said. "We were able to rescue him."

"Rescue him!" Rayce said. "I'm sure your story will be most interesting. Until we developed our rules, the Sephs would sometimes catch our children. Their Facilitators would hide outside our camp—it was before we had houses—and wait for children to wander too far away. We lost one or two every year. It got so that we stopped naming our children until they were five years old. Made it seem easier to lose them, somehow."

"So the Sephs know you're out here?" Mid asked.

"I'm not sure what they know now. They know someone's out here—Facilitators that come too close to our village, well, let's say that they go 'missing.' It's harsh, I know, but necessary. We track the Facilitators' movements, and when they get too close, we move the village. We can pack the entire village and disappear without a trace in less than an hour. Keeps them guessing. As far as the Sephs know, their Facilitators simply disappear into The Fel."

"Serves… serves them… right!" Lery said. "Stupid… *Fessals*."

Rayce eyed Lery curiously, then chuckled. "Yes, I'm truly looking forward to hearing your story. Now, if you'll excuse me—" He left quietly and closed the door behind him.

"It was a short walk to the Fel People's village…"

— 25 —

THE LONGHOUSE

WE CLEANED OURSELVES up and put ourselves in order as best we could. Lery handed out another round of biscuits. I wondered how he managed to fit so many in that bag and made a mental note to ask him later. A washstand with a bowl and pitcher stood against one wall. We washed our faces, straightened our hair, and smoothed our clothes.

Mid ambled around the room, studying the roof and walls. "This is fantastic, Cheff! These people have perfected the grass house. The supports are made of long, stiff reeds of some sort. The woven grass panels are tied on. The walls must weigh practically nothing, yet they keep the wind out. Fascinating! And look at this weaving! The textures, the designs, the colors. It's more than good—it's an art!"

Several women came in. One carried a soup pot and some bowls, another brought a jug of hot tea, and the others held several plates of various foods. They served the soup, then lit the oil lamps hanging from the roof beams.

Cheff tasted the soup. "Mmm, this is wonderful! If you don't mind me asking, what's in it?"

"Oh," one woman said, "a little bit of this and a little bit of that. It changes according to what we catch. This one has some Bonna fish, a bit of eel, and some marsh pig."

"And some roots and vegetables that we gather in the marsh," said another.

"We've learned to eat just about everything," a third added. "We have to, if we are to survive."

"Even rats," the first said, "when we must. It's not our first choice."

I agreed silently. Rats were our primary source of meat in the Labor Compound. Cheff's Aunt Dee was a wizard at spicing rat meat, and she'd taught my mother, but… rat is rat. Still, it could have been worse.

We finished our soup and stacked the bowls and spoons. Lery had his grub sack open and some of his spice packets in his hand. He and a woman were sniffing them and chatting.

"Thank you," Cheff said. "That was truly delicious."

The rest of us added our thanks, too.

"I'm glad you enjoyed it," the first woman said. "It's time for us to leave you now. The council will be here shortly. If there's anything else you need, stick your head out the door and call me. I'm Sorma."

"Nice to meet you, Sorma," Cheff said.

"Come on, ladies," Sorma said to her companions. "We have things to do. It's going to be a big night."

I wondered what she meant by that, then I figured that I was going to find out soon enough.

"Good soup," Lery said. "That… woman told me about… some of the spices they… use here. I gave her some… of mine… to try."

"Maybe she'll give you some, too, later," Mid said.

Lery smiled. "She said… that she… would."

The door opened, and a group of older men and women, mostly Torphs, filed in. We stood and greeted them respectfully. They seated themselves in a circle around the charcoal brazier and invited us to do the same. Two large Torph men escorted Brex to the circle and sat her down, then stood behind her with their arms crossed.

When we were all seated, Rayce said, "Council members, these are the youngsters I found outside the village today. Their leader is Cheff." Cheff raised his hand. "The others are Cheff's sister, Buttons, Mid, Lery, Books, and Sable. They are from Fellstone City. They are in trouble and have come to ask our assistance. One of their group, a young Lora woman named Carra, is missing, possibly taken by a Fessal hunting party. I propose that we hear their story, then decide if we can help them and whether we should."

There was a murmur of assent among the council, then an elderly woman with long, silky white braids spoke. "I am Morsana, the chief of our council. Cheff, can you please tell us why all of you came to The Fel in the first place?"

"Carra was sent from Tumberland to gather the herb rovaldia," Cheff said. "The rest of us were sent to help her."

"Sent by whom?" an older man asked.

"I… I'm sorry, but I'm not allowed to say. But I think I can say that it's for a good cause. Some… people we know think it can help us fight against the Sephs."

"Ah, I understand," a middle-aged man said. "You're FRM. Kind of young, aren't you?"

Cheff gawped. "You know about the FRM?"

"Of course we do," the middle-aged man said. "Many of us here *are* FRM, or at least we used to be. It's an open secret in the village. It's one of the main reasons a lot of us are out here."

Brex screamed, "I knew it! I knew it the whole time, you rotten traitor!"

"And that one is *not* FRM," said a youngish woman.

Everyone laughed. One tall man, a black-and-white Mountain Lora like Buttons, said, "Looks to me like you're the traitor, young woman. What's a Torph doing in the Bluebands, working against others of her own species?"

"For shame," an elderly Torph woman said. "You should be ashamed of yourself."

"I'm *not* ashamed," Brex said. "I'm *proud* of what I am. I've shown all of Andaran that a Torph can be as good a servant of our beloved Emperor Pallador as anyone from any species!"

"I'll bet you have," said a spiky-haired Lildur woman. "You have the look."

"What look?" Brex demanded. "What are you talking about?"

But the Lildur woman didn't respond.

"Answer me, filth!" Brex screamed and leaped to her feet.

Her Torph escorts shoved her roughly back to the floor.

Rayce said, "Miss Averith Brex, is it? You will remain silent until spoken to, or I will have the guards bind and gag you. Do you understand?"

Brex glared daggers at Rayce, but nodded grudgingly.

The Lora woman asked Cheff, "This one was sent to spy on you?"

"I'm not sure," Cheff said, "but I think so. We didn't know she was following us until Mr. Rayce spotted her outside the village. She is well known in the Fellstone Labor Compound as a loyal Blueband. I'm afraid she could cause you much harm."

Rayce said, "We'll see about that in due course. Meanwhile, let's continue with your story."

"There's not much more to tell," Cheff said. "Our missing girl is from Tumberland. She's a Lora, like me and Buttons, and an FRM agent, too. I guess it's all right to tell you that."

"I had already surmised as much. What do you want with rovaldia? Apart from its rather pretty flowers, it's not good for much. It's just a weed."

"The laboratory in Tumberland thinks there's something in rovaldia that will help neutralize the effects of jexan. Do you know what that is?"

"Yes," Rayce said. "We have heard of it. The Sephs give it to their victims before they feed."

"That's right," Cheff said. "But they're also putting it in the food supply. Everyone's food. Anything white, like flour or sugar."

"This we did not know," Rayce said. "It must be something new."

"I think so," Cheff said. "As far as we know, it's only being used in Fellstone City."

"And Tumberland," I said. "And some other places a friend of ours mentioned."

"Then it will soon be all over Andaran," Rayce said. "I'm sure there's much more to your story, and we'd love to hear all the details—we don't get much news out here in The Fel—but I think we've heard enough to make our decision. Before we vote, does anyone have questions?"

The elderly Torph woman with the long braids said, "Aren't they awfully young to be FRM agents? Back in my day, one had to be an adult to be invited to join the FRM."

"We are young, ma'am," Cheff said. "We were invited under… um… special circumstances. I can't talk about it, I'm sorry."

The Lildur man said, "Special circumstances? What special circumstances?" He considered, then snapped his fingers. "Why, they must be the ones who—"

"Telus, please." Rayce flicked his eyes toward Brex. "Some things should not be spoken of, especially in front of—"

"Of course, of course," Telus said. "Plenty of time for that later."

"Any other questions?" Rayce asked. "No? In that case, I propose a threefold solution. First, we get their companion, the girl, Carra, back from the Sephs before they eat her. Second, we load her up with all the rovaldia she can carry. Third, we see her well on her way back to Tumberland. All in favor?"

An enthusiastic round of 'aye' came from the council.

"Opposed?"

No one was opposed.

"What about that nasty Blueband brat you pulled out of the mud?" the youngish woman asked.

"You're all a bunch of liars," Brex hissed. "Sephs don't eat people! That's malicious Torph propaganda." One of her escorts prodded her with his toe. She subsided.

"Let's keep her here until we get back with Carra. After that, we can decide what to do with her," Rayce said.

"Poor girl's been brainwashed," Telus said. "Why else would she be loyal to a murderer?"

"I think she should go with us," the elderly Torph said. "Let her see for herself what's being done to her own kind, and by whom. Then she'll know who the liar is."

There was another round of assent.

"So be it," Rayce said. "Okay, people. Let's get moving. We have much to do before dark."

The sound of a commotion came from the street. We all, except Brex and her escorts, went out the door to see what was happening. In the middle of the village, right in front of the longhouse, Mr. Grumbles sat on his haunches with a beatific smile on his bear face. All the children in the village had gathered around and were petting him all over and feeding him little bits of meat and berries.

"Your bear has made himself quite the spectacle," Rayce said.

"What about him?" Cheff asked. "How are we going to keep him from following us to the hunting lodge?"

"Why would we?" Rayce said. "He's a free agent. He can go where he pleases. He has so far, hasn't he?"

"Well, yes, but—"

"Let it be, youngster," Morsana said, "let it be. The creatures of Andaran have their own logic and their own purposes. Let The Fel bear be a Fel bear." She hobbled toward one of the grass houses, then turned and said over her shoulder, "Better get crackin', sonny. Daylight's burning!"

"By the way," Rayce said, "see the man getting some meat from the grill? That's your old friend, Boran. Why not go over and say hello?"

As I went down the stairs, a group of girls, led by a Torph girl perhaps ten years old, came tearing around the longhouse. The one in front ran straight into Lery, while the other girls skidded to a halt. The leader stepped back and stared up into Lery's face. Then she drew back her fist and socked Lery in his belly with all her might.

"Oof!" Lery grabbed his belly with both hands, gasping for breath.

"Grahsi!" Rayce called. "Behave yourself!"

Without a word, Grahsi turned and ran off across the village, her friends right behind her, laughing and giggling.

"I'm sorry about that," Rayce said. "I don't know what came over her."

"I do," Buttons said. "The ponies say that Grahsi's in love!"

"I'd… I'd hate to think what… she'd do… if she hated me," Lery said.

"Silly boys!" Buttons said to Sable. "They don't understand girls at all."

"Hopeless," Sable agreed.

OPERATION LOCKDOWN

— **26** —

CANOE RIDE

THE WORD MUST have spread quickly because soon the entire village was in motion. We watched from the front steps of the longhouse while men, women, and older children alike packed backpacks and strapped on weapons and other gear.

A few minutes later, Rayce came by to collect us. "You youngsters ready to ride?"

"Sure," Cheff said.

"Wait—ride?" Mid said. "Ride what?"

"Canoes, of course," Rayce said. "It's the only way to get around in The Fel if you're in a hurry. I'm surprised that you came on foot."

Mr. Grumbles waddled up and sat down on Cheff's feet. Cheff idly scratched his ears. "I guess we have a lot to learn about The Fel. For that matter, we've learned quite a lot already."

"Indeed you have, youngster. Now, follow me."

We joined the queue of dozens of Fel People heading down the path to the waterline. The children followed, chattering happily. Even the marsh pigs came to see us off.

At the tail end of the line, Brex was escorted by two tall Torph guards. She kicked savagely at a little marsh pig that was sniffing her, but a guard blocked the kick with his spear, then leaned over and said something to her that we couldn't hear. After that, she kept her feet to herself.

At the waterline, some large canoes were tied to the bank, waiting for us. They were mostly made of reeds tied together, but some were made from leather. They were all wide with flat bottoms.

Rayce explained, "The leather canoes are faster than the ones made of reeds. Usually, we only use the leather ones for hunting or tracking the Facilitators, but tonight is an exception. This is no ordinary hunting trip, and we're going to need all the canoes we can muster."

He directed us to a large reed canoe that already held several Torphs, paddles in hand. "Hop in, kids, and get settled. We'll be launching any time now." He stepped into the canoe and took a seat.

We climbed in after him and stowed our gear under our seats. The canoe smelled good, a combination of reeds and the pitch coating that covered the outside. I thought of the last time the six of us were together in a boat—it was a wooden steam launch, a proper fishing boat, quite different from this reed canoe. And we had been crossing Fellstone Bay, not slogging through a muddy marsh. But that steam launch would never have been able to navigate the shallow waterways of The Fel.

After we were seated, Brex and her two guards stepped in and sat down.

"Why, Miss Averith Brex!" Cheff said. "Welcome."

"Oh, shut up, Karfendek," Brex growled.

One of the guards gave her a poke in the ribs. "Quiet, traitor."

Brex looked pointedly away from us and stared out at the reeds lining the waterway.

Mr. Grumbles came over and sniffed the canoe. He put his huge paw on the prow, then took it away again when the canoe rocked. He whined and paced back and forth.

Buttons called, "It's okay, Mr. Grumbles. You can't come on this trip because you don't fit in a canoe. You'll have to wait here, but don't worry, we'll be back soon."

Mr. Grumbles was far from satisfied. He sat down in the mud and whimpered. A few of the younger children ran up and petted him. One said, "It's all right, Mr. Bear. We can't go, either, because we're too young. You can stay with us, and we'll play."

Mr. Grumbles lay down in the mud, closed his eyes, and rumbled grumpily.

Soon, everyone who was going was seated in a canoe. Rayce stood up and whistled, then shouted. "Launch!"

The paddlers in each canoe pushed off, and we paddled south down the winding waterway. Those canoes fairly flew through The Fel. Mr. Rayce was right—it was much faster than walking.

"How do you know where the Hunting Lodge is?" Cheff asked.

"It's a big log building on some high ground far to the southeast of here," Rayce said. "We've known about it for a long while. Our scouts found it years ago, and we check on it from time to time. We needed to know where it is, if for no other reason than to stay well away from it. Anyway, don't worry—we know these waterways like city people know their streets. Might as well settle back and enjoy the ride, youngsters—it's going to be a while."

So we settled back and watched The Fel go by. There wasn't much to see at first, since the tall grass and reeds made high walls on either side of us. But in some places, the grass gave way to vast, open spaces filled with wildlife of all sorts.

We saw many different kinds of birds. Some had long legs and long beaks which they used to dredge for food. One long-legged white bird with a pointy beak scooped up a frog and swallowed it whole. From time to time, schools of tiny pink fish darted about beneath the surface, and once a group of slippery eels wriggled by.

There were occasional families of marsh pigs, too, wild marsh pigs with huge tusks. We steered clear of them. Sometimes they howled as we passed, but other times they ignored us completely. On one small island, a family of river otters played with their babies, leaping and splashing in the water.

Once, Buttons pointed at the shore. A dark, shadowy figure was barely visible through the tall grass. "Look, Cheff! Is that Mr. Grumbles? I think he's following us."

"I don't know, Sis. He might be, but it's a long way and we're moving fast. It seems unlikely to me, but you never know."

"It was him," Buttons said firmly. "The ponies are certain."

The warm air was thick with buzzing insects. The steady rhythm of the paddlers was almost hypnotic. I closed my eyes—only for a minute, I told myself.

"Books! Wake up!"

"What is it, Cheff?" I sat up and rubbed my eyes. "Was I sleeping? How long?"

"Long enough," Cheff said. "We're getting close now. Rayce wants us to have a bite to eat before we get there, to keep up our strength."

Buttons helped Rayce pass out some little buns. I bit into one and found it was full of meat and vegetables. Delicious, juicy meat. Next, he handed out little green squares of pressed, dried, leaves.

"It's dried felmoss," Rayce said. "Don't eat it. Chew it a little bit, then stuff it between your lip and your gum. It'll help you stay alert and keep your strength up. It's an old Fel trick."

One of the paddlers said, "It's why we can paddle so far and not get tired."

"It's like drinking felmoss tea," Rayce said, "except it's more concentrated."

"Think I should take some back for Mr. Rishten?" I asked Cheff.

He chuckled. "I don't think so—he's already had enough felmoss tea."

We laughed.

Shortly after we'd eaten our meat buns, Rayce said, "Okay, youngsters, look sharp—this is it." He stood and moved deftly to the prow. The paddlers turned the canoes abruptly and ran them into the muddy bank. Rayce hopped off and dragged the canoe as far onto the bank as he could. "Everybody out!"

We exited the canoe carefully so as not to cause an upset. Up and down the bank, all the Fel People in the other canoes were doing the same. When each canoe was empty, its paddlers pulled it onto dry ground.

Brex's guards dragged her roughly from her canoe and forced her to follow along as Rayce led the way down a grass-lined path. We had hiked only a short distance when he whistled again. This time, his whistle sounded like one of the birds we'd seen earlier.

"We're there," he said softly. "Keep your heads down and follow me."

We crouched and followed him to the edge of a big clearing. In the center of the clearing, on the crest of a small hill, stood an imposing structure made entirely of long, straight logs. It was big, much bigger than the longhouse. In the center, a section with a peaked roof had large double doors that exited onto a wide porch, or veranda, with long ramps called 'slitherways' leading down to the grass. Two long wings extended from each side of the center section. At each end of the building, right at the peak of the ridgeline, was mounted a mind-control dish similar to the ones we had seen at the Iron Fortress.

"Where did all those logs come from," Mid asked. "Did fir trees grow here in The Fel, once?"

"Not that we know of," Rayce said. "Our best guess is that they were trucked to the edge of The Fel, then floated the rest of the way here. No one knows for sure, though—it's been many decades since the hunting lodge was built."

"Why not use grass," Cheff asked, "like the houses in the village?"

"Too cold for Sephs," Rayce said. "Sephs like to keep warm. See that chimney?" He pointed at the south end of the center section, where a column of smoke arose from a stone chimney. "There's a huge fireplace inside. The logs act as natural insulators."

"Makes sense," Mid said.

"What next?" Cheff asked. "What's our plan?"

"Our plan is simple," Rayce said. "We run up to the house, break in, and kill everyone inside, except the girl."

We stared at him.

"What?" he said. "You have a better idea?"

"Lure," Sable said. "Ambush."

"What's she talking about?" Rayce asked.

Cheff said, "Sable is suggesting that we lure as many of the Fessal Facilitators as possible out of the lodge, then ambush them one or two at a time. It'll take a little longer, but when we finally break in, there will be a lot less resistance."

"We don't have time for that," Rayce said. "It'll be dark soon. Look, the sun is almost touching the mountains."

"Darkness is our friend," Sable said.

Rayce thought that over. "She has a point. If we can do it her way, we're a lot less likely to get ourselves killed."

"The ponies say, not getting killed is good," Buttons said.

"So," Mid asked, "how are we going to lure them out?"

"And how do we know how many are in there?" I asked.

"Windows," Sable said.

It was true. There were large windows all around the entire lodge.

"Apparently," Cheff said, "the Sephs like sunshine, too. Rayce, do you have scouts that can look in those windows?"

"Too risky in the daylight," Rayce said. "After dark, maybe."

"Or," Sable said, "just ask."

"Those canoes fairly flew through The Fel."

— 27 —

JUST ASK

"**A**SK?" RAYCE FROWNED. "I don't understand. But go ahead."

Cheff grinned. He selected a stone from the ground, placed it carefully in the pouch of his hunting sling, whirled it over his head, and released it toward the hunting lodge. The stone bounced off the logs with a resounding *thonk!*

We waited. No response. Cheff selected another stone.

"Careful, Cheff," Mid said. "Don't hit a window."

Cheff slung the second stone. *Thonk!*

This time, the front door opened, and a uniformed Fessal Facilitator came out, stepped to the edge of the porch, shaded his eyes, and scanned the clearing. His uniform was identical to the ones the Fessal Facilitators wore the night of the banquet in the basement of the Iron Fortress: dark-green pants, light-green jackets trimmed in dark green to match the pants, and shiny black boots. The pants sported silver stripes down the sides. The jackets featured white epaulets and silver buttons. I shivered, remembering.

When the Facilitator turned to go back inside, Cheff coughed loudly and shook a handful of reeds. The Facilitator paused and

229

scanned the clearing again. Cheff coughed a second time, louder, and shook the reeds even harder.

The Facilitator came halfway down the slitherway toward us. "Who's there?"

Cheff coughed again, then said, "Arglebum woffet mumfy."

Buttons giggled. Cheff clamped his hand over her mouth.

"Who is that?" the Fessal Facilitator called. "Show yourself, right now!"

"Ders fon wernorknots. Duckfel izzum runklepod," Cheff growled loudly, then coughed once more.

The Fessal Facilitator went back inside, then came back with a rifle in his hand, followed by a second Fessal, also carrying a rifle.

"Heh," Cheff said. "Two for the price of one." He rattled the reeds once more.

"Stay where you are!" the first Fessal demanded. The two Facilitators charged into the bushes straight to where we were crouched.

Except for Cheff and Rayce, we scrambled back into the gloom.

The Facilitators leveled their guns at Cheff and Rayce. "What's going on here? Who are you people? What do you want?"

"Why," said Cheff, "we're the Fantastic Fel Fellows Four, of course. We're your entertainment for the evening. Or, rather, your masters' entertainment. Didn't they tell you? No? Keep things from you, do they? What a shame." He shook his head sadly.

The first Facilitator deliberately mouthed the words to himself, "Fantastic… Fel… Fellows… Four—hey! There are only two of you. Where are the other two?"

"They had to, you know, *go*," Cheff said. "Look, here they come now." He pointed back toward the waterline. The Facilitators took a few steps farther into the reeds and craned their necks. Two burly paddlers brought the edges of their paddles down sharply on the backs of the Facilitators' heads. *Wham! Wham!* The two Facilitators whooshed like punctured tires, then settled down for a little nap in the mud.

"There," Cheff said. "How easy was that? And no one hurt, so far. Let's see if one of our new Facilitator friends might be willing to help us. Could you get some water for us, please, Lery?"

"Okay." Lery took a small bottle from his pouch and trotted down to the waterline. He was back in a flash with his bottle filled and Mr. Grumbles right behind him. Mr. Grumbles nuzzled Lery's pack, looking for another handout. Lery found him a biscuit, which he accepted eagerly. "Look who… I found."

"Mr. Grumbles!" Buttons said, and threw her arms around the bear's shaggy neck. "I knew it was you! Did you come to help?"

Mr. Grumbles finished his biscuit, sat down, and addressed an itch behind his left ear.

"Let me have that water," Cheff said. He poured a little on the first Facilitator's face and said sweetly, "Wake up, sleepyhead!"

The Fessal groaned and turned his head.

Cheff slapped him gently on the cheek. "Wakey, wakey!"

The Facilitator sat up abruptly. "What? Who? Ow!" He rubbed the rapidly swelling knot on the back of his head as he slowly looked around at Rayce, the two paddlers, the six of us kids, and Mr. Grumbles. "You're not the Fantastic… whatever you said, are you?"

"Attaboy," Cheff said. "Now you're catching on. No, we're not the Fantastic Fel Fellows Four, although we are entertainers of a sort. And we may turn out to be the evening's entertainment after all."

"What? What are you talking about? What sort? Are you tumblers? Musicians? Where are your instruments?" He furrowed his brow and put his hand to his temple.

"Easy does it, smart guy," Cheff said. "Don't strain yourself. It's like this: in order to plan a proper evening's entertainment, we need to know exactly how many we'll be entertaining. So we need you to tell us how many Sephs are in the hunting lodge, and how many Facilitators."

The Fessal stared at Cheff, then narrowed his eyes. "I'm not supposed to tell you anything." He folded his arms across his chest. "And you can't make me, either."

Mr. Grumbles ambled over to inspect the newcomers. He sniffed the terrified Fessal from head to toe, then did the same with the second Facilitator, who was still unconscious.

"That… that… that's a *bear*!" the Facilitator said.

"And they say Fessals are slow," Cheff said, shaking his head. "No offense, Lery."

"None taken… Friend Cheff." Lery chuckled. "Stupid… Fessals."

"Now," Cheff said, "you were about to tell me who all is in the hunting lodge."

The Fessal set his jaw and shook his head. "I know nothing. *Nothing!*"

Cheff turned to the bear. "Hear that, Mr. Grumbles? He knows nothing, nothing. I don't think he's our friend, do you?"

Mr. Grumbles looked at Cheff, then went to the Facilitator and licked his face.

The Facilitator started shaking and crying and trying to scoot backward on his backside through the mud, to no avail.

Mr. Grumbles followed, towering over him, and continued licking his face.

"Well?" Cheff asked. "Are you going to tell us about the Sephs' little dinner party, or should I tell Mr. Grumbles that you're going to be *his* guest for dinner?" Cheff licked his chops, then drew a finger across his neck. "If you know what I mean."

"Okay! I'll tell you everything! There are many… many… Facil—" He started choking and gasping for air. "I… can't… breathe…"

"He's turning blue, Cheff," Mid said.

Rayce and Sable rushed in, cleared his airways, tried to resuscitate the poor man, but nothing they did helped. The Facilitator's eyes went wide and he grabbed at his throat, convulsed violently several times, then went limp.

Sable put her ear to his chest. "Dead."

"Dead?" Cheff asked. "How can that be? We didn't hurt him—we just scared him a little."

"Mind control," Sable said, pointing at the dishes on the roof of the lodge.

"I think she's right," Rayce said, "about the mind control, I mean. From time to time we've captured a Facilitator, and they all died the same way. They were fine until they tried to answer our questions, then they died, like him."

"It serves that traitor right!" Brex said from where she'd watched the entire scene play out. "Death to all traitors!"

Two husky Torphs dragged the second Facilitator, still unconscious, off into the grass. No one asked what would become of him. We already knew.

"Well," Cheff said, "so much for just asking. I guess it's back to Plan A."

"Anyway," Rayce said, "there are two less we'll have to contend with when we get inside."

"Is there any way we can lure out more of them, do you think?" Cheff asked.

"Maybe," Rayce said, "but I'm going to guess not. The Sephs have some kind of bond with their Facilitators. It has something to do with how they use their Ability to completely control them."

"Is it like mind reading?" Buttons asked.

"We don't know much about it," Rayce said, "not much at all. But we don't think it's mind reading. It's more like, once a Seph controls a Fessal Facilitator, the Seph is always aware of the Facilitator's presence."

I said, "Cheff, remember the first day I was with you in Mr. Rishten's class? He said something about Fessals being especially suited for voluntary—what was it Mr. Rishten called it?—Imperial Mental Adjustment."

"That's right," Cheff said, "mental adjustment. I think we might be on to something here. I'll report it to—"

"Cheff," Mid said, and gestured toward Brex and her guards.

"Right," Cheff said. "Thanks. Well, it's worth a shot, anyway. Lery, try a few more rocks, if you please, and let's see what we get for our trouble. Remember, don't hit the windows."

Lery chucked another dozen rocks at the hunting lodge, but there was no response.

"I think we've established that they know we're out here," Mid said.

"I agree," Rayce said.

"Okay," Cheff said. "What's next?"

"Excuse me," Mid said, "but if you don't mind, I'd like to try something."

"What would that be?" Rayce asked.

"It's a little something I've been experimenting with," Mid said. "It might draw another one or two Facilitators outside."

"Fine with me," Rayce said. "Let's see what you've got."

"If I may, Mr. Rayce," Mid said, "I'd like to station several of the paddlers right inside the grass line. I'm going to try to lure some Facilitators into the grass."

Rayce gave orders to the paddlers.

Mid took his Amazing Voice Changer from his tech bag, adjusted the settings, and took his position. He raised the AVC to his lips. His voice came out deep and commanding. "THIS IS THE FEL RANGERS! YOUR IMMEDIATE ASSISTANCE IS REQUIRED! THERE ARE TWO INJURED FACILITATORS DOWN BY THE WATERLINE. COME AT ONCE, REPEAT, COME AT ONCE!"

Rayce grinned at Mid. "Hey, that's amazing!"

I took my fingers out of my ears. "And loud, too."

Cheff was laughing. "Fel Rangers? Is that like the Swamp Sheriff?"

Buttons giggled. "Or the Marsh Marshal?"

I said, "How about the Wetlands Watchers?"

Mid shrugged. "Do you think they'll buy it?"

"We're about to find out," Cheff said.

We watched the double doors of the lodge. A minute later, a crack of light appeared between them.

"Who is that?" a Facilitator called out.

Mid raised his AVC again. "THIS IS THE FEL RANGERS. COME AT ONCE, BY IMPERIAL ORDER! IMMEDIATE ASSISTANCE IS REQUIRED. BRING FIRST AID."

The door closed, but opened again almost immediately, and two armed Facilitators came out. One carried a bag that looked like a medical kit.

"DOWN HERE, BY THE WATERLINE!"

"Here they come," Rayce said. "Mid, get back. Paddlers, stand ready!"

Mid moved back to where we were crouched. The two Facilitators dashed down the little path and without even slowing ran right into the grass.

Wham! Wham! The two Facilitators went down, and the paddlers dragged them toward the canoes.

"Excellent! Well done, Mid!" Rayce said. "That's another pair we won't have to deal with inside."

Sable said, "Rifles."

Cheff said, "That's right—we have four rifles that we didn't have before."

"Small advantages add up," Rayce said. "I'll get these in the hands of our best marksmen."

— 28 —

THE HUNTING LODGE

"**W**HAT NEXT?" CHEFF asked. "I don't think we're likely to lure any more Facilitators out here."

"Dark," Sable said.

"She's right—it's nearly dark now," Rayce said, "dark enough to send some scouts to have a look in those windows. Scouts, go have a look at that lodge. Youngsters, let's watch them."

We resumed our position at the edge of the clearing. The two Torph scouts pulled their hoods over their faces, crouched low, and crept toward the house.

They crept forward a few dozen steps, then came to a complete stop. They tried several times to continue toward the lodge, but it was as if they had run into an invisible wall. Finally, the scouts gave up and came back.

"What is it?" Rayce asked them.

"We don't know. We couldn't go any farther."

"I'll try," Sable said.

She crouched and started toward the lodge. She got farther than the Torph scouts, but she, too, was stopped and had to return.

"Mind control," Sable said. "I felt it."

"Why doesn't their Torph Ability shield them from Seph control?" I asked.

"Amplifiers," Sable said.

"Those dishes on either end of the roof," Mid explained. "They're connected to Ability Amplifiers to enhance Seph Ability. They are much too strong for normal Torph Ability to neutralize."

"Great," Cheff said. "Now what? We're running out of options, here."

"Cheff," Mid said, "remember what Carra told us about the rovaldia? That the lab in Tumberland thinks that refining rovaldia could provide an antidote for jexan? Do you think it could help against the Sephs' mind-control Ability?"

"Maybe," Cheff said. "Do we have any with us, or did Carra put it all in her bag?"

"I have… some," Lery said.

"Give it to me," Sable said.

Lery handed her his waterproof rovaldia bag.

Sable tasted a piece, then tore off a sizeable chunk and chewed it. Nothing happened for five minutes or so, then she said, "I feel it."

"Feel what?" Cheff asked.

"Don't know," Sable said. "Something."

She waited another few minutes, then tried crossing the clearing to the hunting lodge. When she reached the spot where she'd been stopped on her first try, she hesitated, then pushed on. She reached the hunting lodge with some apparent difficulty. One by one, she pulled herself up to each windowsill and looked inside. She disappeared around the back for a long while, then came around the far side. Finally, she went up the slitherway to the porch and tried the door. She dropped into a crouch and returned to our position.

"How does it look?" Rayce asked.

"Three large rooms: the one in the center behind the double doors, and a big room on each end. Four Sephs, two in each of the side-chambers, coiled on cushions. Many Fessal Facilitators in the center room, preparing food for the Sephs."

That was the most I'd ever heard Sable say on a single occasion.

"Food?" Mid asked. "What kind of food?"

"Marsh pigs. Two bears. In cages."

"What about Carra?" Cheff asked.

"Cage. Near the marsh pigs."

"Good work, Sable," Rayce said. "Now we know what we're up against."

"Door is unlocked."

"What?" Cheff said. "Sable, are you sure?"

Sable merely looked at Cheff.

"Of course you are," Cheff said. "Sorry."

"They're relying on their Ability," Mid said. "They think they're safe."

"Why, how *very* careless of them," Cheff said, grinning. "Tsk, tsk, tsk."

"Do you think the rovaldia will work on Torphs?" I asked.

"We'll soon find out," Rayce said. "Let me have some of that, Lery." Rayce broke off a piece somewhat larger than Sable had tried. After a few minutes, he said, "I think it's working. Let's find out."

He crossed the clearing without hesitation, touched the side of the lodge, then returned. "Seems to be working." Rayce smiled for the first time since we met him. "I can still feel the mind control, but I… don't care!" His eyes were unnaturally bright. "I'll go tell the troops to gather all the rovaldia they can find, and how much to munch. How much to munch, much to munch," he repeated, then bounced off to the waterline.

"'Much to munch?'" Cheff asked. "I don't like the sound of that."

"Maybe he's just happy to have a plan?" Mid asked.

"Maybe," Cheff said. "I hope that's all it is." He glanced over at Sable, who was squatting, motionless, a big smile on her face.

Sable said, "I feel… good!"

"I have a bad feeling about this," Cheff said.

"Should we eat some rovaldia now?" Buttons asked.

"I think we should wait for Rayce to give the word," Cheff said.

A half-hour later, Rayce returned, with thirty or more warriors. His smile was even bigger than before. "Ladies and gentlemen, take your rovaldia!"

Lery handed out portions to each of us. Buttons' portion was smaller, Lery's was bigger.

"What… about… Miss Brex?" Lery asked.

"Give her some, too," Cheff said.

Lery took a portion to Brex, who slapped it out of his hand. Without a word, one of her guards picked it up and brushed the mud off, mostly. Her other guard tipped her head back and forced her wide Torph mouth open. The first guard pushed the rovaldia in, then held her mouth and nose closed until she swallowed. She gagged and choked when they let her go, but it was too late—the rovaldia was inside.

"Okay, people!" Rayce said. "Five minutes, then we go! Warriors, split into two groups, one for each side-chamber. Take out the Facilitators first, then the Sephs. Youngsters, concentrate on rescuing Carra. I don't want you getting involved in the fighting."

The rovaldia leaves tasted good, like sweet licorice, with a bitter aftertaste that made me want to eat more rovaldia to get the sweetness back. I didn't feel anything at first, but after a minute or so, starting right behind my bellybutton, a warm, golden glow started to grow. The golden glow grew bigger and bigger, filling me up inside until I had to smile. All my fear of danger and fighting the Sephs was gone. I felt like I could do anything, anything at all!

Mid finished counting off the five minutes by his watch, then gave Rayce a thumbs-up. Mid was smiling, too.

It's hard to describe what happened next because a lot happened all at once. Rayce whistled, long and shrill, and with one accord the Fel warriors rushed for the hunting lodge's porch. We followed right behind them, with Mr. Grumbles right behind us. Brex and her guards brought up the rear, followed by all the rest of the Fel People.

The lodge door wasn't locked, but it wouldn't have mattered if it was. The Fel People hit that door running, and it flew open. We swarmed inside, all of us who could fit. The lodge was too small for all the Fel People. Those who were left outside howled and screamed. Some threw rocks at the walls and windows. Others beat on the walls with sticks. Moonlight sparkled on the broken glass scattered on the grass outside.

Rayce watched them for a heartbeat, then said, "I may have given them too much of the rovaldia."

But he didn't have time to think about rovaldia right then. With a ferocious battle cry, the Fel warriors charged the Facilitators. The four Torph marksmen with the captured rifles found it difficult to get a clear shot in the crowd, so they turned their rifles around and used the rifle butts as clubs. The Fel warriors fought fiercely, but the Facilitators used their firearms to good effect, and soon a dozen Fel warriors lay dead or wounded on the floor. There was neither mercy nor pity on either side.

However, as Rayce pointed out later, firearms are only good until the ammunition runs out, but spears keep right on killing. Unfortunately for the Facilitators, their ammunition didn't last long, and the Fel warriors had their chance.

One Facilitator stopped to reload his sidearm next to Lery, who unhooked his mighty pipe wrench from his tool belt and knocked the Facilitator unconscious. An instant later, a Fel warrior pierced the fallen Facilitator's heart with a spear.

We rushed to the far wall, dodging Fel warriors and Facilitators alike, where Carra and the other captives were imprisoned. Buttons opened the animal cages, and soon marsh pigs and assorted small animals squealed and yipped and roared, running in wild circles under everyone's feet. Mr. Grumbles followed

Buttons, snapping and clawing at anyone who got close to her. When Buttons came to the cage with the two Fel bears, Mr. Grumbles whined and pawed at the cage door. Buttons released the Fel bears, who nosed Mr. Grumbles and roared their thanks. Then the two bears charged into the fray, snapping furiously at the Fessals and adding to the general confusion.

At the sight of Carra in a food cage, Brex's eyes went wide open. "She's… she's…they… the Sephs—they're going to EAT her!"

"That's right, traitor," one of her guards growled. "That's where our children go, and that's probably where your parents went."

"But it's not possible! I mean, they're only rumors, aren't they?"

"Use your eyes, traitor," the other guard said. "Look for yourself and learn!"

We didn't have time to educate Brex right then. In a flash, Lery walloped the padlock off Carra's cage with his pipe wrench. She was barely conscious, moaning, waving her arms, and kicking. I guessed that she had been given a large dose of jexan, just as Cheff's Uncle Karf had been given three weeks earlier, before being swallowed. Carra lurched drunkenly and tried to fight us. We tried to hold her down—Cheff sat on her legs, Lery held one arm, Sable the other, and Buttons and I tried to sit on her middle, but it was no use. It was like trying to hold a windmill.

Several times, Carra broke loose and joined the chaos in the room, running around screaming and waving her arms. Lery grabbed her, hoisted her over his shoulder, and carried her out the door, her arms still swinging crazily. Sable, Buttons, and I followed. Cheff and Mid remained at the lodge.

As we left, a cheer went up among the Fel People. All the Facilitators were down. The Fel warriors split into two groups. One broke for the east wing, the other to the west. We joined in the cheer, then dashed across the clearing, back to our observation post.

Lery set Carra gently on the ground. Sable and Buttons fussed over her, giving her water and encouraging her to be calm, to try to sleep. Once she was settled, Lery and I returned to the hunting lodge to find Cheff and Mid, while Sable and Buttons stayed to watch over Carra.

— 29 —

TORPH ABILITY

RAYCE STOOD ON the lodge's porch, calling for the still-raving Fel People to calm down and retreat to their canoes, but they didn't respond at all. They rushed around frantically, gathering reeds and dry grass, piling them against the walls of the lodge, and lighting them with their torches.

Lery and I joined Cheff and Mid next to Rayce. Cheff called out, "Wait, stop! There are Fel People inside! We have to get everyone out first! Wait!"

But the Fel People heaped more brush against the lodge walls, and the flames leaped higher, illuminating the entire clearing. The brush fires roared and the logs of the lodge started to catch fire. It wouldn't be long before the entire structure would become a raging inferno.

Cheff said to Rayce, "Your Fel People have gone completely insane. The rovaldia must work differently on Torphs."

Rayce looked worried. "I think you may be right."

"The lodge is still full of Fel People." Mid said. "If we can't get them out of there, they'll all be burned to death."

"Mid," Cheff said, "the AVC."

Mid pulled the AVC from his bag and stepped inside the lodge. His voice, loud and deep, rang out, "FIRE! FIRE! EVERYONE TO THE CANOES. FIRE! EVERYONE TO THE CANOES. GO! GO! GO!"

That did the trick. Mid jumped out of the way as the Fel People rushed from the main hall and ran for the waterline. A few of the Fel People gathered some of the bodies of the fallen warriors and carried them down to the canoes.

"This is crazy," Cheff said. "Where's Brex? Did you see her run out?"

"No," Mid said.

"She was still inside when we got Carra," I said.

"We have to find her. Hurry!" Cheff led the three of us through the front door of the lodge. "Where is she?"

"I don't know," I said. "She was here when we left."

"C'mon," Cheff said. "It's only a matter of time before the inside of this place catches fire, too!"

It was getting hotter inside the lodge, but the thick log walls were not actually in flames—yet.

Mid pointed at two dead Fel warriors lying together near the cages. "Aren't those Brex's guards?"

"I don't know," I said. "Maybe. It's hard to tell."

"Brex must be here somewhere. Let's try the side-chambers."

We cautiously peeked into the east side-chamber. Two Sephs lay dead on the floor, dozens of spears piercing their soft underbellies. Their yellow fangs still dripped venom. The bodies of many Fel warriors and Facilitators lay near the dead Sephs. The cries of the wounded and dying were horrible.

A Facilitator groaned, grabbed Mid's ankle, and tried to raise himself on one elbow. Quick as lightning, Lery dispatched him with one swing of his pipe wrench. Lery's lips were set in a tight, straight, line. "Stupid Fessal."

"Brex must be in the west side-chamber," Cheff said. "Let's go!"

We tore across the lodge to the west side-chamber, opened the door a crack, and looked in. The floor here, too, was littered with the fallen. One Seph was dead, but the other was still fighting five fierce Fel warriors. And there was Brex, standing motionless by the window, staring out at the rising flames.

Over and over again, the fighters plunged their spears into the Seph's vulnerable underside. The Seph thrashed and snapped wildly. Although the Fel warriors dodged and weaved expertly, from time to time the Seph pierced one with his sharp, poisonous fangs, and down he went. The Seph snapped one final time, and the last of the Fel warriors was dead.

"Wait here," Cheff commanded, then he opened the door quietly and slipped inside. Mid, Lery, and I followed right behind him. No way were we going to wait in the main hall alone!

The Seph was wounded and bleeding, but very much alive. He weaved and bobbed hypnotically, great gouts of blood spurting from dozens of belly wounds.

His gaze was fixed on Brex, and he spoke to her in a quiet, sing-song voice, "Brexsss, my daughter, welcome to my home. You are my loyal ssservant, yesss?"

"Yes, my lord," Brex answered. Her eyes were glazed over, and she seemed oblivious to our presence.

"Brex!" Cheff hissed. "Come on! Let's get out of here!"

Brex ignored him, her eyes fixed on the Seph.

"Are thessse your friendsss, Brexsss?"

"No, my lord. They are traitors."

"Neverthelesss, they are welcome."

I felt the most amazing sensation in the back of my brain as a surge of love for the Seph welled up inside me, a warm glow not unlike that of the Rovaldia, only different somehow. I shook it off. "Come on, Cheff," I said. "Let's get out of here. The Seph is trying to control us."

Cheff wore a stupid smile. "But, Books, he wants us to stay."

"He's going to kill us, Cheff."

"No, he isn't, Books. He loves us. He won't hurt us."

Lery's pipe wrench slipped from his hands to the bloody floor with a thump.

Mid, too, stared at the Seph. He held both hands to his head, trying hard to clear his mind.

I smacked Cheff's face as hard as I could, then smacked him again.

Cheff shook his head. "Right. Thanks, Books—that's better." He turned and smacked Mid. "Snap out of it, Old Son."

Mid staggered, but recovered. "I'm... I'm okay, I think."

"We need to get out of here," I said. "Let's go."

"We can't leave without Brex," Cheff said. "Even if she is, well, you know. It wouldn't be right."

"She'sss fine," the Seph intoned. "I'll take care of her. She'sss my daughter, aren't you, dear one?"

"Yes, my lord," Brex said.

Cheff grabbed her by the shoulders and spun her around. "Come *on*, Brex, shake it off. Use your Torph Ability."

"I don't know what you mean, Karfendek," Brex snapped, then returned her gaze to the Seph.

"I told you, my ssson, Brexsss isss mine, now."

"Oh, no, she's not!" Cheff said. "Not if I can help it. Let her go, you filthy worm!"

"How isss it that you resssisssst me?" the Seph asked. Sephs can't show emotion in their rigid faces, but if he could have, I'll bet this one would've looked puzzled.

Cheff ignored him. "Come on, Brex, you can do it. Look inside yourself, deep down. You don't have to listen to him. Find your Ability. Use it!"

Brex frowned, then shook her head. "I can't, Cheff. I don't know how."

"Of course you do. It's who you *are*. Look deep inside. This monster might be the same Seph who ate your parents. Resist him! Do it! Use your Ability."

"I can't, Cheff, I can't!"

"You can! Remember who you are! You're Miss Averith Brex. No one owns you."

Brex clenched her fists and squeezed her eyes shut.

"There you are," Cheff said. "You *can* do it. Use your Ability, Brex, *use it!*"

"No, Brexsss, you will not. You are mine. You love me, remember? You are mine, your friendsss are mine. Sssubmit…"

The heavy feeling grew even heavier. There was nothing I could do. In that instant, I loved that Seph with all my heart.

"He ate your parents, Brex!" Cheff shouted. "Use your Ability—NOW!"

Brex's eyes snapped open. Her back arched, then she roared like I'd never heard anyone roar before.

The Seph recoiled as though he had been struck, then collapsed onto his pillow, eyes empty, tongue hanging from his enormous jaws.

"That's it!" Cheff shouted. "That's how you use your Ability! Well done, Brex!"

The heavy feeling was gone. What a relief! A veil was lifted from my mind and heart, and the world looked brighter.

Mid shook his head to clear it. Lery fell to his knees and put both hands to his head. Cheff looked around the room, uncertain of the next move.

Sable bolted into the room. "Cheff! Spear! Now!"

The Seph moaned and writhed a little. He was starting to come around.

Cheff darted forward, picked up one of the fallen warriors' spears, and thrust it into the Seph's open mouth. I grabbed the spear shaft and helped him. Mid got a grip, too, then Sable, and finally Lery. The five of us pushed as hard as we could until the point of the spear came out of the back of the Seph's scaly head.

The Seph's enormous body gave one final twitch. I about jumped out of my skin, but Lery, in one fluid motion, let go of the spear, scooped his pipe wrench from the floor, and bashed the dead Seph right in the snout. The Seph collapsed into an inert heap.

"It's okay, Lery," Mid said. "He's dead."

"Stupid… stupid Seph!" Lery mumbled. Trembling, he cleaned his pipe wrench and put it back on his belt.

"Good job, Brex!" Cheff said. "You saved us all!"

Brex was quivering all over. "But… but… Cheff, I don't understand. He was going to *eat* that girl, the one that was with you!" She turned and vomited. Cheff held her hair out of her face with one hand and patted her gently on her back with the other until her stomach was empty "I'm… I'm so sorry, Cheff. I didn't know they actually ate people. I thought it was only a nasty rumor."

"Not so much," Cheff said. "But let's talk about it later, okay? This place is on fire, and we have to leave. *Now!*"

Brex took a step, then stopped, gripping the log wall for support. "Hold on, Cheff," Brex said. "I feel funny…" Her eyes rolled up in her head, her knees buckled, and she slumped to the floor, unconscious.

Lery scooped Brex up, and we fled the west side-chamber.

Back in the main hall, a crowd of Fel People had re-entered the burning lodge to look for us.

"Time to go," Cheff said.

To my surprise, the Fel People listened to Cheff and started out the door, except for some who took the time to recover the last of the bodies of the Fel warriors. Then they, too, quit the burning lodge and followed us to the waterline.

We joined Rayce in the clearing, where we stood for a while and watched the Sephs' hunting lodge burn. The Fel People were calmer—the effects of the rovaldia seemed to be wearing off.

"What happened after you went back in, Cheff?" Buttons asked.

Cheff briefly filled them in. When he got to the part where they killed the Seph, Buttons' eyes grew round, but she didn't say anything, merely reached out and took her brother's hand and squeezed it tightly.

The flames rose high into the dark night, and the sparks and the black, greasy smoke even higher. We watched until the roof of the lodge collapsed into the heart of the flames, then Rayce said, "Okay, people. Let's go home. There's nothing left to see here."

The Fel People went down to the waterline, some of them solemnly carrying the fallen warriors. We waited respectfully until they had passed, then followed. We found our canoe, took our seats, and rode back to the Fel Village.

"The five of us pushed as hard as we could…"

— 30 —

RETURN TO THE FEL VILLAGE

I DON'T KNOW HOW the paddlers found their way in the pitch darkness, but, in due course, we pulled our canoes up to the waterline at the little landing spot outside the village. Someone had stuck torches in the ground to mark the place. Rayce led the way, followed by the fallen warriors borne by their companions. As they walked slowly into the village, we heard the wails of their loved ones. The dead were placed in the clearing in front of the longhouse and arranged respectfully. The villagers who had stayed at home joined those who were returning until all were assembled.

Rayce mounted the steps of the longhouse. "Friends, there is good news and bad news! The bad news is before you." He gestured toward the fallen warriors. "We lost many of our bravest and most beloved warriors this day."

A collective moan arose from the crowd.

"The good news is that their deaths were not in vain. For the first time ever, with the help of our new friends, we were completely victorious over the Sephs."

The villagers cheered.

"It's true, my friends. The young woman was rescued. Four Seph lords were killed, along with their Fessal Facilitators."

A much louder cheer!

"That is not all, people. The Seph hunting lodge that has plagued our village, murdered our people, and stolen our children for decades was completely destroyed. Burned to the ground!"

A cheer that rocked the village!

"It was not easy, friends. The hunting lodge was protected by roof-mounted mind-control-enhancing dishes. It created an uncrossable barrier that kept us at a distance."

One villager called out from the crowd, "How did you get past it?"

"That's where our new friends came in. They brought some news from our fellow resistance fighters in Tumberland, up north. We now have a method of resisting Seph control. I will discuss the particulars at a later time. For now, suffice it to say that the tide may have turned at last. For the first time since our village was established four decades ago, the Sephs no longer dominate The Fel."

Another rousing cheer!

"We must move the village again, of course."

A groan.

"I know, I know, but it has to be done—there's too much evidence that could lead any investigating agents to this place. And there will be investigating agents. But not tonight! Tonight, we say farewell to our brave comrades, then... we... CELEBRATE!" Rayce clasped his hands above his head.

The villagers clapped and shouted and cheered and whistled. As the applause died down, someone yelled, "Did you bring back any Seph meat?"

"No, sorry," Rayce said. "Our people were a little... um... agitated, shall we say? The Sephs were burned to ashes inside the lodge. Maybe next time."

Everyone laughed, then the assembly broke up as the villagers went to prepare for the celebration.

We sat on the longhouse steps. Rayce came and sat with us. "Well, I must say, you acquitted yourselves well tonight. You truly are amazing youngsters."

"Um, Mr. Rayce," Buttons asked, "that man was joking about Seph meat, right?"

Rayce chuckled. "Well, Sephs *are* a lot like eels, only bigger, aren't they? And meat *is* hard to come by out here in The Fel." Then he rose and went to join his family. He stopped briefly, turned, and said, "You might want to go on into the longhouse. Your missing friend is inside being looked after."

Buttons stared after Rayce. "Cheff?"

"I don't know, Sis. I just don't know. But, you have to admit, turnabout's fair play."

"Ewww." Buttons shuddered. "The ponies just lost their appetite. And so did I!"

"No worries, Buttons," Mid said. "Rayce said they didn't save any Seph meat tonight. I think you're safe."

We went up the steps and into the longhouse. Carra lay on the floor, covered with an old gray blanket. Two village women knelt beside her sleeping mat.

"She's unconscious," one said. "But I think she'll be coming around soon. She's been moaning a little and tossing. Come, sit with us."

We sat in a circle around Carra and watched silently. After a while, she blinked a few times, then looked around at us. "You!" she growled. "Where were you people? You nearly got me killed!"

Cheff started to reply, but his mouth wouldn't work. He stared at her.

"How could you go off and leave me like that?"

"Say, what?" Cheff asked. "We—"

"There I was, collecting rovaldia by the waterline, and you all went off and left me there! How *could* you?"

"But you said you had to—"

"Then *they* came. They grabbed me and hit me on the head. When I woke up, I was tied up in a canoe with two"—she wrinkled her nose—"filthy Fessals paddling it. They took me to some kind of log house and put me in a cage. Do you hear me, Cheff Karfendek? They put me in a stinking *cage!*"

"I'm sorry, Carra, we didn't mean—"

"There were all manner of horrible creatures in other cages. Animals, Cheff. I was caged with *animals.*"

"But, Carra—"

"They made me eat something, something nasty, I don't know what it was. Then I passed out again."

"Jexan," Cheff said. "They force-fed you jexan. They were going to—"

"Shut up, Cheff—I'm not finished yet. Then I woke up here. With these... outlandish *people* hovering over me."

"Hey, be nice," Buttons said. "These ladies have been taking care of you."

"Well, they wouldn't have had to take care of me if you'd been doing your *job*, now would they?" She turned her face away from Cheff. "And you call yourselves FRM agents. Hah! Pack of idiots, that's what you are. You couldn't be real FRM agents in a million years, no matter how hard you tried."

"But, Carra—" Cheff tried again.

"At least we have the rovaldia," Carra said. "Otherwise, this mission would be a complete failure."

"Not so much," Mid said. "The rovaldia's all gone."

Cheff shot Mid a look. "Thanks a lot, Mid."

Mid shrugged. "Well, it is."

"Look, Carra," Cheff said, "I can explain. We used the rovaldia to—"

"I don't want to talk anymore, Cheff. Leave me alone. I'm going back to sleep. And when I wake up, you're going to take me back to Meltern's. I don't want to spend another single, solitary minute with you… you… *pretenders*." She rolled so that her back was toward Cheff, then closed her eyes.

We looked at each other in silence for a few minutes.

"That went well," Buttons said.

Lery laughed. "I… I think… she's… mad at you… Friend Cheff."

"You think so? How could you tell?"

"Call it… call it a… hunch," Lery said.

In spite of everything, we laughed a little.

"Don't worry, young fellow," one of her caregivers said. "She's still confused from the jexan. Let her sleep. You can set all things straight in the morning."

"Yeah, Cheff," Buttons said. "You can tell her about the raid on the Iron Fortress. That'll show her that we're real FRM agents."

"Buttons, hush," Cheff said. "Not here."

"Oh, it's all right, young man," the second caregiver said. "The whole village knows all about it, anyway."

"The whole village knows what, exactly?" Cheff asked.

"That you're FRM agents. That you're the ones who raided the Iron Fortress. Your blond-headed Torph in the detention cell has been blabbing her head off all morning. And, well, people talk."

"Andaran's bones!" Cheff said. "Whatever happened to 'need to know?' And anyway, Brex didn't know anything about the Iron Fortress."

"Seriously, young fellow," the first caregiver said. "Our heads aren't carved out of Fel-oak wood. We're capable of putting two and two together."

"Anyway," the second caregiver added, "your little sister here just confirmed it, didn't she?"

"Sorry, Cheff," Buttons said in a small voice.

Cheff slumped. "Oh, boy."

"Small village," Sable said.

"Sable's right, Cheff," Mid said. "There are no secrets in small villages. I know—I used to live in one. Besides, what are we going to do about it?"

Buttons held Starry and Moka to her ear. "The ponies say they don't even see how it's our problem. *We* didn't tell them. Mostly."

"I guess," Cheff said. "Still…"

"It's too late, anyway," Mid said. "Seems like everybody knows all about us. I'd say let it go. What else is there?"

"Everybody knows," Cheff echoed. "And that brings us back to—"

"Brex," Sable said.

Cheff clapped a hand to his forehead. "What are we going to do about Brex? She's seen and heard everything."

"I don't know, Cheff," Mid said. "Maybe we should leave her here with The Fel People? She seemed to have had a change of heart—last night, anyway."

"She had something, that's for sure," Cheff said. "We should talk it over with Rayce. Or, I suppose we could go talk to Brex, see where she stands. Maybe that will give us some ideas."

We left the longhouse in search of Brex. A huge bonfire roared in the middle of the common area. I guessed they weren't worried about anyone finding the village tonight. Cheff asked one of the warriors by the bonfire, and he directed us to the place where Brex was being held. Blazing torches lined the paths.

She was in a small grass house off the main clearing. Two guards stood at the door, but they let us go in without a word. Brex sat in a cage in the middle of the room, much like Carra's cage in the hunting lodge, except this one was larger, tall enough for Brex to stand up in. Two more guards stood on either side of the cage.

Brex stood up when she saw us come in.

"Hello, Miss Brex," Cheff said.

"Karfendek," Brex said, looking sour. "I suppose you're proud of yourself."

"I'm sorry they have you in a cage," Cheff said. "I'll speak to Rayce and see if we can do something about it. Why did you follow us into The Fel, Miss Brex?"

"In that meeting of Blueband squad leaders the night before you left the labor camp, your name came up as a suspicious person. I was directed to keep an eye on you. When I realized the call to the administration tent was phony, the same as the one in the schoolyard, I got suspicious."

Cheff gave Mid a stern look.

Mid mouthed, "Sorry."

"Please continue, Miss Brex," Cheff said.

"So, when that horrible fat man stopped at the mess area, I got in his filthy truck."

"Horrible man?" Buttons said. "Zeek's not horrible. He's nice!"

Brex ignored her. "And I was right, too. I knew all along you were up to something. You and your little friends, here, you're all in it together, aren't you?"

"We are," Cheff said.

"You're FRM agents, like your traitor parents."

"True," Cheff said. "But by now, I'm sure you know all about it. After all, you've seen and heard everything we've said and done for the last two days."

"That's right, Karfendek. I know everything. I know you're all FRM agents. I know you were involved in that raid on the Iron Fortress a few weeks ago. I know you were sent out here to The Fel to gather rovaldia, whatever that is. I know that Zeek is an FRM agent, too, and probably that man, Meltern, who runs the guest house in Old City. I know that these sad, pathetic Fel People are hiding from the Imperium and that some of them, or maybe all of them, are, or were, FRM agents, too."

Cheff frowned. "And we know something about you, too, Miss Brex. We know you have the Torph Ability whether you like it or not, and whether or not you'll admit it to yourself. We saw you use it last night to counteract the Seph's mind control in the hunting lodge. We watched you reach down deep inside yourself,

Miss Brex, and find your Ability, and use it. It's how we were able to kill the Seph. In fact, you saved us all, 'traitors' though you believe us to be. So tell me, Miss Brex, how does it feel to be the thing you've hated all your life? And to be responsible for your 'beloved lord's' death? Hmm?"

Brex sat down heavily on the floor of the cage, but remained silent.

"What's the matter, Miss Brex?" Buttons asked. "Haven't got anything to say, for once?"

"Quiet, Sis," Cheff said. "It's not right to taunt her while she's in a cage."

"Taunt all you want," Brex said. "I'll be out of here soon enough and I'll have plenty to say then."

"Will you, Miss Brex?" Cheff asked. "And what exactly will you say? Will you tell the authorities that you have the Ability after all? Will you voluntarily present yourself for testing? Will you request a transfer to a Torph Camp? Does your loyalty go that far? Well, does it, Miss Brex?"

"And what if I don't?" Brex demanded. "Are you going to turn me in? Because I'll bring you all down first. Every last one of you. And which do you think they'll believe? Children of political prisoners? Or a loyal Blueband squad leader with years of excellent service and a spotless record?"

"I think they'll believe their tests," Cheff said.

Brex was thinking that over when the door to the little hut opened, and a middle-aged Torph couple entered. They walked up to the cage and looked in. The man said, "Averith? Avie? Is that you?"

Brex leaped to her feet, horrified. "Dad? Mom? What are you doing here? I thought you'd been eaten—er, I mean, taken to a Torph Camp years ago."

The woman said, "Oh, my dear, sweet little Avie! I've missed you so much. It's been so long." She started to weep.

Her husband put his arms around her and patted her gently. "There, now, sweetheart. Everything's going to be all right. We have our Avie back, at last." He turned to us. "Are you the ones who brought her here?"

"After a fashion," Cheff said. "Brex followed me and my friends."

"Thank you, thank you all so much!" Brex's mother said. "We never thought we'd see her again in this life. There aren't words to tell you how grateful we are."

"We haven't seen her for years," Brex's father said. "Not since the day we were reported, and the soldiers came and took us away."

"Poor Avie," her mother said. "She was left all alone, and at such a young age. We weren't even sure she'd survive."

"We'll take our leave," Cheff said. "I'm sure the three of you have much to talk about. Come on, gang, let's join the party for a while."

We went back out into the night and joined the crowd at the bonfire.

"They don't know, Cheff," Buttons said. "They don't know that Brex is the one who turned them in."

"They'll figure out she's a Blueband," Cheff said, "as soon as they clean the mud off her uniform."

"That's going to be an awkward conversation," Mid said, then grinned. "I wonder if we can arrange to overhear it?"

"Why, Mid!" Cheff put his hands to his cheeks in mock horror. "Eavesdropping? I'm shocked!" He looked thoughtful. "Still, that's maybe not such a bad idea. Brex is going to have to be dealt with, and sooner rather than later. Perhaps a little eavesdropping might not be a bad thing."

Brex's mother and father burst from the little grass house and ran past us. Her mother was sobbing.

"Looks like we missed it," Mid said.

"Looks like," Cheff agreed. "Let's keep an eye on those two, in case they have another conversation. Buttons, maybe you and the ponies could tag along with them, see if you can learn anything."

Buttons beamed. "Sure, Cheff. Thanks! The ponies are always happy to help." She disappeared after them into the crowd.

OPERATION LOCKDOWN

— **31** —

VICTORY CELEBRATION

HE REST OF us went down to the big bonfire in the common area. Several marsh pigs roasted on spits over the fire. An amazing fragrance rose from a bubbling cauldron near the fire's edge.

"That smells wonderful!" Mid said.

"I'm… going to… to talk to the… the cooks…" Lery said. "Maybe… I can learn… something."

A musical group was forming on the steps of the longhouse: three varieties of stringed instruments, a couple of pipes I didn't recognize, and a small hand-held drum played with a double-ended drumstick. They spent a few minutes tuning up, then began to play. I didn't know the tune, but it had the sound of a victory march.

The villagers formed a parade of sorts and marched slowly around the bonfire. As they started their second round, an elderly woman stopped and pulled Cheff by the sleeve. "Come, join us, youngster. It's your victory march, too. Come, all of you, march with us."

The six of us, plus Mr. Grumbles, fell in with the others. The march continued for a second slow circuit, then a third. At the beginning of the fourth round, the parade left the village by a side path, through the reeds to another clearing, freshly cut out of the tall grass. In the center of the clearing, all the fallen warriors had been placed on funeral pyres. By each pyre stood a Torph warrior holding a lighted torch, wearing full battle attire: leather armor, leather helmet, and camouflage face paint. Fallen female warriors were attended by a female torch bearer, male warriors by a male torch bearer.

The entire village was present, including Carra, who was wrapped in a blanket and escorted by her two nurses. Brex was there, too, escorted by two burly guards, hands tied behind her back. Near Brex stood her mother and father. Buttons held Brex's mother's hand. In her other hand, she held Starry and Moka against her chest.

When all were assembled, Rayce raised a hand for silence. "We now bid farewell to our brave warriors. Thank you, dear comrades, for your sacrifice on our behalf. It was not in vain. You claimed four Seph lords and many Facilitators, and saved the life of a young woman, an ally and fellow agent. You will be sorely missed, and you will be long remembered. We will sing songs and tell tales of your great deeds to our children and our children's children. Farewell!"

The torch-bearers lit the pyres, which burst into flames. We watched, respectfully, as the flames did their work, the sparks rising high in the night sky. Even Mr. Grumbles sat quietly at Sable's feet, sucking on his hairy paw.

The Fel villagers wept openly, but their eyes shone with pride and hope. They, like us, felt the warriors' sacrifice was worthwhile. And I'm not ashamed to say that we wept, too, all six of us.

When the fires began to die down, we made our way solemnly back down the path to the village, with Mr. Grumbles waddling along behind.

Our mood remained solemn until Rayce once more ascended the steps of the longhouse and addressed the entire village, who had gravitated to the common area. "Dear friends, we've said our farewells. Let us now celebrate our victory as our departed warriors would have if they were yet with us. Where are the musicians? Play us a cheerful tune, lads. Let us eat, drink, and rejoice in honor of our warriors, living and dead, and in celebration of our magnificent victory tonight."

The villagers cheered and shouted, "Hurrah!"

"And let's not forget our new friends. Take time to speak with them, for in the morning they must leave us."

"Awww!"

"Though we must acknowledge that they leave us richer than we were before they came."

"Hurrah!"

Soon, the cooks handed out bowls of steaming stew and slabs of roast marsh pig. We ate until we could eat no more. Even Mr. Grumbles seemed sated, for once. Then, little by little, the villagers retired to their homes for the night. Brex was taken back to her house of detention. Buttons said goodnight to Brex's mother and father, then came to stand with us. She seemed somewhat subdued and took Sable's hand without a word. Carra's nurses guided her back inside the longhouse. She still seemed dazed, but she was quiet and cooperative.

At last, only the six of us remained with Rayce, sitting on the steps, while Mr. Grumbles snored softly at the foot of the stairs, content after his enormous supper.

Buttons asked, "What's going to happen to Brex, Mr. Rayce?"

"I'm not sure, yet, Buttons. I've been thinking it over. There are several possible outcomes. I'm afraid a lot depends on Brex herself."

Buttons frowned. "I don't understand."

"I saw you with Brex's mother," Rayce said. "What did you learn?"

Buttons blushed. "I *was* eavesdropping, but for a good reason. We wanted to learn all we could before we had to deal with Brex in the morning."

"Wise," Rayce said.

"But I wasn't pretending—I was sad for them, especially Brex's mother, and I wanted to help her feel better."

Rayce smiled. "Of course you did, Miss Buttons. You have a kind heart, I know."

Buttons looked stricken.

"But I promise not to tell anyone," Rayce added quickly, and Buttons brightened again. "It's all right," Rayce said, "we all have our reputations to maintain. Tell us what you learned."

"Well, they were talking about what happened after we left Brex. They… she… they didn't know that it was Brex who turned them in. And they didn't know that Brex had become a Blueband. Brex said some pretty mean things to them. Called them traitors, and worse. They're overly sad. Arla, that's Brex's mom, can't stop crying. They think it's their fault, somehow, that Brex went bad."

"I see," Rayce said. "How tragic for them. What do you think should be done with Brex, Buttons?"

"I don't know, sir."

"How about the rest of you? Cheff?"

"It's complicated, sir. I'm afraid that Brex's life, as she has been imagining it, is over, one way or the other."

"How so?"

"On the one hand, her suspicions about us have been confirmed. She knows that we're FRM. She knows about this village. She knows about, or at least suspects, that Meltern is FRM, and our friend Zeek, too. Do you know them? Meltern and Zeek?"

Rayce said enigmatically, "Let's say that we've met, on occasion."

"So," Cheff said, "if we let Brex return to her normal life, we'll put a lot of good people in danger."

"Right so far," Rayce said.

"On the other hand," Mid said, "we know that she has the Torph Ability. She has likely had it for some time, whether she admits it or not—if she even knows she has it. *We* know she has it—Cheff and Books and Lery and I saw her use it. But, her continued survival as a Blueband squad leader depends on her being Ability-free. If she goes back to being a Blueband, she'll be caught, sooner or later, and taken to a Torph Camp for testing, which she is bound to fail. She'll be imprisoned for life."

"Not so," Rayce said. "There are no Torph Camps."

"What?" Cheff asked. "I thought that Torphs with the Ability are taken to special camps, somewhere out west, where they live happy and productive—oh, I see."

"See what, Cheff?" Buttons asked.

"A lie," Sable said.

"Another piece of lying propaganda from our beloved Emperor," Mid said.

"So," Cheff said thoughtfully, "all the Torphs that were rounded up and tested, the ones with Ability, they were all—"

"Killed," Rayce said. "Every last one, save a few kept for experimentation. Or they were eaten. That's why everyone who could get away is out here in this village."

"Wait," Cheff said, "that means that Lhuk's parents—"

"He's a Torph schoolmate of ours," Buttons said.

"—are dead, almost certainly," Rayce said.

"Oh, no," Buttons wailed. "Poor Lhuk! He's... been so looking forward to being with them again."

"So, then..." Cheff mulled this over. "All the Torphs here in The Fel have the Ability?"

"Well reasoned," Rayce said. "Yes, almost all of us have the Ability to some extent. A few without Ability came with their husbands, wives, or children. And, as I'm sure you noticed, there are members of the other Peoples here, too. They are also under a death sentence, wanted for one thing or another. We don't discriminate, youngsters. Anyone can live here if they're in danger from the Imperium and if they swear to keep our little village a secret. It's a good arrangement—it has worked out rather well, so far. But the question remains: what is to be done with Brex?"

We were silent for a while, until Rayce said, "It's been a long day, children, and a full one. Brex's fate doesn't have to be decided tonight. I suggest we get as much sleep as we can—sleep is our friend—and wait for the council meeting in the morning, after breakfast. We'll figure out what to do about Brex, then we'll see about getting you youngsters on your way home. You can sleep in the longhouse tonight. The women caring for Carra have made up some sleeping mats for you."

Mid yawned. "Sounds good to me."

We said goodnight to Rayce, then went inside. Mr. Grumbles heaved himself to his feet and started to follow us in.

"No, Mr. Grumbles," Buttons said. "You have to sleep outside and keep watch."

Mr. Grumbles didn't care much for that idea. He tried to nose his way through the longhouse door.

"Ehem," Rayce said. "Mr. Grumbles."

Mr. Grumbles turned and looked at Rayce, who had a peculiar look on his face. I got the strangest feeling that I'd seen that same look recently—*very* recently. Rayce and Mr. Grumbles looked at each other for a little while, then the look was over. Mr. Grumbles ambled over to the bonfire, where he curled up into a furry ball by the embers, heaved a great ursine sigh, then closed his eyes. I got the impression he was smiling. Rayce slipped me a wink. I smiled, too, then joined the others in the longhouse and found my sleeping mat.

Even though we were as quiet as we could be, Carra opened her eyes. "Cheff," she said. "What are you doing here? I'm sorry I was so mean, before. The nurses told me what you did for me. Thank you, Cheff." She closed her eyes and was instantly asleep again.

Mid raised the back of his hand to his forehead and looked heavenward. "Am I going mad? Or did Carra Trenta Wolcutt—of the Tumberland Wolcutts, no less—say something nice to Cheff?"

Everyone laughed. Even Sable smiled.

"All right, all right, cut it out, gang," Cheff said. "Let's get some shuteye. We've got another big day ahead of us tomorrow."

"Not as big as today, I bet," Buttons said.

"I sure hope not, Sis, I sure hope not."

— 32 —

FAREWELL TO MR. GRUMBLES

I SAT UP ABRUPTLY and blinked into the semi-darkness. It took me a second or two to recognize where I was: inside the longhouse in the Fel village. Cheff's bedroll was empty, but the others were still sleeping. Carra was sleeping, too, in-between her two caretakers. Yellow beams of sunlight filtered through the grass roof.

When I stood up, I felt a little dizzy, but I shook it off and tip-toed out the longhouse door into the common area. Cheff sat on the longhouse steps, watching the village wake up.

I sat next to him. "Hey, Cheff."

"Hey, Books." His voice was flat.

"Everything okay?"

"Sure, I guess."

"What's the matter, Cheff? You can tell me."

"Well… yesterday was the first time I ever killed a sentient be-ing. Sure, I've hunted, but never another… you know… *person.*"

Mid came out of the longhouse, blinked at the morning sun, put on his sunglasses, and sat on the other side of Cheff. "What's up?"

I said, "Cheff's feeling bad about killing a sentient."

"Not bad, exactly," Cheff said. "More like… strange."

"You mean the Seph lord?" Mid asked.

Cheff nodded.

"Well," Mid said, "I don't see that we had much choice. He was certainly going to kill us. Eat us, probably."

Cheff's mood didn't seem to improve. We sat quietly for a while, then Lery joined us on the porch, and shortly thereafter, Sable and Buttons.

Buttons looked at Cheff, then at me and Mid. "What's going on, Cheff?"

Mid said, "Cheff's having some misgivings about killing that Seph lord last night."

"I've never killed before," Cheff said.

"Sure you have," Buttons said. "You hunt for meat all the time."

"Sure, Sis, for meat. But this is the first time I've killed a *person*."

Buttons frowned, but said nothing.

Rayce found us on the porch and sat down with us. "What's up, children?"

No one spoke, so I said, "We're talking about taking the life of a sentient being."

"Ah," Rayce said. "I see." He turned to Cheff. "Yesterday was your first time?"

Cheff said, "Not only mine, though. Books, Mid, Sable, and Lery—we did it together."

Rayce pondered this. "It is good that you consider taking a sentient life to be such a serious matter. It's something that should never have to happen to anyone."

Cheff didn't respond.

"Sadly," Rayce continued, "the actions of others sometimes make it unavoidable."

"Necessary," Sable murmured.

"I… I have… killed," Lery said. "In the… army."

"I thought you were a cook in the army?" I asked.

"That was… later. After they… found out I… could cook… a little. Before that… I was a… a soldier."

Cheff stared at him. "So you killed people?"

"Yes… Friend Cheff. That… is what soldiers… do."

"It is," Sable murmured.

The rest of us sat motionless. Of course, we knew that Lery had been a soldier, but we hadn't made the connection.

Rayce said, "Thank you, Lery. I don't think we need the details of that. Let's all be grateful that you became a cook."

Lery said happily, "I like… cooking… better than… well… you know."

"Anyway, Cheff," Mid said, "it was him or us. I don't see that as a choice."

"It's true," Rayce said. "Sometimes choices are forced upon us against our will."

"I helped," I said. "I grabbed that spear and pushed as hard as I could. And I'm not sorry. That Seph was going to kill us all."

"And eat Carra," Buttons added.

"They had it coming, Old Man," Mid said, "fair and square."

Cheff took a breath. "You're right, of course—we didn't ask for any of this. They started it when they kidnapped Carra. I guess, if Sephs don't want to be killed, they'd best not capture our friends and make them the main course of their evening meal."

Mid pounded Cheff on the back. "Now you're talking, Old Man. On their own heads be it!" He sniffed the morning breeze. "Let's get ourselves on the outside of some grub."

Cheff stood up and smoothed his clothes. "Thank you, everyone. You helped a lot. By all means, let's eat. I'm starving." He took off toward the communal campfire.

"Good idea," Rayce said. "The world is brighter with sufficient sleep and a full belly. Let's go see what's cooking. I need to speak with some folks, anyway."

The rest of us split up and went to forage for breakfast.

Mr. Grumbles still snored contentedly at the edge of the bonfire. When I approached, he roused, sniffed my hand, licked it, then nuzzled my pockets looking for a handout. "Hungry, Mr. Grumbles? Come on, let's go see what's cooking."

Mr. Grumbles and I strolled over to where a few women cooked over a small bed of coals, all that was left of last night's bonfire. Strips of smoked meat sizzled on an iron griddle. A soup cauldron bubbled, producing a wonderful aroma. In another spot, a man cooked some golden griddle cakes.

"Good morning, Mr. Boy," the woman said. "Good morning, Mr. Bear. I'm Daedy. Hungry?"

"Yes, ma'am, Daedy," I said.

Mr. Grumbles raised himself on his haunches and clapped his paws together. The woman tossed him a strip of meat, which he caught in the air and practically inhaled. She tossed him another, which he also scarfed, then waddled over to beg for a griddle cake.

"That was some fine work you did yesterday," the woman said. She filled a soup bowl and handed it to me, then put a few meat strips on top. "Go get some griddle cakes, Mr. Boy. Harn is an expert with griddle cakes."

"Thank you, ma'am," I said. I got some cakes from Harn, then went back to the longhouse and sat on the steps. Mr. Grumbles didn't follow me—he was busy trying to coax another strip of meat or two from Daedy.

I was finishing my soup when the longhouse door opened and Carra came out, supported by her nurses.

Cheff and the rest of the gang returned with full plates, sat down, and addressed their breakfasts with a will.

"Good morning, everyone," Carra said softly. She inhaled the enticing fragrances wafting from the cooking fire. "What's for breakfast? I just realized that I'm terribly hungry. I don't think I ate at all yesterday."

"Soup, smoked something, and griddle cakes." I gestured toward the camp kitchen, where Mr. Grumbles was still begging for treats. "It's pretty tasty. You should grab some."

"He's right, you should!" Cheff said. "I'm starved, too. I'll bet I could eat an entire Fel bear by myself!"

"Shh, Cheff, Mr. Grumbles will hear you," Buttons said.

"Mr. Grumbles looks pretty busy to me," Mid said. "You'd better hurry, Carra, before he gets it all."

"You can… wait… here… Miss Carra…" Lery said. "I'll get… you some…"

"Thank you, Lery," Carra said.

"Good morning, Carra," I said. "Are you feeling better this morning?"

"Hi, Books," Carra said. Her caregivers helped her to sit down beside me. "My head still hurts pretty bad, and I ache all over, but I'm better than I was yesterday."

"And she seems to have her appetite back," one of the caregivers said.

"That's a good sign," the other added.

"Listen, Books," Carra said. "Yesterday, when you all came to see me, I wasn't quite myself. I don't remember much, but the nurses told me that I said some pretty harsh things. I'm sorry if I hurt your feelings."

"It's okay, Carra," I said. "We know you were under the influence of the jexan. But you're right, you did say some things… mostly to Cheff, though. When you have a chance, you might want to have a word with him."

"Thank you, Books. I appreciate that." She patted my hand. "You're a good friend." She glanced at Cheff, who was pointedly looking the other way, but said nothing.

Lery gave Carra her breakfast and helped her get started, then went back to get himself seconds. When he returned, Mr. Grumbles followed him, sniffing his pouch. Lery found him a biscuit, and he settled down to enjoy it. We chatted for a while as we ate, then Mid said, "Here comes Rayce. I wonder what he'll have to say this morning."

Rayce sat down on the steps. "Good morning, everyone. You're all looking not too much worse for wear. That was quite a night we had, wasn't it?"

Mr. Grumbles finished his biscuit and begged another one from Lery.

"Have you thought about what you're going to do with Mr. Grumbles?" Rayce asked.

"Not yet," Cheff said. "We didn't ask him to follow us, you know. He just… did."

"Is that right?" Rayce asked. "That's unusual for a Fel bear. They're not usually that friendly. Smart, though."

"Mr. Grumbles is friendly," Buttons said.

Rayce chuckled. "He is, indeed. Still, I don't suppose you're planning to take him back to Fellstone City with you, are you?"

"No," Cheff said, "of course not."

"But, Cheff," Buttons said, "he's our friend. And the *ponies* like him. And besides" —she glanced sideways at Carra—"he *did* help save Carra."

Carra looked startled and queried Cheff with her eyes.

Cheff shrugged. "He did, that's true, but—"

"But think about it, Buttons," Mid said. "Even if we could take him back to Fellstone City with us, what would happen to him?"

Buttons frowned and stared at her lap. "I know you're right. If we took him with us, someone would probably eat him. And that would upset the ponies, Cheff. *Really* upset them." A tear leaked out of the corner of her eye. She wiped it away quickly with her sleeve.

"Fel bear," Sable said.

"Sable's right," Cheff said. "Mr. Grumbles is a *Fel* bear, not a *Fellstone* bear. The best thing would be for him to stay out here in The Fel and live a happy life as a Fel bear."

"Easily said, Cheff," Mid said. "But how are we going to arrange that? You going to have a word with him?"

"Rayce," Sable murmured.

Rayce glanced at Sable. "Sable's right. If you want me to, I could help you with him."

"With your Ability?" Buttons asked.

Cheff said, "If Mr. Rayce can help Mr. Grumbles, I think we should let him."

"Agreed," Mid said.

"Okay, Cheff, if you say so. But the ponies are going to be keeping an eye on Mr. Rayce." She held Starry and Moka so they could observe the proceedings.

Rayce stood up and fixed his eyes on Mr. Grumbles. He got that same look on his face as he'd had the night before.

Mr. Grumbles stopped scratching and looked up.

Rayce said, "We thank you for your help yesterday, Mr. Grumbles, and we've enjoyed your company. But now it's time for these youngsters to go back to their homes in Fellstone City, and for you to go back to your home, too. Say goodbye, now."

Mr. Grumbles heaved himself to his feet and, one by one, nuzzled each of us, and let us scratch his head. Even Carra thanked him and gave him a pat. He nuzzled Buttons last.

She threw her arms around him. "Goodbye, Mr. Grumbles. I wish you didn't have to go. Have a happy life, okay? Who knows, maybe we'll see you again sometime." She buried her face in his shaggy fur. "The ponies will miss you. *I'll* miss you!" She hugged him tight once more, then jumped up and ran into the longhouse.

"Okay, Mr. Grumbles," Rayce said, the strange look still on his face. "Time to go."

Mr. Grumbles gave a small roar, then went down the steps and across the square. When he was about halfway across, the longhouse door opened, and Buttons stood on the top step. She waved. "Goodbye, Mr. Grumbles."

Mr. Grumbles turned, stood on his hind legs, and roared a mighty roar, his massive paws raised high above his head.

We waved back, and called, "Goodbye, goodbye."

He dropped to all fours, then ambled out of the village and disappeared into the tall grass.

"Good bear," Buttons whispered. She went and stood next to Rayce. "Did you use your Ability to make him do that?"

"I didn't *make* him do that, little Buttons," Rayce said. "I just made him *want* to do that."

We stared at each other. We'd heard that phrase before.

"We have a friend, a Torph boy, in the Labor Compound," Buttons said. "His name is Lhuk. He has a pet mouse named Squeaky."

"We asked him how he makes Squeaky do his tricks," Mid said, "and he said the same thing: he doesn't *make* Squeaky do tricks, he just makes him *want* to do tricks."

Rayce and Buttons sat down with the rest of us on the steps. "How old is Lhuk?" Rayce asked.

"Same as me," Buttons said.

"So young," Rayce said, "and he already has the Ability. He could be in a lot of danger. If anyone ever suspects, he could be taken and killed. You might want to consider encouraging him to join us here in The Fel."

"Excuse me, Mr. Rayce," I said. "Our teacher, Mr. Rishten, the one who drinks felmoss tea all day, told us that the Torph Ability was a kind of shield against Seph mind control, not a way to control others."

"Although," Cheff said, "he did say that the Torphs used their Ability to subjugate the other races. But I don't believe that."

"The Torph Ability is not merely one thing," Rayce said. "It's different for every Torph. Resisting Seph mind control is something that all Torphs with the Ability have in common, though some more than others. Some Torphs barely have any Ability, while in others it is quite strong. Something they probably didn't teach you in school: the Torph Ability is the strongest in the royal line."

"The royal line? I thought that was another myth," Mid said.

"Although," Cheff said, "we did swear to help find the rightful heir when we joined the FRM."

"That's true," Mid said. "I guess I didn't connect it."

"Most myths have some basis in reality," Rayce said, "though today it's not popular to believe such. People today would rather believe that the old stories are pure fantasy."

"But what about what you did with Mr. Grumbles?" Cheff asked.

"A few Torphs, including me, have a somewhat limited Ability to influence the lower creatures. Apparently, your friend Lhuk has it too."

"Brex has the Ability," I said. "Cheff, Lery, Mid, and I watched her use it on the Seph."

"It's true," Mid said. "We were all paralyzed to one degree or another. Lery was completely paralyzed, Cheff could still move and talk, but he believed that the Seph loved us. Books and I were influenced too, but we were able to shake it off."

"I shook it off, too," Cheff said, "with a little help from my friend Books, here." He grinned and rubbed his cheek where I'd hit him.

"Fessals are the most severely affected by Seph mind controls," Rayce said. "Other species are affected too, but to a lesser degree."

"Cheff kept yelling at Brex to use her Ability," I said. "Then she screamed, and the Seph fell unconscious."

Rayce looked grave as he pondered this. "A Torph able to render a Seph unconscious isn't unheard of, but there hasn't been any report of such a thing since The Fall, over a hundred years ago. In fact, the last report of such an occurrence was during the final battle of The Fall, when Queen Brindshale II used her Ability on an attacking Seph. What little we know suggests that she was only partially successful. You see, children—" He stopped and thought. "Remember when I said that the Torph Ability is different from one Torph to the next? It's rare for a Torph to be able to influence animals. Disabling a Seph is rarer still. Most Torphs have only enough Ability to protect themselves from Seph control. Some can shield others around them."

"What about Brex, then?" Cheff asked. "She disabled a Seph. That means she has the rarest Ability. What's going to happen to her? Are you going to keep her here?"

"It hasn't been decided yet. The council wants to talk to you youngsters first."

"Can't you use your Ability to make Brex *want* to be a decent person?" Buttons asked.

"No, little Buttons," Rayce said, shaking his head sadly. "The Ability only works that way on animals, not people. But even if it did work that way on people, we still wouldn't do it. Everyone deserves to be able to think their own thoughts, even if they are bad ones. If we were to use our Ability on people, we'd be exactly as evil as Emperor Pallador, wouldn't we?"

"I… I guess so," Buttons said. "I hadn't thought of it like that."

"It's a big part of what's wrong with Andaran," Rayce said. "The Sephs have the Ability to control the minds of others, and they use it to our detriment. Their signal amplifiers and jexan and other drugs simply make it easier for them to do what they have done for centuries. In part, the Seph Ability is what caused The Fall of the Sixth Kingdom, over a century ago."

"Why are Torphs the only species with the Ability to resist the Sephs?" Mid asked.

"Good question," Rayce said. "I wish we knew the answer to that. Maybe, long ago, someone knew, but no one knows anymore. But the fact remains that we Torphs do have the Ability, and it's our responsibility to use it well, for the benefit of all the Peoples, and never, ever, to manipulate or control anyone."

Cheff nodded slowly. "I see. I think I see. So, for better or for worse, Brex's fate is up to Brex."

"Not entirely true. She's in our custody now. Our council will decide what we will do with Brex, based on what she herself decides. Here they come now."

"She buried her face in his shaggy fur."

— 33 —

BREX

THE COUNCIL MEMBERS who had met with us on the previous day strode purposefully across the square. Brex, escorted by two guards, followed behind. Brex had been cleaned up somewhat, and her hair was something like combed.

We stood as they approached. They climbed the steps and entered the longhouse without a word. Rayce said, "Us, too, youngsters. Are you ready?"

"We're ready," Cheff said.

We followed Rayce into the longhouse and took our seats around the council fire. Carra was already seated between her two caregivers. Brex didn't want to sit, but her guards pushed her firmly to the floor. Council Chief Morsana said, "Miss Brex, if you won't behave, we'll have your cage brought here. Is that what you want?"

"No," she spat. "I'll *behave*."

"Very well."

The longhouse door opened, and Brex's mother and father entered. "Please," Brex's father said, "if it's all right with the council, we would like to observe."

Morsana looked around the council. There was no objection. "It's all right with us, for now. But you'll observe only, not participate."

"Yes, Morsana, we understand." They took their seats.

"Thank you. We have invited the young woman called Carra to this council, because even though she was unconscious or not present for most of the events in question, her future will also be affected by our decision today. Youngsters, if you disagree with anything said during this proceeding, or if you have something to add, please wait until we're finished."

"Yes, ma'am," Cheff said.

"Good," Morsana said. "Then let us begin. Ladies and gentlemen of the council, we have a decision to make concerning this unfortunate young woman, Averith Brex. Here are the facts as we understand them:

"Item One: the person in question is Averith Brex, a female of the Torph species, daughter of Zerra Brex and Arla Brex, who are present today.

"Item Two: Averith Brex was separated from her parents when they were arrested on suspicion of having Torph Ability when Brex was a young child. Her parents escaped and eventually made their way to us here in The Fel.

"Item Three: Averith Brex was raised by a Fessal woman in the Fellstone Labor Compound along with the Fessal woman's children.

"Item Four: Averith Brex completed Basic School and is currently attending Regular School, with a focus on Military Service.

"Item Five: Averith Brex is a member of the paramilitary order known as Bluebands and holds the rank of squad leader.

"Item Six: Averith Brex has demonstrated before witnesses that she has the Torph Ability, and a strong one, at that, having faced a Seph lord and won.

"Item Seven: Averith Brex is now aware of the existence of us and our village, and is oath-bound to report us to Imperial authorities." She glanced at Brex, who was seething. "And I have no doubt that she will."

She turned to Cheff. "Do you or your people have any corrections or additions?"

"Yes, ma'am. Brex, er, I mean Averith Brex, has suspected for some time and is now fully aware, that I and my associates, and Carra, are FRM agents. And possibly Meltern, too."

"And Zeek," Sable said.

"Good, thank you," Morsana said. "We'll call that Item Eight. It certainly will have a bearing on our decision. As to her fate, there are several possibilities. Who will offer suggestions?"

A council member growled, "Kill her, toss her body into The Fel."

Brex's eyes widened and she started to speak, but one of her guards prodded her roughly on the shoulder with the blunt end of his spear. She subsided.

Brex's mother began to cry. Brex's father put his arm around his wife.

Another council member offered, "If we simply send her back to her old life, she'd be a threat to many good people. That's not an option."

A third said, "Two of our non-Torph villagers could escort her to a guard station, and denounce her for her Ability."

"It would be kinder to kill her outright," Morsana said.

"Excuse me," Buttons said. "Mr. Rayce, are you sure you couldn't make Brex an exception to the rule? Maybe adjust her mind a tiny little bit? Just this once?"

"No, little Buttons," Rayce said. "I'm sorry. Torph Ability simply doesn't work that way on sentient creatures. But even if it did, it would be unethical. Which is right—otherwise we'd be no better than the Sephs. We talked about this, remember?"

"Buttons has a point, though," Mid said. "If Brex hadn't climbed into Zeek's truck, if she hadn't followed us, she'd never have known any of this. She'd be the way she always was. Sure, she'd still be trying to spy on us at the salvage camp and making a general nuisance of herself, but she wouldn't be dangerous. She has good parents, obviously. Who knows? In time she might come to recognize the truth about Pallador and the Imperium."

"But she did get in the truck," Morsana said gently. "And she did follow you. We can't ever go back. None of us can."

"Excuse me, Morsana," a councilman said. "But there is a way to go back."

Morsana said, "Are you referring to the ancient technique of Fara Amma, The Forgetting."

"I am," the councilman replied. "Averith Brex appears to me to be a special case. She is the daughter of two of our most dear. She is strong in the Ability—and to waste such a bloodline is foolhardy. But most of all, she is young and deluded. Who knows what she might become with time and opportunity?"

The council member who had suggested killing Brex outright said, "It's not ethical! And it most certainly isn't safe! We have no idea whether this Fara Amma will work or not. Or if it does work, how long the effects will last."

"True, Councilman Baese," Morsana said. "I agree it's ethically questionable, at best. But we wouldn't be controlling her, only resetting her life to a point before it became a death sentence. It would be a chance, albeit a slim one, of saving the daughter of two of our own."

"It hasn't been used for a long time," a councilwoman said. "Does anyone still know how to do it?"

"Send for Rosca," Morsana said, then turned to Cheff. "She's our village's healer. If such a thing is possible, she'll know."

A guard left and soon returned with Rosca. As they entered the longhouse, a hush fell over the council, followed by a low murmuring which quickly subsided.

Morsana explained the circumstances and the problem, then said, "It has been suggested that the ancient technique of Fara Amma might be employed in Brex's case. Can it be done?"

"It can," Rosca said. "It will require certain ingredients, but I have most of them on hand. I will make preparations and come back at noon."

"Can you guarantee results, Rosca?" Councilman Baese asked.

Rosca shook her head. "Of course not! I've never performed the Fara Amma myself. But it's at least as ethical as killing the young girl outright. If it doesn't work, you can always kill her later."

Brex looked shocked, briefly, but composed her face into a mask of indifference.

Councilman Baese started to object, but Rayce rose to his feet and spoke for the first time. "Morsana, if I may make a suggestion?"

"Of course, Rayce. What is it?"

"We have a contact in Fellstone Old City, the one who—"

"The details need not be mentioned, Rayce."

"Of course, Morsana. What I mean to say is, I can put the word out to keep an eye on the girl after she's back home, to make sure she isn't remembering."

"Thank you, Rayce," Morsana said. "That's a fine idea. Council?"

Most of the council were in agreement.

"It's settled, then. Rayce, speak to your contact. Anyone else?"

"Morsana, ma'am," Cheff said. "I have a question for Rosca."

"What is it, youngster?"

"Is there any indication that her memory loss will be permanent? It could become awkward if Brex were to start piecing things together later. Especially for the six of us."

"Good question," Rosca said. "Unfortunately, the answer is that I'm not sure at all." She considered briefly. "But if I had to guess, I'd say that if Brex did begin to remember, the memories would come gradually, not all at once. And they'd likely be vague and jumbled at first, like a dream."

Rayce said, "Leave that to me, Cheff. I'll make sure my contact has a clear line of communication with you through your regular chain of command. If you see any signs that Averith Brex is regaining her memory, report it immediately to your supervisor. See?"

"I see," Cheff said. "Thank you." He frowned.

"Do you have another concern, young… Cheff, is it?" Morsana asked.

"Yes, ma'am. It's just that… well… if we're going to tamper with Brex's mind, shouldn't we ask Brex what she wants?"

Morsana said, "You make a good point, Cheff. We can ask her. But I'll remind you, the final decision belongs to the council."

"Yes, Morsana. We understand."

"Well," Morsana said, "what about it, Miss Averith Brex? What do you have to say for yourself?"

"You're all traitors!" Brex snarled. "All of you. Do whatever you want with me. I can't stop you, you filthy Torph vermin! You're a pack of liars, accusing me of having your disgusting, sick, perverted, *disloyal* Ability."

"Miss Brex," Cheff said. "Please, try to calm down and be reasonable. We were there with you. The Seph was going to kill you, and me, and Books, and Lery, and you stopped him. You saved us. Don't you remember?"

"Never happened, Karfendek. But I saw you *murder* that Seph lord, you and your fellow assassins. You and these grubby villagers murdered all four Seph lords and their Facilitators. They were having a little hunting vacation in The Fel, and you all slaughtered them."

"But, Miss Brex, what about Carra? Don't you remember that the Sephs were going to eat her? They force-fed her jexan."

Brex jumped to her feet, though still held by the guards. "Sephs don't eat people, you fool. It's a dirty, rotten lie! And there's no such thing as jexan, either. They probably picked that stupid girl up when she wandered off into The Fel and were going to take her back to Fellstone City. The same thing goes for your stupid village children—they wandered off into The Fel and were eaten by marsh bears or Fel pigs or who knows what. Pallador is *love*,

Karfendek. You felt that love in the Seph lord's presence. I know you did—I could see it in your eyes. But you, you're so full of hate that you wouldn't know love if you saw it. You *are* full of hate, Karfendek—hate for Emperor Pallador, hate for the Imperium, hate for loyal Facilitators, hate for Andaran, hate for *everything* that matters! And so, in return, I hate *you*! Someday I'll get you, all of you, if it's the last thing I ever do!"

"All right, that's enough from you, Averith Brex!" Morsana said. "I think we're fairly clear on where you stand. Guards, please take Brex back to detention. I think our point has been made. Zerra Brex, Arla Brex, I'm so sorry, we all are, but you've seen how it is. Do you have anything you'd like to say?"

Zerra Brex stood. "As parents, of course, we beg you to save the life of our daughter, if you can. As members of this village and of the resistance, we will accede to whatever the council decides." He sat back down and took his wife in his arms.

"Well spoken," Morsana said. "Ladies and gentlemen of the council, I propose we go forward with the attempt to perform the Fara Amma. If it works, we will return Averith Brex to her life. If not… then we will do what we must. All in favor?"

A chorus of 'aye'.

"It is decided. Thank you, everyone. This meeting is adjourned. We will meet back here at noon. "

OPERATION LOCKDOWN

— 34 —

THE FORGETTING

WE LEFT THE longhouse and rambled around the village for a while, exchanging pleasantries with the Fel People and snacking on little bits of Lery's biscuits, plus whatever was cooking at the community kitchen in the common area. Although Rayce had said that meat was scarce in The Fel, there was always some tasty bit of dried meat, pickled eel, or spicy sausage available. I wondered if that was because of our presence or if it was normally like that. I thought over what Rayce had said about Sephs being much like large eels and decided I'd stick with the dried marsh-pig meat.

We ate in the shade of a beautiful Fel oak. When she had finished, Buttons said, "I just don't understand."

"Understand what?" Cheff asked through a mouthful of pickled eel.

"How Brex got it all turned around in her mind. She was there. She saw what we saw. But today she remembers everything completely sideways!"

Sable murmured, "Choice."

"What choice?" Buttons asked.

Cheff explained, "Sable means that we all choose our own reality. When we experience something, anything, we can choose to remember it the way it was, or we can tell our minds some other story."

Sable nodded her agreement, then added, "Blind."

"That's right," Cheff said. "If we want to believe something strongly enough, we can—all of us can—blind our own minds to the truth."

Mid added, "Brex's entire life, her very existence, is based on what she believes about Pallador's rule."

"What do you mean?" Buttons asked.

Mid said, "All Brex's life, she has believed that Pallador is the ideal ruler: Pallador rewards the faithful, Pallador cares for his subjects. To Brex, loyalty is everything. For all those things to remain true in her mind, Brex must remember accordingly."

"Everyone," Sable said.

"Sable's right," Cheff elaborated, "everyone has to choose between reality and the way we want things to be."

Lery said, "The way… that it is… *is* the way that… it is."

"Exactly!" Cheff said. "Well done, Lery. Does that help any, Sis?"

"Not really, Cheff. I mean, I get it, but the ponies say if you don't deal with things the way they are, you can't deal with them at all."

"True," Sable agreed.

"And then," Mid said, "an entire village ends up having to decide for you, whether to let you go, let you live, or merely erase your mind."

Cheff thumped Mid on the shoulder. "Well said, Old Son!"

* * *

When noontime came around, we returned to the longhouse. The council of elders was already there, sitting in a circle around the council fire. Carra sat quietly between her two attendants, still subdued and looking somewhat disoriented. Brex was there, too, but in her cage this time, and escorted by six guards. Brex's parents, Zerra and Arla, sat together holding hands, looking resolute. Arla cried quietly.

Rosca tended a bubbling concoction that she was brewing over the council fire. From time to time she'd taste it, then add a pinch of this or that mysterious powder she kept in a pouch. Finally, she was satisfied, and asked, "How many days of forgetting are desired?"

Rayce turned to us. "What about it, youngsters? How far back do we go?"

Cheff thought it over. "I think we should go back to before she got into Willam the Wheezer. What do you think?" he asked us.

Mid said, "Sounds right to me. That way, she won't even remember that she followed us at all."

The rest of us concurred.

"Okay, how long is that?" Cheff counted on his fingers. "There's this morning, all day yesterday, and all day the day before yesterday, right? That makes two full days and a half day.

Buttons asked, "How are we going to explain a two-and-a-half-day gap in her memory?"

"Good question, Sis," Cheff said. "I don't have a clue. We'll think of something, though, I'm sure. Maybe Zeek will have an idea."

"So," Rosca said. "Two and a half days. Are you sure? Last chance."

We were sure.

She measured out a purplish powder from a glass vial into her hand. She made two little piles, and a half pile, put a few pinches back into the vial, then emptied her hand into the pot. "It'll be ready in about ten minutes," she said. "That's the final touch. It's important to add it last, directly before administering the potion to the subject."

A purple mist filled the room. It smelled the way feet smell when you haven't changed your socks for a week. My eyes watered.

"Yes," Rosca said to me, smiling, "it is strong. That's how you know it will work."

"Okay," I said. I wiped my streaming eyes with my sleeve. "We want it to work."

By the end of the ten minutes, everyone in the room was wiping their eyes and coughing. Rosca said, "It is time. Averith Brex's parents should leave now. Guards? Please escort Zerra and Arla to the door. They don't need to see what comes next."

When they were gone, the six guards pulled the struggling, frenzied Brex from her cage. "No! You can't do this to me! I'm a loyal servant of our beloved Emperor! I have rights!"

The guards ignored her and stretched her on the floor, face up. Two guards held her feet, two more held her arms, and two held her head still.

Rosca made sure the concoction was cool enough that it wouldn't burn Brex, then produced a funnel with a tube attached. She held the funnel in one hand and the end of the tube near Brex's mouth. "Averith Brex, open your mouth. Or would you prefer to do this the hard way?"

"Let me go, you monster!" Brex screamed, then clenched her jaws tight.

Rosca shrugged. "The hard way it is. Guards, if you please."

One of the guards held Brex's head in a vice-like grip. The other forced her jaws apart. Rosca slowly and gently inserted the tube into Brex's throat. She raised the funnel as high as it would go, then slowly poured the mixture into it.

After a few seconds, Brex stopped squirming. Her eyelids fluttered a few times, and she was asleep.

Rosca retrieved the funnel and the tube. "Thank you, guards. She'll be asleep for a day, maybe longer. Your work is done here."

"A moment, please, Morsana," Rayce said. "We're going to need a team of four to carry Brex back to the pickup point." He turned to the guards. "If any of you would care to accompany us, we would be grateful. If not, please ask around the village."

The guards put their heads together and conferred, then one said, "Please, Rayce, if it's all right with you, all six of us would like to accompany you. We can spell each other."

"Very well," Rayce said. "The more the merrier, eh, gentlemen?" Then he turned to us. "Youngsters, your time among the Fel People has nearly reached its end. Are you ready to return to Fellstone City?"

"Yes, sir," Cheff said. "We're well fed, rested, all packed up, and ready to head out. I guess we can collect what rovaldia we find along the way."

"Excellent!" Rayce said. "Best say your goodbyes, then."

We went out to the square, Carra with us, blinking our eyes against the bright, midday sunlight. Mid put his dark glasses on.

To our surprise, a crowd of villagers was waiting for us. One stepped forward and handed Cheff a large sack, stuffed full. "Rayce said you needed rovaldia to help fight the Sephs. While you were sleeping, we picked some for you. We hope it's enough."

Carra stared at the bundle. While she was staring, a second villager handed her another large sack, then came a third. Carra stammered, "Why, this is wonderful! Thank you, thank you so much. This is plenty, more than we could possibly have hoped for. I assure you, your fellow resistance fighters in Tumberland will put it to good use."

The villagers cheered.

When the cheers subsided, Cheff said, "On behalf of Carra and all of us, we thank you for your help and your generous hospitality. We could not have completed our mission without you. We will think of you well, and often, and return to you when we can."

Another tremendous cheer. We smiled and waved.

"Well spoken, youngster," Rayce said to Cheff. "You have the makings of a fine leader. Of course, you have helped us, too, by ridding the Fel of the Sephs' foul hunting lodge. It will be a long time before they can rebuild it, if they ever do. Who knows? Maybe they'll go bother someone else for a while. Perhaps far away in the Great Western Desert. In any case, it goes without saying that you, all of you, are always and ever welcome in our village."

Rayce looked the seven of us over, then checked with the guards. Two of them carried Brex on a stretcher.

Lery had a final word with his new friends, the cooks, who handed him several packets and bundles, which he tucked into his cooking pouch. In return, he gave them several folded paper envelopes.

Carra said goodbye to her nurses and kissed each one on the cheek. "Thank you, thank you. You've been so kind. I appreciate it more than I can say."

"All right, youngsters," Rayce said. "Looks like that about wraps it up. Let's march!"

The crowd parted as we crossed the square, Rayce in the lead. There was one final cheer as we went down to the canoes.

On the outskirts of the village, a little girl in a washtub poked her head up as we passed by. Her mother was shampooing her hair. When the girl recognized Lery, she narrowed her eyes and blew a huge raspberry.

"Oh, Grahsi!" Her mother pushed her head under the water and smiled an apology to Lery, who smiled in return. That was the last we saw of Grahsi and of the Fel village.

"Definitely in love," Buttons said to Sable.

"Definitely," Sable agreed.

Lery blushed. "Please… Miss Buttons… Friend Sable…"

We laughed.

We reached the waterline and boarded the canoes. Rayce, Cheff, two guards, and I were in the lead canoe. Two more guards escorted Brex, Carra, Buttons, and Sable in the middle canoe. The last canoe carried two more guards, plus Lery and Mid and the three huge bundles of rovaldia.

Rayce whistled, and the paddlers pushed off. We glided along the waterway between high walls of grass and reeds.

"This sure beats walking," I said to Cheff. "Think we'll be at the big Fel oak by sundown to meet Zeek?"

"I hope so," Cheff said. "Otherwise we'll have to camp another night." He looked at the sky, then considered the speed of the canoes. "It's strange to think it, but I believe we will paddle in a few hours what it took us two days to walk."

"Destination known," Sable murmured.

"That's right," Cheff said. "This time we don't have to guess which way to go."

"We'll be there by sundown," Rayce said. "Nothing to it."

"That settles it," I said. "The next time I come to The Fel, I'm bringing a canoe."

"It's the only way to travel in The Fel," Rayce said. "Comfort, grace, style, and speed. Who could ask for more?"

* * *

Rayce was right. Well before sundown, our canoes pulled up a few hundred yards from the big Oak. We shouldered our packs and hiked the rest of the way, accompanied by Rayce and two of the guards carrying Brex. The other four guards waited with the canoes. We hid in the tall grass by the big Fel oak and chatted pleasantly.

Along about sundown, we first saw the plume of smoke, then heard the characteristic wheezing and groaning of Willam the Wheezer. We gathered our belongings and moved to the edge of the road, leaving the still-sleeping Brex in the care of the guards.

Zeek brought Willam to a screeching, groaning halt and jumped out. "There you are, children! I'm so glad to see you. One more day, and I would have had to start searching The Fel."

Pally, too, had jumped out and was sniffing everyone all over, including the two little ponies, who each received a rather wet lick. When he was satisfied that everyone was all right, he took his station in the back of the truck.

Buttons threw her arms around Zeek. "Hi, Zeek! The ponies are so glad to see you! They missed you!"

"And I missed them, too, Miss Buttons." He spotted Rayce and crushed him in an enormous bear hug. "Rayce, my old friend! Good to see you. How long has it been? I hoped my children would run into you, though I didn't expect it. I wasn't sure if you were still out there."

"We're out there," Rayce assured him, "as good as we ever were. Better now, for the visit of these youngsters. Have they got a story to tell you!"

"Oh?" Zeek said. "I take it that your mission did not go exactly as planned?"

"Not entirely," Cheff said, grinning. "We did get the rovaldia, though, thanks to Mr. Rayce and his villagers." Lery held up the three sacks full.

Zeek's eyebrows shot up. "That's the rovaldia? You got that much, truly?"

"As I was saying," Cheff said, "we had help. A lot of help."

"We burned down the hunting lodge," Buttons blurted, "and killed all the Sephs, and their Facilitators, too!"

"You did?" Zeek said. "That's amazing!" He looked at Rayce for confirmation.

"They did all that," Rayce said, "and more. It turns out that rovaldia has some rather remarkable properties. I'm sure they'll tell you all about it."

"I'm looking forward to it," Zeek said. "I wouldn't miss it for the world. I'm glad your mission went well."

"Me, too," Cheff said. "How about you? Everything okay back in the salvage camp?"

"Yes, yes, indeed," Zeek said. "No trouble at all." He stroked his chin. "It's a funny thing—you were all so worried about that Blueband girl, Brex, poking her nose into our salvage operation, but I didn't see her the whole time you were gone. Not even once."

"About that..." Cheff beckoned to the guards waiting in the grass by the big Fel oak tree. They brought Brex on her stretcher and set her down gently near the venerable steam truck.

Zeek clapped his hand to his forehead. "Andaran's bones, children! What in the world has been going on out here? Never mind, you can tell me later. Let's get her off the road and into Willam."

Zeek and the guards loaded Brex into Willam's spacious back seat, and Carra propped her up so it looked like she was sleeping. Meanwhile, Mid and Lery helped the guards load the three bags of rovaldia into Willam's coal bin, hiding them under the coal. Next, Mid checked the water level while Lery stoked the boiler, with Pally supervising the operation. Finally, Mid and Lery jumped down.

"Everything's in order, Zeek!" Mid reported.

"Excellent! Well, children," Zeek asked, "are you ready to go? Yes? Then let's load up and get rolling!"

"Goodbye, goodbye," we called to Rayce and the guards, who waved one last time, then disappeared into the tall grass. We took our places in Willam's warm and spacious cab.

"Andaran's bones, children," Zeek said again, "it sounds as if you've had quite an adventure! What's all this about killing Sephs and Facilitators? How did you find Rayce? And what in Andaran is Brex doing out here in The Fel?"

We all started talking at once, so Zeek said, "Whoa, there children. You're going to have to tell it slowly. I'm old now, and I don't listen as fast as I used to."

We laughed.

Zeek continued, "I know just the thing. On the way back, we should stop at Meltern's Guest House and have a nice dinner, the specialty of the house, whatever that is tonight, and some more of his delicious cider. I'm sure Meltern will let us use his back room, and he may even want to join us. Then you can tell the story slowly and in order. How does that sound?"

It sounded wonderful, of course, and we told Zeek so in no uncertain terms.

"Fine, then, children, that's settled. Let's get rolling, shall we? Are you ready to shove that shifter, sister?"

"Ready, Zeek!" Buttons giggled, then shoved the shifter into first gear, and just like that, we left The Fel behind.

— **35** —

LINEN AND ROVALDIA

WE GOT TO Meltern's Guest House early in the evening, just about supper time. Zeek parked Willam around the corner on the side street rather than on the Boulevard. Brex was still sleeping, propped upright against a window. She was only slightly visible from the street, but we decided to lay her down and cover her with a blanket, just in case someone got curious enough about Willam to climb up and take a look inside.

We knocked on the back door of the Guest House. Meltern looked happy to see us. "Come in, come in! Let me count you! Seven! Good, we didn't lose anyone. I'm most happy to see you, children. Come, let's go into the back, the meeting room this time. Roe! Bring a round of cider, right away, if you please. We'll quench your thirst first, then we can see about getting some supper into you."

We followed him into the meeting room, one we'd never been in before. A dozen padded wooden chairs surrounded a long, polished, wooden table. Zeek took a seat at the foot, Meltern at the head, and the seven of us on the sides.

Was it possible that we'd left Meltern's only two days ago? Surely not! But it was true: a mere two days earlier, we'd left this Guest House for our first afternoon in The Fel. On the second day in The Fel, Carra was captured and then rescued that same night, with the victory celebration afterward. And then came today: this morning was Brex's forgetting, followed by an afternoon canoe ride to the big Fel oak where we'd met Zeek just before sunset. Amazing!

Roe brought a tray full of frosty cider mugs and served everyone. I drank half of mine in a single gulp. Roe surveyed us and shook his head, bewildered. He seemed about to comment, but Meltern gave him a warning look, and he left the room without saying a word. I suppose we were quite a sight—dirty, rumpled, and unkempt. The Fel can do that to you.

We drank our cider in silence, grateful for the comfort the Guest House afforded. Roe came back with a large stone pitcher from which he refilled all our mugs.

When he was gone again, Meltern leaned forward and rested his elbows on the table. "Tell me all about it, children. Did we accomplish our mission? Did you get the rovaldia? Why are you so muddy? I'm dying to hear!"

"Me, too," Zeek said. "We were too excited to talk much about it in Willam. Besides, your excellent cider has a way of making a good story flow."

Meltern nodded his thanks to Zeek.

Cheff began, "After we left here, Zeek dropped us off near a big Fel oak tree. We headed southeastward into the grass." He recounted the highlights of the last two days. Every once in a while, one or another of us would chip in with a detail or two.

When Cheff mentioned Rayce, Meltern broke in, "You found Rayce! He used to be an FRM agent, you know. Still is, though unofficially, of course. Had to leave when Pallador's terror squads started rounding up the Torphs. I'm glad he's okay—haven't heard from him in ages."

When he heard about the total destruction of the hunting lodge, Meltern frowned. "You children *are* a menace, aren't you? I'm going to have to be careful where I send you from now on."

"Send them to the Silver Palace, Mel," Zeek said. "The way they're going, that would just about finish off Pallador's entire Imperium!"

Zeek and Meltern laughed heartily over this, but the rest of us didn't find it all that funny.

Carra leaned over and whispered to Cheff, "What's he talking about?"

Cheff just shook his head. "Not important."

Roe and two helpers came in with our supper plates piled high. It looked amazing—a nice change from marsh pig jerky and pickled eel.

While we ate, Cheff told about how Brex had stowed away in Willam's side-panel, and how she met her parents.

"I knew them, too," Meltern said. "Good people. They must be heartbroken."

"They are," Cheff said. "It made me pretty angry, the way she spoke to them. At least she *has* parents. I'd give anything to have my mother and father back."

"What are we going to do with her?" Meltern asked.

"Not sure," Zeek said. "Cheff?"

"Rayce said she'd sleep until tomorrow, and that she wouldn't remember anything, not even getting into Zeek's truck. The hard part will be when she notices that she's missing three days."

"Maybe we could get Lery to knock her on her head with his mighty pipe wrench," Mid said, "then tell her she fell onto some scrap metal at the salvage camp."

Lery grinned. "The right tools…"

"Or better yet," Buttons said, "tell her that while she was snooping around Zeek's truck some scrap metal fell onto her head. That'll teach her to come nosing around here. Anyway, she already has a bump on her head. Several, in fact." She smacked Starry against her palm.

"Buttons!" Cheff said. "Did you—?"

"Of course not, Cheff," Buttons said. "She got them all by herself, fair and square."

Cheff didn't look convinced, but let it go.

"Woods," Sable said. "Leave her."

"That's a thought," Cheff said. "We could just leave her in the woods outside the camp and not tell her anything. Let her work it out for herself."

"I like it," Mid said. "I don't see how it's our problem, anyway. After what she did and how she acted in the Fel village, she's fortunate that she didn't end up as supper for a family of marsh pigs." He shuddered.

Cheff looked around at us. We gave him our unspoken agreement.

"Good enough," Cheff said. "Then that's our plan."

"Well, children, I must say that you did quite well," Meltern said. "You've shown resourcefulness and adaptability. In my opinion, you've justified Madame Entigy's confidence in you, and I'll tell her so the next time I make contact. As for you, Carra Trenta Wolcutt, it pains me to say it, but it seems to me that you still have a lot of things to learn. Things like teamwork, communication, and cooperation. You nearly caused this mission to fail completely on more than a few occasions."

Carra tightened her lips, but said nothing.

"For all your rich-girl resources, you could learn many a lesson from Cheff and his crew. In the meantime, I'll ask Madame Entigy to pass a message on to your father, to tell him that you have the rovaldia and you're heading home."

"Thank you, sir," Carra said. She didn't look happy, and I had a feeling that we were going to hear more of this before we sent her on her way back to Tumberland.

"Speaking of which," Meltern went on, "let's get that rovaldia inside and package it for travel. Roe, clear the table, if you please, then bring something we can use for wrappers."

Zeek and Lery brought the three large bags of rovaldia from Willam and emptied them onto the table. Meltern picked up a leaf and smelled it, then broke off a piece and tasted it.

"Be careful with that, sir," Cheff said. "Remember what we said about the unusual side-effects."

"And it seems to work rather quickly," Mid added.

"You don't want to burn down the Guest House for no reason," Buttons said. "The ponies say they'd miss your cider."

"We'd all miss your cider," Zeek said, laughing.

"Mr. Meltern," Mid said, "if you don't mind, I'd like to have a small amount of that rovaldia for myself. I have some ideas I'd like to try out."

"Of course, Mid," Meltern said. "It looks like we have plenty. Be sure to report whatever you discover, no matter how insignificant it may seem. We'll pass your results on to the lab boys in Tumberland, and they can add them to their research. With this kind of thing, you never know what will trigger a breakthrough."

"Yes, sir," Mid said, "I'll be sure to do that."

Roe arrived with a stack of cloth napkins and a large bowl of water.

"Seriously?" Meltern asked. "That's all you could find, my best linen?"

"Sorry, Mel," Roe said. "It's what there is on such short notice."

Meltern frowned, then sighed. "Oh, well, it's for a good cause, I suppose. I'm sure the Tumberland boys will find a use for them."

He dipped a napkin in the water, then showed us how to wrap the rovaldia leaves so they wouldn't break. "The moisture will keep them fresh until they get to Tumberland. Set aside any of the plants with their roots still on. We'll package them separately. Maybe they can figure out how to grow rovaldia in the lab."

When we were finished, there were several dozen bundles of leaves and one large bundle of about twenty whole plants with roots. Meltern handed Mid two of the bundles, and five of the live specimens wrapped separately. "Will that be enough for your experiments?"

"Yes, sir, I think that will be plenty. Anyway, now we know where we can get more."

"Don't even think about going back into The Fel," Meltern growled, "without my express permission, Mid! Understand me? That goes for all of you."

"Yes, sir," Mid said. "We understand."

"Good," Meltern said. "We don't want to be taking unnecessary chances with our newest, and extremely effective, agents."

Carra frowned at this, but again, didn't comment.

"As for you, Carra, do you think you can manage this much rovaldia? Yes? Good. It would be a shame to lose it after all you went through. I assume you have arrangements for someone to pick you up somewhere on the other side of the bay?"

"Yes, sir. When you tell them I'm coming, they'll know when and where."

"Excellent." Meltern stood up. "All right, people. It's time to get you back on the road."

We gathered our gear and the rovaldia. Meltern shook each one of our hands, including Carra's. "Chin up, Carra," he said kindly, "and be brave. The rest of this mission is in your hands alone. The FRM is counting on you. All of Andaran is depending on you, even though most of them don't know it. Stay alert, use good judgment, and keep your... *self*... off the skyline. You'll be fine. Okay?"

Their eyes met and held, then Carra said, "Yes, sir. Thank you."

"Thank *you*, Miss Wolcutt," Meltern said. "I'll be waiting to hear of your safe arrival."

We went out the back door and climbed into Willam's spacious cab. Sable and Buttons once again rearranged Brex, who was still fast asleep and snoring softly, back to a vertical position. It was strange—asleep, she was softer, somehow, almost pretty.

Almost.

"Time to get Carra on her way," Zeek said. "I think we can get pretty close to her canoe by road. Let's roll!"

Operation Lockdown

— 36 —

DISPOSITIONS

WE DECIDED TO drop Brex off first. She'd been twitching in her sleep and moaning a little. We didn't want her to wake up in Willam. Zeek passed the stub road that led to the salvage camp and kept going north for another half mile (800m) or so. He pulled over to the side of the road and brought Willam to a stop. "How's Brex doing?"

"Still sleeping," Mid said, "but she's stirring a little. We'd best hurry."

"Good," Zeek said. "Let's get her into the woods and park her where she can see the salvage camp. Come on, Lery, this is a job for you, I think."

Lery grinned and slid off his seat to the ground. He went around to the door where Brex was sleeping and opened it carefully so Brex wouldn't fall out. He hoisted her over his shoulder like a sack of potatoes and followed Zeek into the brush. They were gone only a few minutes, then returned, Brex-less.

"She'll be fine," Zeek said. "She's not far from the northern fence line. As soon as she stands up, she'll be able to see the lights from the salvage camp."

"I wish I could see her face when she wakes up," Buttons said.

"You might, if you get back to the camp soon enough," Zeek said. "We put her a short distance north of our tents. If she walks straight into the camp from there, we'll likely be the first ones she sees."

"That's a happy thought," Mid said.

We drove north until we calculated we were more-or-less even with Carra's campsite, then Zeek let us out. "Hurry back to the salvage camp, children. We have much to do before we can go home. Come in from the northwest, so you don't run into Brex. And watch out for the guards along the fence."

It was an about an hour after moonrise, so we could see pretty well in the dark without our lanterns. Lery shouldered the bundles of rovaldia. The rest of us put on our packs, pouches, and other gear. We hiked due west until we spotted the little pond where Carra had set up her camp.

Carra said, "You know, it seems a long time ago that you found me here, but it was only a couple of days. I sure was surprised to see you."

"I'll bet you were," Cheff muttered.

We circled the camp, trying to pick up our two-day-old trail back to where we'd stored Carra's canoe, but it was too dark in the woods. We took a chance and lit a lantern. When we found the trail, Carra stopped and had a last look at the clearing and the pond. "You sure had me fooled," she said. "When we first met, I mean. I thought you were going to kill me and bury me in the woods. Of course, now I know that you were only kidding me."

No one said anything.

Carra looked at us, then frowned. "You *were* kidding, right?"

We looked back at her, then Cheff shook his head. "Yeah, sure, right. Kidding. Let's go." He looked disgusted. As we fell in behind Sable, he muttered under his breath, "Slow learner."

"Looks like romance is dead," Buttons murmured to Sable.

It didn't take long before we found Carra's canoe near the beach. We removed the camouflage, dragged it to the water's edge, and loaded Carra's gear and the rovaldia. Lery held the canoe steady by its stern while Carra climbed in and got herself and her things situated.

"Before I go," she said, "I have to say something: I'm sorry I said you weren't real FRM agents. For little kids, you did pretty okay."

Cheff raised his eyebrows. "*Pretty* okay? Is that all? We're *so* glad you think so."

"Yeah," Mid said. "Thanks a bunch."

"No, I'm being sincere," Carra said. "When you grow up and become *real* FRM agents, instead of, what is it? BIS?"

"BSI," Cheff said, deadpan.

"Yes, that's it, BSI. When you become *real* FRM agents, and not merely BSI, I'm sure you'll be pretty okay at it."

Buttons started slapping Starry against her palm.

I thought it was too bad that Carra didn't know that Starry was stuffed full of ball bearings and sand.

"Wait a minute," Carra said. "I just thought of something. When I was coming out of the jexan fog, somebody said something—was it you, Buttons?—about real FRM agents and the raid on the Iron Fortress."

Buttons narrowed her eyes and slapped Starry against her hand even harder. "Please, Cheff, please let me, just one time? Just a little one?"

"Tempting, Sis," Cheff said, "but… no."

Carra frowned. "I can't quite get the memory back, but I seem to remember that someone said… that… you…" Her eyebrows arched. "That you were the ones who raided the Iron Fortress? That can't be right, can it? Surely not."

Sable bared her fangs in a wicked grin.

"I guess," Mid said, "that we *fake* FRM agents were simply too stupid to realize that it couldn't be done. Goodbye, Carra."

"But—"

Lery shoved the stern of the canoe as hard as he could into the surf. For the next few minutes, Carra was too busy trying to keep from capsizing to think of anything else.

When she finally got her little craft under control, she turned back and yelled something to us, but the current had taken her and she was too far away for us to make out what she said.

"Good riddance," Cheff said.

Lery laughed, then waved at Carra. "And don't... don't... come back!" he shouted.

Carra waved back cheerfully, then started paddling across the bay toward the Fellstone Light.

Buttons made Starry and Moka wave goodbye, then she grinned. "You know, Cheff, the ponies don't like her at all!"

* * *

We quick-marched down the beach and slid under the fence into the salvage camp not too far from our tents. There was no sign of Brex.

We cleaned ourselves up, then ambled over to the mess tent. Zeek was already there with his three helpers, industriously reducing heaping plates of chow. I don't know how Zeek did it—I was still full of Meltern's delicious supper. Willam was parked on the edge of the mess area, fully loaded with scrap.

Zeek waved at us and shouted. "Oh, there you are, children! Just in time for supper. Grab your food and come sit with me."

We headed for the chow line. "Pile it on," Cheff said. "It'll likely be a long time before we'll eat like this again. Whatever you can't eat, we'll pack up and take it home with us tomorrow. Our families will appreciate it." We heaped our plates high and returned to Zeek's table. We'd no sooner sat down than Tocette appeared, wringing her hands.

"And how is the Beautiful and Intrepid Tocette tonight?" Cheff asked.

"I'm so worried, Cheff," she said. "I haven't seen Brex for two days! I looked everywhere. She didn't even come back to our tent to sleep. Whipple is going crazy." She wiped her face on her sleeve. "I couldn't find you guys, either. Do you know where Brex is?"

"Sure don't, Tocette. Haven't seen her. We've been down at the stern section, mostly—even slept there one night. And we went to Fellstone City a few times to help Zeek unload, so maybe that's why you couldn't find us."

"Don't worry, Tocette," Mid said. "I'm sure she'll turn up before too long."

"Maybe you should make her a plate of food," Buttons said. "If she misses supper, she'll be sad."

"Oh. Well… okay," Tocette said, but she looked doubtful.

"Don't worry," Cheff said. "She's bound to show up sooner or later. Why don't you go fix her a bowl of something, then come back and sit with us?"

"Okay," Tocette said, and trundled off toward the chow line. When she returned, she was carrying a bowl of food for Brex plus three plates of dessert for herself. Without a word, she plowed into the first dessert.

We watched her eat for a while, then Lery pointed toward the north edge of the camp. "Look! Here she… comes… now."

Sure enough, Brex was stumbling our way, holding her head.

Tocette ran over. "Miss Brex! Are you okay? You look terrible! Where have you been?"

Brex glared at Tocette, then cleared her throat. "Stop screaming at once, imbecile," she rasped. "My head aches, and I hurt all over. And my throat is sore."

"Maybe you're getting the flu," Tocette said in a stage whisper. "Here, sit down. I'll go get you some felmoss tea." She gently guided Brex to our table and helped her sit down, then rushed back to the chow line.

Brex put her elbows on the table and rested her head in her hands.

Buttons quietly slid down the bench and sat opposite Brex. She whispered softly, "What happened to you, Miss Brex? You don't look so good and you have a nasty bump on your head. Did you have an accident with falling scrap metal or something?"

"I… I don't know," Brex said. "I woke up in the woods north of camp. I don't know how I got there."

"Can I get you anything?" Buttons asked.

"No, please, shut up and leave me alone."

Buttons shrugged and scooted back to her seat next to Zeek.

Tocette returned with a mug of steaming tea, which she set down in front of Brex.

"Oh, no… that smell…" Brex said. "I think I'm going to—" She rushed to the edge of the mess area and emptied the contents of her stomach into a bush.

Tocette followed Brex, put her arm around Brex's shoulders, and helped her back to the table. "I've been looking for you for three days, Miss Brex. I was so worried."

"Three days?" Brex asked, frowning. "What day *is* this?"

"Sixth day, Miss Brex. Time to go home."

"It can't be, Cadet Moron. You're mistaken."

"No, Miss. I'm sure."

"Tocette is right, Miss Brex," Zeek said. "Salvage is over." He pointed toward Willam. "That's my last load, all ready to go to my scrapyard. Willam's all watered and stoked and ready to roll. We were about to go pack up our gear when you showed up. If you like, you can ride back to the Labor Compound with us."

"Ride? With you? In that disgusting old truck?" She shivered. "No… no, thank you. I'd better find the rest of my group. Come with me, Tocette. Help me back to my tent."

Tocette took Brex's elbow and they left for the south side of the camp. On her way out of the mess area, Brex gave Willam the Wheezer a peculiar look, shivered again, then shook her head to clear it.

"Think she'll figure it out?" Mid asked.

"Dunno," Cheff said. "It'll be in her own best interests to minimize her absence. I'm not sure how she'll explain herself, but it'll be fun to find out. Are we about ready? Let's go get our stuff before Pallador's Corps of Engineers comes and packs up the tents."

We gathered our gear, piled into Willam, and headed for home.

— 37 —

GIFTS OF HOME

When we got back to the Labor Compound, Zeek said, "Don't worry about unloading tonight. It's getting late. I'll take care of this load tomorrow." He went into his little shack and came out with Fentor Rignish's peddler's pack. "Here, you take this. It's full of all sorts of things I'm sure you'll find a use for. You can figure out how to divvy it up. Old Rignish would be pleased to know that it went to good use."

Lery took the bundle and slung it over his shoulder.

"Oh, and Lery, I forgot to tell you: I petitioned the administration office and got approval to hire you full-time. Full-time *after* school, that is. Permanent job as my assistant, you see. If you want it, of course."

Lery beamed. "I'll see… see you… tomorrow… after school… Boss."

Zeek chuckled. "Good, I'll be glad for the help. Between the two of us, we'll get this junk heap under control. Oh, and children, I have one more surprise for you. Come with me." He led us through the mounds of scrap metal into a shop building on the northeast corner of the scrap yard, near the smelter. We went inside, and Zeek turned on the light. "Look at this, children, I think you'll like it."

"A stack of empty steel drums?" Mid asked. "Um, sure, Zeek, it's… nice."

"Don't be such a smart aleck," Zeek said. "These are no ordinary oil drums. Watch!"

He reached under one of the drums and flipped a latch, then pushed gently with one finger. The entire pile of drums tilted back on hinges, revealing a ladder going down into a pit. Zeek shone his lantern down the hole. "See? A BSI special! Your own private access to the storm drains from Zeek's Emporium of Scrap! Complete with a counterbalance to make operation easy. How do you like that, eh? I spoke with Meltern while you were in The Fel, and he told me about your new headquarters, and so I thought I'd surprise you. Now, down you go. Take that bundle to your headquarters before you go home. You don't want to have to explain to the Bluebands what's in that pack. Here, take this with you, too." Zeek handed Cheff his lantern. "Don't worry, I have plenty. Now go!"

We followed Cheff down the ladder and found ourselves in an unfamiliar tunnel. Zeek called down after us, "Go east until you get to a bigger tunnel, then turn north. Your new headquarters will be on your left. Good night, children."

The oil-drum trap door clanged shut above us. We followed Zeek's directions and shortly were at the old rusty door to our new headquarters.

Sable climbed in first. Lery handed her the peddler's pack. The rest of us climbed in after. Cheff set Zeek's lantern on a dusty table. We gathered some chairs and sat in a circle.

Cheff sighed contentedly. "Well, gang, here we are, after our first official BSI mission—"

"Successful mission," Buttons added.

"—resting in the new official BSI headquarters. It isn't much, so far, but it's ours."

"We can leave Fentor Rignish's pack here," Mid said, "and go through it later."

"No hurry," Cheff said. "I have a feeling we'll be spending some considerable time here, many afternoons to come."

"Home," Sable said.

"The ponies say it feels like home, too, Cheff. We need to get busy and fix it up."

"That's exactly what we'll do, Sis," Cheff said.

"There's… a stove…" Lery said. "If we… fix it up… I can cook… for us…"

"Chef Lery's Fine Home Cooking," Mid said, which made Lery giggle.

"How about a cup of tea, Lery?" Cheff asked. "Can you coax that much out of the stove tonight?"

"I… I'll… try, Friend Cheff."

In a few minutes, we sipped hot, steaming mugs of bitter fel-moss tea.

"Well," Cheff said, "that was quite a week. Overall, I'd call it a success."

"We did find Mr. Rignish," I said.

"And that horrible Carra person," Buttons added.

"And we helped the Fel People get the Sephs out of their back-yard," Mid added.

"Anti-jexan," Sable murmured.

"That's right," Cheff said. "Maybe we helped the FRM develop the beginnings of an anti-jexan drug."

"I'd like to commandeer one of the side rooms for a laborato-ry," Mid said. "I have some ideas of my own about how to refine the rovaldia."

Lery said, "That… would be… good. Jexan is… *bad*."

Buttons added, "Let's keep that rovaldia away from Lhuk!"

"Speaking of Lhuk," I asked, "are we going to tell Lhuk about his parents? He still thinks they were sent away to a Torph Camp out west."

"I've been thinking about Lhuk," Cheff said. "It seems to me that the BSI might be able to use someone with that kind of Ability."

"I suppose that's true," Mid said. "It would help with the next Mr. Grumbles we meet or any other critter we run across."

"The… the marsh pigs…" Lery said.

"Carra!" Buttons said, and we laughed.

"Yeah," Cheff said, "Carra… what a… a…"

Sable put her hand on Cheff's shoulder. "Sephs."

"Of course," Cheff said. "If it weren't for Brex's Ability…"

"Do you think Lhuk could do what Brex did to that Seph?" Mid asked. "He's so young."

"He's older than I am," Buttons said.

We thought this over, then I said, "Meltern did say we should look for new members. Maybe Lhuk is our first candidate? I like the idea."

"Everyone agree?" Cheff asked.

"Agree," Sable said at once.

Lery and Mid exchanged a glance, then Mid said, "Well, I'm not so sure. He *is* young, even if he's older than Buttons. And he's a Torph. Having a Torph in the group will only make us more of an obvious target for Brex and her Bluebands. On the other hand, I agree that his Ability may prove to be useful. So, okay, I guess so."

"Fair enough," Cheff said. "Lery?"

"As long as… as he doesn't… use his… Ability… on me," Lery said.

"You heard what Rayce said about using the Ability, right? The Torph Ability doesn't work on people except for the Sephs. And animals. I don't think it's going to be a problem. Okay?"

"Okay… Friend Cheff."

"How about you, Sis?"

Starry and Moka looked at each other inquiringly. "The ponies think inviting Lhuk is a great idea, Cheff!" Buttons said. "And so do I."

"Glad to hear it," Cheff said. "Lery can let Zeek know tomorrow after school, and Zeek can relay the message to Meltern the next time he goes to town. Okay, Lery?"

"Okay."

"But remember, everyone, don't say anything to Lhuk until we get clearance from Meltern. On a more serious note," Cheff said, "Zeek whispered to me to get ourselves ready for the next mission. He said it will start as soon as the lockdown is lifted."

"Ooh! Where's it going to be this time, Cheff?" Buttons asked.

"I don't know, Sis."

Buttons consulted the ponies. "Well, we sure hope it's going to be someplace drier than The Fel! We've had enough dampness to last quite a while."

"Why did he only tell you, Cheff?" Mid asked.

"He said it was 'need to know,' but I think we need to know as soon as possible. No matter how many eventually join the BSI, we'll always be the First Six. And the First Six will always need to know together."

That sounded pretty good to me.

Cheff drained the last of his felmoss tea. "Well, gang, shall we get ourselves home? Tomorrow's coming around pretty soon. Books' mom, Mid's mom, and Aunt Dee will be expecting us, and Sable's people, too. Marsh pigs we can deal with. Fel bears? No problem! Even Seph lords we can handle—but we sure don't want to get Aunt Dee riled at us! That simply wouldn't do at all."

OPERATION SHIFTING SANDS

Book Three

by

Liam Kincaid

An ordinary school field trip turns into a daring mission for the Bayside Insurgents when they discover that Imperial Agents have infiltrated Xanparthur Monastery, home of over four hundred peaceful Sephs. When one ancient, demented Seph lord demands that the BSI retrieve a spherical crystal artifactfrom a mysterious tower, Master Vessslu, the head of the Monastery, sends them on a covert mission deep into the desert.

Will the BSI find the artifact in time to save Xanparthur Monastery?

Read on for a special preview of

OPERATION SHIFTING SANDS

OPERATION SHIFTING SANDS

"Excellent," Attan said. "You plead guilty. That will save us much time and trouble."

"Guilty? Not me! I'm too cute to be guilty!" Buttons said. "The ponies object!"

"Hey!" Mid said. "We didn't confess to anything!"

Attan slowly turned his gaze on Mid. "I thought I told you to keep quiet."

"Why should I, if you're only going to kill us anyway?" Mid asked.

It seemed a fair question.

"Why, indeed?" Attan said. "For one thing, we haven't yet discussed the means of your deaths. It could be quick, possibly even painless, or relatively so. On the other hand, you could end up like that little goat I sent to Kahph earlier this evening. I had one myself. He was delicious. I love it when they wriggle inside. But he was so small, and I'm so sharpishly hungry." He opened his jaws wide enough to show his fangs, then flicked his forked tongue almost into Mid's face. "Mmm… Troh! It's been a long time since I tasted a chubby little Troh boy!"

"Hey!" Mid said.

"Master Vessslu is expecting us," Cheff said. "You'll never get away with it."

"Get away with it?" Attan asked. "Me? You mean Kahph, don't you? I assure you, I will be most sincerely sad when I report that Kahph devoured the lot of you before escaping." He chuckled. "Oh, yes, I can see it now. How sad we'll all be to learn that the old villain, Kahph, has once again taken sentient lives. I'm sure that the memorial service will be quite… touching."

Cheff was stumped—we all were. Then once again I felt the sensation of being drowned in honey. Attan was using his Ability. I tried to move but my feet felt as though they were stuck to the floor.

"Go ahead, eat me, I don't care," Mid said. "You don't scare me, you big bully! I hope I get stuck in your throat and you choke!"

"I don't frighten you?" Attan asked. "What a pity. You must either be exceptionally brave, or consummately stupid. Or maybe you simply don't care about yourself. I wonder how much you care about your friends." He lowered his head until his face nearly touched the end of Buttons' nose. His ugly purple tongue flicked again. "How nice! A little girl, a little Lora girl. I hope you don't taste too much like fish. Loras always taste fishy."

Cheff was struggling to break free of Attan's Ability, but to no avail. "You filthy cannibal!"

"So, you care about this little one, do you? That's good to know. Is she your nest mate? Your sister, perhaps? All the better! I shall begin with her." He turned to Buttons. "Step inside, little girl."

He unhinged his jaw and lowered it until it touched the cold stone floor of the corridor. At first, nothing happened. Then Buttons, in spite of her struggling, took a step forward, then another, then she put her head inside Attan's mouth.

"Don't do it, Buttons!" Cheff yelled. "Don't let him make you do anything."

"I can't help it, Cheff. My feet won't listen to me anymore." She lifted her right leg and put a knee inside.

Attan was clearly enjoying her discomfort. He drooled until it spilled over his scaly lips onto the floor.

Buttons lifted her other knee and put it inside, too. "Help me, Cheff!"

"I can't move!"

Attan ran his slimy tongue over her face. "Mmm… delicious."

"Lhuk! Do something!" Cheff yelled.

"Like what? I'm stuck, too."

"Use your Ability! Make him not want to eat Buttons!"

Lhuk's eyes were scrunched tight. "I'm trying, I'm trying. It's not working."

"Try harder!"

"I can't! He's too powerful!"

"Forget that, make him not want *anything*!"

Lhuk's eyes scrunched tighter, and his face grew red. "No good! I'm sorry, Cheff!"

"Concentrate!"

Attan's slavering jaws started to close. Buttons screamed. "Nooo! Don't. Hurt. My. *Ponies!!!*"

Don't miss

OPERATION
SHIFTING SANDS

Book Three

by

Liam Kincaid

The fun isn't over! Visit:

https://FellstoneTales.com

**for news, updates, illustrations,
charts, and maps!**

ABOUT THE AUTHOR

Liam Kincaid was born to parents of Scottish descent on December 30, 1953, in a boxcar in the high Sierra Nevadas during a raging snowstorm. After graduating from high school, Liam declined a medical scholarship to Stanford University and a musical scholarship to Julliard.

Instead, Liam served for a time in the United States Air Force, then traveled the world working at many jobs, including professional wood-worker and stilts maker, maintenance supply specialist for Pacific Southwest Airlines, kelp processor for Kelco, hot-air balloon pilot, cow clipper (for one day), house painter, time-share salesman in Mexico, hospital housekeeper, school bus driver, wrestling-arena peanut vendor, street musician, English teacher in the Dominican Republic, ranch hand, e-zine publisher, bio-diesel manufacturer, carpet cleaner, pig photographer, and computer programmer.

When his roaming days were over, he longed for the wholesome science-fiction adventure stories of his youth, so he decided to try his hand at writing some. Having raised four sons, he was inspired by the powerful, astounding feats a group of intelligent, determined children can accomplish.

Liam welcomes correspondence from his readers and does his best to answer each one personally. E-mail him at: LiamKincaid@WorldHeartEpic.com

About the Artist

Daniel Wood is a freelance artist and illustrator based in Richmond, Virginia.

He honed his skills at Virginia Commonwealth University, where he earned a Bachelor of Fine Arts degree in Communication Arts. Drawing is the love of his life, so much so that he often spends his spare time drawing the day away.

Skilled in many forms of illustration, including concept art, comic art, book illustrations, and game art, both colored and black-and-white, he specializes in fantasy, science-fiction, and all of their more specific subgenres. Every project is a joyful challenge to transform the author's concepts into compelling visual imagery.

Daniel welcomes discussions regarding new projects. See more of his work at DanielWoodArt.com, or e-mail him at woodillustration@gmail.com.

WE NEED YOUR HELP!

Dear Reader,

We depend on your reviews and word-of-mouth.

If you enjoyed this book, please help spread the word through Twitter, Facebook, and other social media, and please consider giving us five stars and writing a brief review on Amazon.com and Goodreads.com, or your favorite book-review venue.

Thank you very much!

Liam Kincaid
North California Coast,
March 2024

To view full-size, full-color maps and illustrations,
and to learn more about Fellstone and its peoples, visit:

https://FellstoneTales.com

www.ingramcontent.com/pod-product-compliance
Lightning Source LLC
Chambersburg PA
CBHW060233100726
47907CB00003B/615